UNFINISHED BUSINESS

Katharine Anne Prescott Millholland is an up-and-coming young lawyer from one of Chicago's oldest families—until she finds herself at the death scene of her richest client. Now she not only has to deal with the dead man's affairs, she's also a suspect in his killing.

Bart Hexter is a legend in the Chicago futures market. In an industry where greed, guile, and naked aggression are considered assets to be cultivated, he has no peer, few friends, and plenty of enemies.

Torey Lloyd, a beautiful young runner on the trading floor, is having an affair with Hexter. She loves him, certainly. But does she love him better dead than alive?

Margot Hexter is Bart's outspoken and unstable daughter. All his children despise him, but is Margot driven enough to kill him?

"Mr. Silver" is the mysterious cosignator on several of Hexter's hidden Bermuda bank accounts. Who is he, and what other secrets did he and Hexter share?

Also by Gini Hartzmark
Published by Fawcett Books:

PRINCIPAL DEFENSE

FINAL OPTION

Gini Hartzmark

IVY BOOKS • NEW YORK

Ivy Books
Published by Ballantine Books
Copyright © 1994 by Gini Hartzmark

Library of Congress Catalog Card Number: 93-91730

ISBN 0-8041-1227-4

Manufactured in the United States of America

First Edition: March 1994

10 9 8 7 6 5 4 3 2 1

To Sam, Jonathan, and JoAnna

Acknowledgments

I am tremendously grateful to the busy people who generously made time to help me with the research for this novel. Mark Kollar of Knight-Ridder Financial News shared his experiences and gave me an overview of the futures industry, as did Roger Rutz and Thom Thompson at the Chicago Board of Trade. Jim Porter of Chicago Research & Trading Group, Ltd., was kind enough to discuss the special alchemy of his firm.

Thanks also go to friends Dr. Mike Rocco, Rick Cooper, Chuck Zellmer, Ruth Berggren, Larry Barker, Michael Bader, Emmeline Diller, and Scott and Jodi Schumann for sharing their technical expertise over the kitchen table or the garden fence. And heartfelt thanks to Nancy Love; Leon Danco; Jan Harayda; my editor, Susan Randol; my friend, Ann Rocco; and especially my husband, Michael, for their unflagging support.

And while I thank all these special people for their input and advice, I must be quick to absolve them from errors of fact and any other misdemeanors I may have committed.

CHAPTER

1

From the very first time I met him, Bart Hexter had been playing games with me. This morning was no exception, just another aggravation added to an already long list. Hexter was my client, a powerful futures trader who was a legend in Chicago—the sort of hard-hitting businessman that this city of big shoulders seems to specialize in. Flamboyant, mercurial, with a huge appetite for risk, he'd earned his nickname, Black Bart, as much for his dark temper as his trademark jet black hair.

But there was a statesmanlike side of the man as well. He was a persuasive spokesman for the futures industry and a lobbyist of no little skill. He and his wife, Pamela, were prominent for their many philanthropic works and held up their dedication to family, community, and each other, as a proud example to those who sought to emulate their success.

Still, there were those who counseled against being taken in by the man's patrician patina. Futures, they insisted, is an industry where greed, guile, and naked aggression are considered assets to be cultivated. For the better part of thirty years, they pointed out, Bart Hexter had been the biggest—and some would contend—the baddest in the game.

Recently, Hexter and his company, Hexter Commodities, found themselves the focus of a government investigation. Most big traders did from time to time, and as his attorney I was not overly concerned. For his part, Hexter was worse than nonchalant. For weeks I'd been begging him for copies of the documents relevant to the government's case, the trading records and account statements that I would need in order to answer the government's charges. But with Hexter Commodities' response due in less than five days, Bart Hexter had yet to produce one scrap of paper.

I was not pleased.

We had scheduled a number of meetings to discuss the matter, but so far Hexter had canceled them all—usually at the last minute. His excuses to date included: an overcrowded schedule, secretarial error, bad markets, and last but not least, a pressing poker game. Our most recently scheduled meeting, set for four o'clock the previous Friday, had been called off with no explanation at all. Furious, I'd phoned Hexter and demanded a weekend meeting. He'd retaliated by insisting that the only time he had available was Sunday morning at eight.

And so I found myself, not comfortably in bed with the reassuring bulk of *The New York Times*, but behind the wheel of my car, dodging construction barrels on the Edens Expressway. This, at least, I reassured myself, was one meeting Bart Hexter was not going to get out of.

Bart Hexter lived on an estate in Lake Forest that had been in his wife's family for four generations. He lived lavishly, with the unabashed enjoyment of material things that springs from early years of want. Hexter had grown up poor even by the working-class standard in the Irish neighborhood of Bridgeport on Chicago's south side. His father was a deckhand on a grain freighter that plied the Great Lakes trade, a faithless husband, and an unrepentant gambler, who only returned to his family when his money or his luck ran out. Bart's mother was a pale and pious woman who bore her husband's perfidy like a cross and raised her sons, Bart and his younger brother, Billy, with equal doses of discipline and religion.

Having survived St. Bernadette's School and three years military service in Korea, Hexter landed a job as a runner at the Board of Trade. He didn't think much of the work at first, but he got off early, with plenty of time to play poker—a game he'd found he had a taste and a talent for in the army. On weekends, Bart occasionally filled in playing trumpet in a friend's dance band, which was how his path crossed that of Miss Pamela Worley Manderson of Lake Forest.

The awkward, sheltered, only child of Letitia and Sterling Manderson, heir to the Manderson meat-packing fortune, Pamela was easily captivated by the Byronic profile and hot brown eyes of the young Irishman. Their marriage, six months later, was the scandal of the year. One could only guess at what tears and entreaties, what threats of elopement and estrangement, had been necessary to extort the grim approval of Pamela's parents to the match.

Despite the scandal, or perhaps because of it, the Mandersons invited the young couple to make their home on their property, building a house for them behind the high hedges of the Manderson estate. Six months after it was completed, Bart Hexter mortgaged the house and used the proceeds to buy a seat on the Chicago Board of Trade.

In less than two years' time, with a one-year-old son and a daughter on the way, Hexter repaid the mortgage and leveled the house that had been his wedding present. In its place he erected another house, this one in the same Tudor style of his in-law's, only four times as large. When construction was complete, Pamela's ample girlhood home stood dwarfed behind it, literally in its shadow.

The drive to Lake Forest from my apartment in the city is a depressing trek up the chain of expressways— the Dan Ryan, the Kennedy, and the Edens—that, feeding into each other, form the suburbanite's daily escape route from the city. Once you're free of the jumble of construction near Wrigley Field, past the tidy bungalows of Skokie, there's a strange stretch, as barren as the moon. Farmland has been asphalted into parking lots, and sleek office buildings sprout like poisonous mushrooms from the flat, empty plain.

But once you leave the expressway and turn onto Route 41, you get to the country as abruptly as turning on a light—at least the expensive and manicured version of the country that passes as Chicago's lush northern suburbs. The ancient elms are huge, meeting above the road in a dark, leafy canopy. There is a muted murmur of vast lawns being mowed in the distance, and if you listen hard enough you can imagine the faint ping of golf balls being hit deep behind the trees.

It was especially warm for April. When I rolled down

the window of my car, the air smelled damp and rich with the progressing spring. I turned onto Deerpath Road and made my shady progress into the bastion of quiet privilege that is Lake Forest. On my right, I passed the city offices, set back from the road like a small college, then past the three blocks of cloyingly cute and shockingly expensive shops that comprise the business district. I crossed the train tracks—the station is so quaint it always makes me think of gingerbread— and turned right onto Parkland Avenue. After a mile or two, I slowed to watch for the twin pillars of red brick that mark the entrance to the Manderson estate.

Hexter's secretary had faxed me detailed directions to the great man's home, including a carefully drawn map, but I'd left them at the office. I didn't need them. I'd grown up less than a mile from his home.

I found the gateposts easily enough and turned onto the drive that was newly paved and deliberately winding. The house, as I recalled, was set quite a distance from the street in what was considered, even by Lake Forest standards, to be a rather grand park.

As I rounded the first turn I was startled to see a car nose down in a gully a little distance from the drive. A whisper of exhaust trailed from the tail pipe. I slowed to a stop.

Everyone knew Hexter's car, a custom-made Rolls Royce Phantom—black with a white top. The license plate read, simply, BART. But what was it doing in the underbrush, with its back wheels cocked absurdly on the bank of a gully and its front butted up against a young birch tree? I got out of the car and squelched my way down the gently sloping bank.

* * *

We may have had a meeting that morning, but Bart Hexter certainly wasn't dressed for business. He waited for me behind the wheel of his Rolls clad only in a pair of red silk pajamas. The window was rolled all the way down on the driver's side and I called his name through it softly. I didn't expect any answer. I was close enough to see clearly the cruel damage of two bullets in his head.

The impact of the shots had knocked him toward the passenger side of the front seat where he sprawled, his head tilted absurdly so that one eye stared up at me with a disquieting mixture of entreaty and astonishment. Below his left temple there was a neat red hole with another larger and more ragged wound beneath it. His arms were limp, with one flung straight back behind his head and the other hanging down from the seat of the car, twisting his neck at an angle that would have been uncomfortable to maintain in life.

Beyond the body the passenger side window was a crimson mess. The white leather of the car's interior was splattered with blood and flecked with what I took to be bits of brain and bone. In a few places, black hairs clung to the goo. Black Irish, I remembered with a shudder, my breath suddenly coming in shallow, little gasps. That's how my mother had always described Hexter, her tone of voice somehow implying that that was the very worst kind. The morning paper, soaked right through, lay near his head.

I do not know for how long I stood looking at the body, transfixed by the tableau before me. I know that I felt a great, mixed-up, paralyzing surge of emotions. Fear, revulsion, and the pure adrenaline rush of shock. But underneath it all there was a vast well of detached curiosity. Some drama had been played out here to a bloody conclusion. One part of me wanted to know how it was that Bart Hexter had come to be here, shot dead at the end of his own driveway.

By the time I heard the whine of the police sirens they were practically upon me, with lights flashing and tires squealing—two squad cars, an ambulance, and a plain white sedan. I stood there, frozen, like a deer caught in the headlights. Since I had not been able to see Bart Hexter's car from the street, I wondered who had called them.

"Stand away from the car," barked an amplified voice as the doors of the various vehicles were flung open. Policemen swarmed out, guns drawn. "Get your hands in the air." Startled, I looked behind me. It took me a second to register that it was me who was being addressed. One of the officers came up to me at a sprint. It wasn't until I was made to "assume the position" against the hood of my car and roughly patted down for a weapon that they got around to asking questions.

"Who are you?" demanded a beefy sergeant, his voice high and loud from tension.

"Kate Millholland."

"What are you doing here?"

"I had a meeting with Mr. Hexter," I stammered.

"What kind of meeting?"

"Business. When I got here I saw his car had gone off the road. I went to see if anything was wrong. He's, he's, he's been shot."

"Shot dead?"

"I think so, yes." My voice, my power of speech was

failing me. I was down to words of one syllable and little more than a whisper.

"What time did you get here?" he barked.

"I'm not sure, my meeting was at eight. I think I was a few minutes early." I looked at my watch. It read close to 8:15.

"I'm going to have to ask you to come with me."

I nodded mutely and allowed myself to be escorted to one of the squad cars for questioning. Out of the corner of my eye I saw a red-haired man climb slowly out of the unmarked car and amble toward the Rolls Royce, his casual bearing in marked contrast to the taut energy of the police officer at my side. The patrolman opened the door of the squad, and I slid into the backseat. It was a Caprice that looked too clean and new to be a real police car, not like the battered Chicago blue and whites that bounce on shot shocks through the streets in my neighborhood. Metal mesh separated the front seat from the back, and before I knew it, I was left alone with the squawk of the police radio. I checked the door. It was locked.

Shock, I decided after a few minutes of quiet contemplation, had turned me into a moron. It was, to say the least, disconcerting to arrive for a meeting at your client's home only to find him shot. But I hadn't even mustered the presence of mind to wonder who, if anybody, had killed him. I thought about it for a while, letting the implications sink in. Why did I automatically assume that someone else had pulled the trigger when suicide was much more likely? In futures markets the payoffs can be profanely high, but the downside is equally steep. If he'd killed himself, I reasoned grimly, Bart Hexter wouldn't have been the first trader who'd found himself sitting on a time bomb of bad trades and eaten a bullet rather than wait for it to go off.

I waited for close to an hour, growing impatient, angry, and finally bored, locked in the back of the Lake Forest police car. Finally the door was opened by a red-haired man in his late forties wearing a shiny blue suit and a tie that was about an inch too wide. He had a thick build, running to fat, and he tapped his blunt fingers impatiently on the roof of the car while I climbed out.

"I'm Detective Ruskowski," he said, not extending his hand to be shaken. He was, I figured, maybe an inch under six feet. We looked at each other eye to eye. There were deep lines in his freckled face, and his ginger hair was liberally sprinkled with gray. On second thought, I decided he must be older than my original estimate; either that, or he'd just lived hard.

"You Kate Millholland?"

"Yes."

"Any relation to the Millhollands that live on Jessup Road?"

"My parents."

I waited for another question, but none came. Neither of us spoke. The quiet lasted long enough to get on my nerves.

"Are you going to tell me what's happened?" I asked, trying hard not to sound testy.

"Why don't you tell me?" answered the detective evenly.

"I had a meeting this morning with Bart Hexter. When I pulled in the drive I saw his car down there in the gully. I stopped to see if there was something wrong. I found him behind the wheel of his car. He was wearing his pajamas. It looked like he'd been shot. I'm pretty sure that he was dead."

"He was the last time I checked," replied Ruskowski. He produced a small notebook from his breast pocket and began flipping through it. We just stood there for a while, the silence growing larger and more awkward with every passing second. I felt puzzled and annoyed. I thought policemen were supposed to ask questions. Maybe Ruskowski thought that if he just let things hang long enough I'd be tempted to blurt something out—a confession perhaps.

"Was it suicide?" I asked, finally ending the game.

"Is that what you'd expect it to be?"

"I expected him to be here, alive, for this meeting," I shot back.

"What was your meeting about?"

"Business."

"What kind of business?"

"Mr. Hexter was a futures trader," I replied, appalled at the speed with which I had slipped into the past tense when it came to Bart Hexter. "The CFTC—that's the Commodity Futures Trading Commission—is considering bringing charges against him and his company for exceeding position limits in soybean contracts in March and April of last year."

"Is that something that might have driven him to take his own life?"

"I wouldn't think so. It's not even a criminal offense," I replied, remembering the time that I'd heard Hexter refer to a twenty-five thousand dollar government fine as a "parking ticket."

"How long ago did you and Mr. Hexter schedule this meeting?"

"Late Friday afternoon."

"Who else knew about it?"

"I don't know. His secretary. My secretary. I'd assume his wife since we were meeting at his home. . . ."

"Have you met Mrs. Hexter?" interjected Ruskowski.

"Yes."

"Friendly with her?"

"Not really. She's more my mother's generation."

"Do you own a gun?"

"No," I lied.

"How long have you known Bart Hexter?"

"He'd been my client less than a year."

"You didn't know him before that? Perhaps socially?"

"I knew of him, of course. I'd seen him at parties, but I didn't really meet him until last spring. He had just fired his attorney and was shopping for new counsel."

"And you got the job."

"Yes."

"Why did he choose you?" inquired Ruskowski. There was something in his tone and the way his eyes raked over me that made my flesh crawl.

"I'm sure he thought I'd do the best job," I answered flatly.

"There wasn't some other reason?" Ruskowski leered.

"Why don't we stick to what's relevant?" I snapped.

"Miss Millholland," barked Ruskowski, "I am a homicide detective, and you are standing at the scene of a crime. That means that on this little piece of earth, what

I say goes. I ask the questions, and you answer them. I don't have to explain myself to you. I don't have to consider your feelings or your reputation. All I have to do is my job, which today means finding the dickhead who shot Bart Hexter. Now, if you don't like my questions, I'd be happy to have you handcuffed and taken to the police station where you can wait around until I find the time to talk to you again."

"It really must be great," I said, my temper rising to run roughshod over my judgment, "to have the kind of job where you can have an ego hard-on like this in public."

This time the silence lasted long enough for me to envision myself spending the rest of the day enjoying the hospitality of the Lake Forest Police Department, harvesting the fruits of my own big mouth.

"Follow me," Ruskowski snapped. Then he turned on his heel and headed briskly down the drive toward the gully.

I followed him, scrambling a bit to catch up, as he made his way down the incline toward Hexter's car. Already they had managed to string yellow police-line-do-not-cross tape around some trees, and a gaggle of policemen were milling around the perimeter.

I faltered a bit as we approached, realizing what Ruskowski had in store for me. It was one thing to stumble on the body unawares, another to go back for a second look.

"Did he kill himself?" I ventured as we ducked under the tape.

"So far," snapped the detective, "all I've got is one dead guy in one damned expensive car."

CHAPTER

2

My mother had long ago pronounced Bart Hexter's house to be the ugliest in Lake Forest. I had never been inside, but these edicts of hers were made with an acid accuracy. I had heard that it was modeled after a famous English manor house, but as I approached it on foot, accompanied by two policemen, it looked only enormous and forbidding. The long drive swept downhill and ended in a wide circle at the front door. In its center was a fountain of carved marble—an elaborate affair of twined dolphins and sea horses blowing high arcs of water into the thin April sunshine.

The police had appropriated a dark and chilly room off the massive entrance hall. It had a stone fireplace that was big enough to stand in and the high ceiling beamed with black oak. The furniture was carved and Elizabethan, with chairs of dark wood upholstered in burgundy and black. An enormous tapestry hung on one wall, so worn I assumed it must be genuine. It was in this vaguely inquisitorial setting that I made my formal statement to Detective Ruskowski.

He took me through it in agonizing detail—every encounter I'd ever had with the dead man, my impressions of him as a person and a businessman, as well as a detailed account of every minute of my last twenty-four hours. Through it all, Ruskowski maintained an attitude of belligerent suspicion, reminding me that policemen, even more than lawyers, live in a world where they expect to be lied to.

When we were done he turned me over to a young woman from the County Crime Lab who cheerily swabbed my hands for a neutron activation test. The test was done to detect the presence of barium and antimony, two substances commonly left behind on the hand after a gun is fired. Then, with the uncomfortable sensation of being in a bad made-for-TV movie, I allowed myself to be fingerprinted.

My business with the police concluded, I went to the powder room to wash my hands. There, in a fire-bowl of hand-painted French wallpaper, I scrubbed off the sticky fingerprint ink. Finished, I reached for a towel and found myself looking at three crisp, monogrammed linen hand towels, the kind people like to give as wedding presents. I stood, frozen in midmotion, hands dripping onto the tile.

I have a whole life packed away in boxes: twenty-four place settings of china, crystal champagne flutes, and Waterford wine goblets. I have table linens and picnic baskets, kitchen gadgets and serving platters, picture frames, silver trays and crisp linen hand towels embroidered with initials that were mine for much too short a time.

I was married once, not so long ago.

Russell and I met in law school, mauling each other in moot court competition during the day and again— much differently—at night in his squeaky Murphy bed.

He was everything I am not: self-made and supremely self-confident. He cruised through everything—law school, job interviews, encounters with my family—like a man with his hand firmly on the throttle. We married the summer after graduation and honeymooned on the isle of Crete. There we sailed and sunned and stayed up late, sipping retsina at an outdoor café, our heads bent together in the light of an oil lamp, making whispered plans for the future.

When we got back to Chicago we reported for work, I as a first-year associate at Callahan Ross, Russell as a clerk for Federal Appeals Judge Myron Wertz. At first we were too busy to pay much attention to the slight limp that Russell had acquired in Greece. It seemed natural to assume that it was nothing—an old soccer injury come back to life—but eventually he was persuaded to see a doctor. Six weeks to the day after our wedding, Russell was diagnosed with brain cancer. I was a widow before my first wedding anniversary.

That was three years ago, and every day I tell myself that the worst is behind me, but still my grief, the throbbing loss, is like a quiet soundtrack to my life. And there are days like this one, when something—the disequilibrium of Hexter's death, my raw encounters with the police, or the sight of an object as ordinary as a carefully pressed rectangle of Irish linen—is enough to let loose a flood of dark emotions.

I looked in the mirror, sternly warning myself against tears, and carefully pulled the pins from my dark hair. I took it down and rewound it with automatic hands into its customary French twist. I splashed cold water on my face, blotting it with a piece of tissue—not trusting myself to touch the towels. Then I took a deep breath and deliberately composed myself back into the hard-working corporate attorney that I carefully presented to the world each day.

The house was cavernous and confusing so I had to search to unearth a member of the Hexter household who was not fully occupied with the police. I finally came upon a sullen-looking young woman in a black maid's uniform who agreed to see if Mrs. Hexter would be available to speak to me. While I awaited her return, I looked out through the leaded panes of a tall window at the front of the house in time to see two squad cars and an ambulance swing quickly around the circular drive—Bart Hexter leaving home for the last time.

Pamela Manderson Hexter received me in a pretty upstairs sitting room in a distant wing of the house. It was a sunny, high-ceilinged spot filled with well-worn Queen Anne furniture upholstered in yellow and cerise—a marked contrast to the rest of the house. I guessed that this room, comfortable and separate, was her private retreat, decorated with cherished pieces from her parents' house. The new widow greeted me from a high-backed armchair set in the wide bay window that overlooked a long, terraced garden.

Pamela and Bart Hexter had shared a very public marriage. Not content to live quietly, Bart Hexter from the first had dragged his shy wife into the spotlight with him, and over time, it became clear that she grew more comfortable there. The couple were active in a number of charities, including a foundation bearing their name that aided families of seriously ill children. In addition, the couple were tireless partygoers, so that very few weeks went by without a mention of the Hexters on the society page.

Pamela was a well-presented blonde of a certain age who had fought the battle of encroaching years with help from the plastic surgeon's knife. Dressed in a simple gray Castelberry suit, her hair, which just grazed her shoulders, had been meticulously arranged and sprayed into immobility. Her face was pale, but her makeup remained undisturbed by tears.

"Mrs. Hexter," I said, crossing the room toward her, "I am so sorry to intrude at such a difficult time."

"Please, call me Pamela," she replied in the clenched-jawed drawl of the upper classes. "After all, I've known your mother practically all my life. I was so surprised when Bart mentioned that you were coming to the house this morning—imagine, Astrid's daughter working as a lawyer. . . ." She motioned me into the chair opposite hers. On a low table between us lay a basket of needlepoint and a notepad. On it was a long list of names written in the loopy script that seems to be acquired at prep school and subsequently applied to a lifetime of invitations and thank-you notes.

"I am so sorry for your loss," I said, falling back upon convention. "This must be a terrible shock."

"I still can't believe it," she replied, her hands folded quietly in her lap, like a schoolgirl reciting a lesson, ankles crossed. "I always assumed . . . I mean, we always thought it would be his heart that would take him. Bart had a heart attack a few years ago—we almost lost him then. It left him with a serious heart condition, though I know I worried about it more than he did. This morning when he didn't come back from getting the newspaper I was worried that he'd forgotten to take the medication for his heart. I went out in my golf cart to see if he was all right. When I saw his car ... The shock ..." Her face clouded over in recollection, and her voice trailed off. I had assumed that I had been the first one to discover Hexter's body. Obviously, Pamela, coming upon him before me, had been the one to call the police.

"Mrs. Hexter ... Pamela," I said. "I hate to have to bring this up at a time like this, but as I'm sure you know, futures is a very volatile, fast-moving business. I'd like your permission to contact the exchanges today. I'm certain they are going to want to take a look at your husband's trading accounts to make sure there's nothing there that might present a problem."

"Whatever you like."

"To your knowledge, was there anything in your husband's business that was worrying him?" I prodded, gently. "Anything that seemed to be causing him special concern?"

"I have no idea," she replied coldly. "As I told the police, I have never taken even the smallest interest in the day-to-day running of my husband's business." It was clear from her tone of voice that Pamela Hexter felt that the rough and tumble of futures was in some way beneath her.

"So you had no reason to believe there was anything at Hexter Commodities that your husband seemed especially concerned about? He didn't seem anxious or preoccupied?"

"Absolutely not. We had a perfectly normal weekend. We had the children for dinner on Friday night. Saturday we hosted an all-day golf outing at the club. We've done it every year. We play eighteen holes of winter rules to kick off the spring season. It was great fun. Last night we went back to the club for a party. As I told the police, there was nothing unusual or out of the ordinary about our weekend. They need to stop prying into our private life and find the lunatic who did this terrible thing."

"Most people are killed by someone they know," I said, gently. Pamela stiffened, and the light of friendliness went out of her eyes.

"Bart was not most people," she snapped. "It would be ludicrous to suggest that anyone we know would be capable of such a thing. It was obviously a madman, someone who stalks public figures, like that man who killed that singer, what was his name, one of the Beatles—Jack Lennon, wasn't it?"

"John Lennon," I corrected her. Certainly she must realize that her private life was the first place the police were going to look for her husband's killer. I changed the subject.

"Do you have any idea how your husband left his business?"

"Everything is divided among the children," she replied. "Our son, Barton Jr., is the executor. I think it's best if you discuss any business matters with him. I, frankly, couldn't care less."

News of Bart Hexter's death was going to send tremors through the financial world. It would move the markets from London to Tokyo. The assets of Hexter Commodities were worth hundreds of millions of dollars and represented the sum of her husband's life's work. What a legacy, a wife who couldn't care less.

"I was wondering if you'd like me to arrange for

some extra security for you. As you say, your husband was a public figure."

"Do you think we'll be bothered by reporters?" she asked, wide-eyed. "It hadn't occurred to me. But, of course, if you think we'll be troubled by trespassers . . ."

"I'd be happy to make the arrangements," I said. Once the story hit the papers it wouldn't just be reporters she'd have to worry about. Parkland Road would be clogged with gawkers coming for a closer look at the house where Bart Hexter had been murdered. Her doorbell would ring with Realtors dropping by to inquire whether she planned to stay in this big house now that she was all alone. And if she was unlucky, enterprising burglars would pay her a call, hoping to hit the house while the family and staff were all safely at the funeral.

"One more thing," I asked. "Your husband was supposed to give me some business papers this morning, documents related to a potential lawsuit. Would you happen to know where he might have left them?"

"They would be in his study. That's where he kept all of his business things when he was at home. Bart liked to smoke a cigar when he worked. I don't permit smoking in the rest of the house."

"Would you mind if I had a look through his study then?" I asked.

"Go right ahead," she said. "The police were in there already, looking for a suicide note."

"Do you know if they found one?" I ventured, fingers crossed.

"Barton would never have killed himself," replied his widow flatly.

"Not even if he'd gotten himself into trading difficulties?" I pressed.

"You didn't know my husband very well, did you? Otherwise you'd understand what kind of person he was. If Bart had gotten himself into trouble trading, he'd have killed every person who had gotten him there before he'd ever think of killing himself."

Pamela Hexter rang the bell for Elena, the maid, to show me the way to her husband's study.

"I can't imagine what could have become of that girl," snapped Mrs. Hexter as we waited in vain.

I could imagine any number of scenarios. Elena on the phone trying to sell her exclusive story to the *Daily Enquirer*. Elena in the garage flirting with a handsome policeman. Elena on the phone, calling friends, serving up the news of her employer's death while it was still piping hot.

In the end I assured Mrs. Hexter that I would be able to find my own way, but once I got downstairs I regretted my optimism. The house was enormous and confusing, a warren of dimly lit hallways and pointlessly overdecorated rooms. Music room, trophy room, gun room, game room, I passed through them all in my quest for the dead man's study. By the process of elimination, I found a hall that I thought would lead me back to the front of the house, but when I came to the end of it, I found myself, inexplicably, in the kitchen. Large and white, the room was as clean, scrubbed, and brightly lit as a surgical suite. At one end I saw a door to what I supposed must be a butler's pantry. Surely, I thought, that must lead into the dining room, which must be in the main section of the house.

But when I opened the pantry door I found my way blocked by the broad back of Detective Ruskowski. He appeared to be engaged in an argument with someone smaller and more soft spoken than himself. When he turned at the sound of my approach, I was surprised to find that that person was Ken Kurlander.

Kurlander was a partner at my firm, a trust and estates attorney who had spent his long career serving his old-moneyed clients, sheltering their fortunes and shepherding their legacies from one generation to the next. Approaching the firm's mandatory retirement age of seventy, Kurlander looked every inch a prince of the law. White-haired, firm-jawed, he was dressed, as always, in a plain black suit. It was a joke at the office that Kurlander's closet was probably one of the darkest places in Chicago.

To say that Ken Kurlander doesn't like me is to tell only a small portion of the story. Ken has always taken my presence at Callahan Ross as a kind of personal affront. To Kurlander, I am nothing less than a traitor to my class. That I have chosen the frankly mercenary world of corporate law seems especially to gall him. It pains him that I spend my day structuring transactions, negotiating mergers, and representing the likes of Bart Hexter, when I should be at the country club, enjoying the sheer restfulness of my good breeding. I, on the other hand, find Kurlander to be a complete pain in the ass.

"Ken," I demanded, with more candor than tact, "What are you doing here?"

"Pamela called me first thing, poor woman," he replied.

"Funny she'd think to call you first," interjected

Ruskowski, not sounding one bit amused. "Most people's first reaction to discovering that their husband has been murdered is to call the police."

"As I've already explained to you, Officer," replied Kurlander in a tone of weary condescension, "under the circumstances, it was only natural for someone in Mrs. Hexter's position to seek advice. Remember, it was I who instructed Mrs. Hexter to dial 911 as soon as she hung up with me."

"Then why don't you go upstairs and instruct Mrs. Hexter to make herself available to the police. I have some more questions to ask her."

"I must insist, as Mrs. Hexter's attorney," replied Kurlander, puffing himself up with indignation as he spoke, "that Mrs. Hexter not be disturbed any further this morning. Her physician has been called. She has already been questioned, graciously consented to having her house searched, and submitted to being finger-printed. You would think it would be common decency to give someone who's just found her husband murdered a bit of privacy."

I saw Ruskowski look at Kurlander the way he had looked at me right before he launched into his diatribe about the prerogatives of a homicide detective. I took hold of one Kurlander's perfectly laundered cuffs.

"Would you mind, Detective, if I had a word in private with my colleague?" I asked. Ruskowski, disgusted, nodded.

I drew Kurlander into the kitchen where we retreated to the farthest corner to confer in whispers.

"What's the problem?" I demanded. "I just talked to Mrs. Hexter. She's very composed. Why not just let her get it over with?"

"It's not me," replied Kurlander. "It's Pamela. That policeman asked her some impertinent questions, and she's terribly offended. She's called Bob Frackman in the mayor's office. She says that until they send out another policeman, she's not answering any more questions."

"She shouldn't be wasting the cops' time with this shit," I said, struck not for the first time by the incredible pigheadedness of the very rich.

"You have to understand that Pamela is very used to being accommodated in all things," explained my colleague.

"And whatever the police are asking her is going to be nothing compared to the heat she's going to draw in the media until they find out whoever did this. Ken, you're her friend. Do all of us a favor and persuade her to cooperate with the police."

Ruskowski waited for me in the pantry. "Where's pencil neck?" he asked.

"He went to talk to Mrs. Hexter."

"It doesn't take much to get his nose out of joint."

"It's not Kurlander's nose, it's Mrs. Hexter's. It seems that some of your questions upset her."

The homicide detective made a noise that might have been a laugh. "I just asked her when she last had sex with her husband."

"That would do it," I replied.

"It's a routine question," replied Ruskowski. "The answer tells you a lot about a relationship. To your knowledge, were Mr. and Mrs. Hexter happily married?"

"I couldn't say. I didn't know them very well. They

seemed to be. I mean, you'd see their picture together everywhere, smiling from the society pages. And they were still married, which says something. Futures traders usually go through wives as fast as they go through money. The Board of Trade has a dance every year called the Harvest Ball, and you can usually count the number of first wives there on one hand."

"So, do you have any idea who might have wanted him dead?"

"Not specifically, no."

"What's that supposed to mean?"

"How much do you know about futures markets?"

"Not much."

"Futures are what is called a zero-sum game," I said. "For every winner, there is a corresponding loser. Every dollar one person earns is lost by somebody else. Bart Hexter had been winning in the market pretty consistently for thirty years. You don't do that without making a few enemies."

"But you don't know of anyone who bore a grudge against Hexter, someone who might have threatened him or attacked him in the past?"

"No, I don't." I said. "I have to notify the exchanges of his death." I looked at my watch. "Are you trying to keep this away from the media?"

"The district attorney is going to make an announcement at two o'clock, but it's just a matter of time before some sap leaks the story. This is going to be a fucking red ball case. Do you know why cops call them red balls?"

"I'm sure you'll tell me."

"Because when you're working on one you feel like you've been sucked into the center of an ever-expanding ball of flames that's being fanned by everyone from the governor on down. It can burn pretty hot until you bring in the killer. The point I'm trying to make, Miss Millholland, is that you'd better not fuck with me on this. If you do, I'll pull you right into the fire with me."

CHAPTER

3

Futures contracts are traded all around the world—in Singapore and Sydney, in Tokyo and New York—but the big leagues are in Chicago, on the trading floors of the Chicago Board of Trade and the Chicago Mercantile Exchange. It is here, in the frenzied trading pits of the CBOT and the Merc, that world prices are set for agricultural commodities like corn, soybeans, and cattle; metals like gold and platinum; financial instruments like treasury and municipal bonds; and foreign currencies like deutschemarks and yen.

A futures contract is simply an agreement to buy or sell a specified amount of a certain commodity at a date in the future for a price agreed upon today. Originated as a way for farmers to lock in prices for their goods, futures are still an important source of liquidity for agricultural producers. For example, for most of the year, a farmer growing soybeans has his assets tied up in his crop. If he needs money before the harvest, how is he going to get it? Banks require collateral, but who knows what price soybeans are going to fetch five months down the line? Banks, after all, are not in the business of gambling on fluctuations in crop prices.

But the trading pits at the Board of Trade and the Merc are filled with gamblers. Well before harvest time a farmer can contract to sell his crop on one of the futures exchanges at a specified date and price in the future. With the sale price locked in, the bank is happy to lend the money with the futures contract as collateral. In the jargon of the pits, the farmer is a hedger.

Any producer troubled by the possibility of swings in prices can hedge. Exxon, queasy at the threat of a drop in oil prices, hedges oil. Nabisco, worried that a rise in sugar prices will cut into its profits on cookies and Kool-Aid, buys futures contracts to lock in a price for sugar to be bought in the future.

Hedgers are, of course, by necessity, only half of the futures equation. People like Bart Hexter and his clients don't grow soybeans, refine oil, or bake cookies. They couldn't care less about actually owning boxcars of pork bellies or bushels of soybeans. They are gamblers, speculators, if you will. What they want to do is make money. They do that by gambling on the direction that commodity prices will move. They take on the risks the hedgers want to get rid of.

Let's say that last February, Bart Hexter had entered into a contract to purchase $10,000 worth of soybeans to be harvested in October. Assume further that in July, a drought had wiped out half of that season's crop, driving prices up so that same quantity of soybeans would sell for $30,000. Hexter would then have been able to sell his contracts, finding himself $20,000 richer without seeing a single soybean. By gambling successfully on the movement of prices he would have earned a hefty reward.

For a big-stakes gambler there is no better game than

futures. The pace is breakneck, and the stakes are huge. What makes the game even headier is the fact that players need only a small amount of cash relative to the actual value of the contract he or she wishes to buy. To purchase a futures contract a speculator need only make a "margin" deposit of five percent of the value of a contract. The principal is called leverage, and it is the powerful tool that allows a man like Bart Hexter to buy ten thousand dollars' worth of soybeans with only five hundred dollars' cash. The trouble, of course, is that when commodity prices rise dramatically, so do the number of dollars that constitute five percent of the contract price. In the futures game, there is, theoretically, no limit to what you can lose.

I once paid a call on Bart Hexter on a day when he'd made more than $600,000 by riding the surging prices in the soybean market like a surfer riding out a riptide. I'd found him in an expansive mood, enjoying a cigar, and looking particularly sleek and well pleased with himself. He'd talked about the zen of trading, of the cunning and intuition and mastery of fear that he felt was required for long-term success in his trade. He said a lot of things that afternoon, but he concluded with something I couldn't help but remember now.

"In this business," he had said with a laugh, "you eat the bear until the bear eats you."

At the time I took his statement as the natural chest-beating of a man who'd had a very good run in the markets, a man who'd looked ruin in the eye and come up a winner. But that morning, just hours after half of his head had been blown off by a bullet, I found myself wondering who it was who'd invited the bear to breakfast.

* * *

Bart Hexter's study was the *Architectural Digest* version of the executive inner sanctum. The walls were covered with bookshelves filled with handsome, calf-bound volumes that Hexter had surely never read. His desk was vast and laden with a full array of presidential cutlery. There were framed photos and a crystal box brimming with smuggled Cuban cigars. The leather swivel chair stood behind it, high-backed like a throne. A library ladder leaned casually against one wall. Beyond a set of intricately paned French doors lay a long, formal garden. The flower beds had been recently turned and lay moist and brown amid the bright grass like newly dug graves.

I took a seat at Hexter's desk and began, with more than a little self-consciousness, to go through the dead man's things. First the piles of papers stacked carelessly on the surface. I found memos and letters, mostly concerning matters of administration at one or the other of the two futures exchanges. Both the CBOT and the Merc are largely self-governing entities, and Hexter was heavily involved in both. There was a thick file pertaining to a proposal to revise the procedure for time coding trades at the CBOT, documents related to Globex, the relatively new twenty-four-hour computer trading system, and a sheaf of correspondence related to the scheduled opening of a second trading floor, sometime in the summer at the Merc.

And then there were bundles of envelopes, bound together with rubber bands, and largely unopened, that looked to be statements from various bank and brokerage accounts. Hexter, it seemed, was a little behind in his mail. I foresaw good times for Kurlander, trying to settle the estate.

I turned my attention to the drawers. They were filled with the usual supplies—pencils, notepads, rubber bands, stamps—all neatly and impersonally arranged. In one drawer Hexter kept buy and sell tickets, and order forms from both exchanges. In another, weather forecasting charts, rolled and banded together. Finally, I found something useful. In a bottom drawer, amid the social directories of half a dozen clubs, were two thin pamphlets listing the home phone numbers of all the members of the Chicago Board of Trade and the Chicago Mercantile Exchange.

The first call I made was to Ricky Sullivan, the current chairman of the CBOT, and a boyhood friend of Hexter's. I caught him just as he was leaving for church. He agreed to set up a meeting at the Board of Trade at noon. Sullivan, it was clear, was shocked by the news of his friend's death, but he had wasted no time indulging it. There would be time for grieving later, for meandering discussions of mortality over a couple of stiff drinks at Butch McGuire's when the trading day was done. But until Ricky Sullivan could be certain that Black Bart hadn't gotten himself into the kind of corner you only get out of with a bullet, his overriding response to the news of his old friend's death was going to be fear.

After a methodical search of Bart Hexter's study I turned up nothing pertaining to the CFTC matter save a pink message slip at the bottom of an otherwise empty briefcase that read: Sunday, 8 A.M., Kate Millholland. There was, however, one drawer in the desk that was locked, so I wandered the Elizabethan halls of Hexter's creepy mansion until I encountered sullen-faced Elena, who agreed to inquire of her mistress where the keys might be. She returned a few minutes later with a bunch of keys on a ring.

It took me a couple of tries, but I eventually found the key that fit the drawer. When I opened it, I was disappointed. The drawer contained little of value or interest: some loose change in a small, shallow tin that had once contained hard candy, a roll of first-class stamps and another for overseas airmail, four cigars—Montclairs—each packed in its own cream-colored sarcophagus, and a cardboard box. I lifted the lid and found it filled to the brim with Bart Hexter's personal stationery. Puzzled, I pushed the drawer closed, and sat staring blankly at the top of Bart Hexter's desk. An array of handsome toddlers stared back at me from their silver frames—Hexter's grandchildren, I assumed.

I had been at it for almost an hour and had found nothing at all. No hint of a financial scandal, no threatening letters, nothing at all of a personal nature. All very well and good, but what troubled me was the absence of material pertaining to the CFTC investigation of Hexter Commodities. It was, I knew, compared to murder, a minor matter. But he had promised to give me all the documents this morning. So where were they?

I picked up the bunch of keys, intending to return them to the maid, but my unanswered questions stopped me. Why on earth would anyone bother to lock up a handful of change, two rolls of stamps, and a box of letter paper, I wondered? Why lock up Montclairs when there was a box crammed with Cuban cigars sitting on top of the desk? I weighed the keys in my hand for a minute, considering, then returned to the drawer and opened it up again.

I opened the plastic cigar containers. Inside I found cigars. I took the box of stationery out and set it on the desk. I removed the lid and found Hexter's letter paper. I lifted it out. Beneath it lay another box.

The money was the first thing that caught my eye—a wad of cash three fingers thick, fastened at the middle with a red rubber band. I picked it up. The bills were all hundreds. I counted until I lost patience—more than $30,000. I turned my attention to the other item in the box—a yellow envelope, five inches by eight.

I laid the envelope on my lap. I put the smaller, empty box back into the larger box and laid the stationery on top, just as I'd found it. I set the money on the desk and closed the drawer. Then I opened the envelope.

Inside were pictures, very different from those of the cherubic toddlers that grinned back at me from the desk-top. I saw more than a dozen in all, black-and-white snapshots, all of the same person, a young woman in her late twenties who wasn't wearing any clothes.

In the first one she was on all fours with her bottom foremost to the camera as she struck an almost feline pose. She looked back over her shoulder toward the camera so that only one eye and the bridge of her nose were visible. Her body was lithe, her hair, long and dark. These, I concluded after flipping through them all, were not the slick product of a professional photographer trying to coax erotica out of a bored model. There was an air of intimacy about them, and the amateurish hand of family photos.

And yet, whoever it was, had allowed herself to be

photographed in all the centerfold poses: back arched, with one hand covering her face in mock ecstasy, the other reaching down between her legs; standing, legs apart, turned away from the camera and bent at the waist so that her dark hair hung to the ground. . . .

It was clear that it was not the woman's face that the photographer had been intent on capturing. There was not one frame in which it was fully visible. And so I sat, looking. Repelled and fascinated, trying unsuccessfully to discern her identity, wondering who had been at the other end of the lens.

When the door handle turned I jumped a foot out of my chair.

"I didn't mean to startle you," stammered the dead man's son, Barton Jr., apologetically.

Quickly, I slipped the photos back into the envelope.

The last time I'd seen Barton Jr. I was nine years old, and he and my brother Teddy were stealing bourbon out of my father's liquor cabinet. Back then he'd been a gangly teenager who'd peered down at me from under a mop of unkempt black hair, dressed in bell-bottoms and a grimy T-shirt, with a scraggly and unsuccessful attempt at a beard.

Time had conspired to turn him into his father. Barton now wore his jet-black hair short, and it was beginning a slow and inexorable retreat from his forehead. He had his father's eyes, the same fair skin, and bushy brows. He was slighter than his father, less burly, and there was a trace of mischief in him that even grief could not completely suppress. Still, the resemblance was eerie.

But the similarities between the two men were purely

physical. Black Bart had grown up with nothing and spent a lifetime trying to put as many dollars as possible between himself and his impoverished beginnings. Barton Jr. had grown up in a sea of materialism and had chosen a path for himself where money and possessions counted for very little.

A professor of theoretical mathematics at Northwestern University, Dr. Barton Hexter, Jr., was an expert in the emerging field of chaos theory, which focuses on the modeling of large, complex systems. While futures markets represent one such system, Barton's interest in his father's business had, much to the elder Hexter's dismay, never gone beyond the academic.

"Ken Kurlander told me I should try to find you," he said after I'd expressed my condolences. "He said you'd want to talk to me."

"I hate to be the one to do this," I began, very conscious of the fact that it was my job to lay a very large burden on the shoulders of a man who had, just an hour ago, learned that his father had been brutally murdered. "I know that Ken will be meeting with all of you in the next day or so to discuss the details of your father's will, but in the meantime, your mother said that you are the executor of the estate."

"I know. Ken told me," he replied. "So what does that mean?"

"Quite a lot of things," I answered slowly. "But right now it means that you're the one who has to call the shots when it comes to Hexter Commodities."

Barton Jr. took a minute to let that one sink in. Hexter Commodities was worth hundreds of millions of dollars. This was not going to be like stepping in and running the family dry-cleaning business.

"I am not a businessman," he said, finally, in a hollow voice.

"You'll have lots of people to help you," I said. "Me, your father's employees, Ken Kurlander. The problem, of course, is that futures is a fast business. There are things that have to be done today, decisions to be made over the next seventy-two hours that can't be postponed, decisions with long-term consequences."

Barton Jr. looked grim.

"I've already contacted the exchanges," I continued. "I have a meeting set up with Ricky Sullivan at noon to go through your father's trading accounts, just to be certain there are no surprises."

"You mean nothing that someone would want to kill him for."

"Among other things. Do you want to come along?"

"No, I think I'm needed here."

"I'm confident I can handle everything," I said. "If not, I'll call you. The exchanges are going to insist that we liquidate your father's positions as quickly as possible."

"But we can't do that until we're sure he's not offsetting himself in other markets," interjected Barton Jr. "I know that lots of times Dad would offset purchases in Chicago with equivalent contracts in Hong Kong." I heard a chorus of quiet hallelujahs. If Barton Jr. knew enough to be worried about offsetting or spread positions, there was a good chance that he and I and Hexter Commodities would survive the weeks ahead.

"With your approval, I'd like to try to get the exchanges to agree to a gradual liquidation schedule, depending on the positions your father was holding, possibly over a week or ten days. That will give us a chance to look for warehouse receipts or confirmation slips from other markets. Do you have any idea where those things might be kept?"

"The person who'd know is my cousin Tim. He was my father's assistant."

"Do you have his phone number?" I asked. "I'd also like to have someone call the people who worked for your dad, spare them hearing about this on the news."

"I don't think you'll be able to reach Tim until dinnertime today. He belongs to a bicycle touring club. They take long rides every Sunday. It's a family joke, every Sunday Tim runs away from Dad. No phones. It's how he stays sane."

"Do you think that your father's head trader might know? Carl Savage? Ricky Sullivan said he'd call him and get him to the meeting."

"I guess so. This is all so strange," he burst out suddenly. "I keep expecting to hear his voice calling me from somewhere else in the house. It's terrifically unreal. When my sister Krissy heard the news she collapsed. They had to sedate her. And yet Mother is upstairs calmly making lists of people to ask back to the house after the funeral. I haven't even been able to reach my wife, Jane. She took the children up to Wisconsin to visit her parents for the weekend. When I called she'd already left to come back home. I had to leave her a note on the kitchen table, but I didn't know what to write. She's eight months' pregnant. I don't want her to be alone when she finds out. I don't want her to hear it on the car radio while she's driving the kids. . . ." His voice trailed off miserably.

Suddenly, the door banged open and a young woman

burst into the room in a flurry of dark hair and jangling bracelets.

"Oh God, Barton," she exclaimed, throwing herself onto him.

"Margot," replied her brother. It was more a statement than a greeting.

Margot Hexter was just a year younger than her brother, but she had an air of immaturity about her that made her seem much younger. She was pretty, in an unusual way, with torrents of curly dark hair and her father's big brown eyes. She was dressed like the graduate student that she was, in a wrinkled T-shirt with the slogan: 'Take Back the Night,' tattered jeans, and a pair of Birkenstock sandals with heavy socks.

"I can't believe it!" exclaimed Margot, apparently oblivious to my presence. "When Krissy called to tell me, it was just amazing. Somebody shot him. Isn't it too much? It's so incredible. Daddy's dead. The relief, the freedom. All the clichés are true. A weight has been lifted; I feel ten feet tall. It's making me dizzy."

"Margot!" exclaimed her brother, horrified. "I wish you'd stop saying the first thing that just pops into your head. Especially in front of other people."

Margot turned around and peered at me like a child seeing a particularly interesting animal at the zoo.

"Who are you?" she demanded.

"Kate Millholland. I was your father's attorney."

"So you're the one who's going to tell us how much?"

"Pardon me?"

"How much money. I thought that's what lawyers do when somebody rich dies. You know, come to the house and read the will."

"I was your father's corporate counsel," I replied in what was intended to be a repressive voice. "I represent Hexter Commodities."

"Jesus Jones. A corporate lawyer. How dull." She plopped down on the couch and addressed herself to her brother. "So who do you think murdered dear old Dad?"

"No one knows what's happened yet," answered Barton, sounding genuinely pained. "The police are investigating."

"Don't go all pompous on me," said Margot. "What's so terrible? The old monster's dead, and we get all his money. You know, the only thing I find really shocking is that he was shot. I mean, frankly, I thought for sure they'd find him naked, in bed with sixteen-year-old twins, and with a pair of scissors in his back."

CHAPTER

4

Once Margot had been successfully prevailed upon to go upstairs to see her mother, I turned the currency I'd found in his father's drawer over to Barton Jr. By anybody's standards it was a lot of money, especially in cash, but for Barton Jr. it was clearly something more. The bullets that had killed his father had, by plan or accident, changed everything for him. Still reeling from the news, with grief so freshly upon him, he couldn't see it yet. But events had placed him at the helm of a vast fortune, one that touched a great many lives. He stood for a time, quietly weighing the stack of bills in his hand, the first tangible sign of the responsibilities that would soon be heaped upon him.

I kept the pictures. Barton had been dealt enough for one day. But I was reluctant to return them to the drawer. Who knows who would be next to stumble across them? Rightfully, they should be turned over to the police. But I found the idea repellent. I remembered how Ruskowski had managed to turn even routine questions into leering insults. How was he going to make Pamela Hexter feel when he asked her about the nude pictures that had turned up in her husband's desk?

I thought about asking Kurlander for his advice, but the thought of discussing pornographic photographs with the senior partner from trusts and estates gave me the willies. Besides, I knew what he would say—burn them, suppress them, do anything but turn them over to the police. The pictures are unpleasant, and it's our job to see to it that unpleasantness is swept under the rug. With this in mind, I sealed them in an envelope along with a hastily scribbled note describing where I'd found them. I gave the envelope to the first policeman I saw with instructions to give them to Detective Ruskowski.

I hadn't realized how glad I'd be to escape the strained atmosphere of the dead man's house. The reactions of his family to the strange crucible of death had seemed odd. But then again, who knew what constituted normal behavior in the wake of such a tragedy?

In the car, on my way to my meeting at the Board of Trade, I called Elliott Abelman. Elliott was a private detective and the first person I could think of who might be able to arrange for protection for the Hexter family. I reached him at home and related the morning's events.

"Talk about being the attorney to the rich and famous," he exclaimed.

"I'm afraid now it's going to be rich and infamous."

"You can say that again. You said he was shot. Did he kill himself?"

"I don't know. He was behind the wheel of his Rolls Royce wearing a pair of red satin pajamas with two bullets in his head."

"Not an outfit I'd choose for my au revoir. Was he connected with organized crime?"

"I don't know. Do you think he might have been?"

"Everyone says that the mafia launders money through the exchanges, but I haven't heard anything specific about Hexter. You have to admit that getting it in the head at the end of your own driveway sounds like a professional hit. Do the police have any suspects?"

"If they do, they aren't telling me."

"Well, I'm sure that Hexter's pissed off a fair number of people over the years. I never believed that pious family man crap. You know, Mr. Philanthropy. You don't make the kind of money he did without screwing people."

"In futures everybody screws everybody else," I sighed. "Try telling me something I don't know already."

The Board of Trade was deserted on a Sunday, the art deco lobby of polished marble presided over by one bored security guard who took my name without raising his head from the sports page. I took the elevator, its doors emblazoned with bronze sheaves of wheat, to the fourteenth floor.

If futures are a game, then it is the Clearing Corporation that makes it possible for the game to be played. Futures contracts are traded face-to-face in a system called open outcry. Traders literally scream to each other across the crowded trading pit, communicating their intentions to buy or sell by a combination of shouting and hand signals, like bookies at an English racetrack. Silos of wheat, boxcars of cattle, hundreds of thousands of dollars all change hands in a split second, often acknowledged by no more than a single word or gesture. There is no time to consider whether the person on the other side of the trade has the money or the actual commodity to complete the transaction.

The Clearing Corporation makes the question of creditworthiness irrelevant to those on the floor by inserting itself in the middle of every transaction. Acting as a sort of central bank, the clearinghouse buys simultaneously from the seller and sells to the buyer. The clearinghouse, by necessity, keeps track of every trade and requires clearing members of the exchange to maintain capital reserves in proportion to the risks assumed in the market.

The head of the Clearing Corporation was a man named Kent Rush. His office was a masterpiece of authority designed to instill confidence in the unwary and convey a sense of unimpeachable integrity, especially to those harboring suspicions that his job, when you came right down to it, was to preside over a glorified gambling den. His desk was even flanked by flags, just like in the Oval Office. Off to one side was a discreet private door for times when escape might serve better than confrontation.

Kent shook my hand, and Ricky Sullivan, the chairman of the exchange, nodded in greeting from his seat on the couch. He was on the phone, rolling calls, breaking the news of Bart Hexter's death, trolling for rumors that might link the murdered trader to trouble. Rush motioned me into a chair and handed me the most up-to-date listing of Hexter's personal holdings. The paper was still warm from its passage through the laser printer.

I had barely begun looking through it when Carl Savage arrived. Savage was a transplanted Texan in his mid-thirties. He was broad-shouldered and bull-necked, and the wide planes of his face were smooth below small, steel blue eyes that were hooded with caution. He wore his dark hair long, slicked back from his forehead into a ponytail that brushed his belt in back.

Hexter's chief of trading operations shook hands all around, accepting murmured condolences before settling down to the task of reviewing the positions his boss had been holding over the weekend. Ricky Sullivan joined us, and we went through them trade by trade, the three men slipping easily into the jargon of the pits. Hexter was big in January wheat, trading the crush in soybeans, and naked short in deutschemarks.

I tried to force myself to follow their discussion, but I found myself seized by an overpowering fatigue, very similar to the vast sleepiness that used to overcome me in geometry class. It struck me still, whenever I was forced into any extensive discussion of accounting. Over time I'd trained myself to feign an alert interest, but my heart was never going to be in the numbers.

Even if the details made my eyes glaze, the big picture that emerged was reassuring—Bart Hexter's holdings were large and complex, but there was nothing in his trades that set off alarm bells of suspicion. Kent Rush, after much analysis, pronounced the dead man's reserves to be adequate relative to his exposure in the markets, and we all breathed a sigh of relief.

When the subject turned to the liquidation of Hexter's trading accounts I sprang to life. I knew that the exchange would insist that all of Bart Hexter's holdings be sold as soon as possible. Such liquidation was a policy of the exchange. But Bart Hexter was no hundred-grand-a-year scalper. In several commodities Hexter held such large positions that selling them too quickly might dramatically destabilize prices in those commodities. There, too, was the real possibility that Hexter was offsetting some of his futures positions with physicals, holding inventories of actual commodities to counter his position in the market or with offshore trades. I didn't want to rush to liquidate completely until we had a chance to unearth warehouse receipts, trade confirmations, and other documents.

In the end there was less haggling than I'd anticipated. I think that the relief of not discovering anything hideous in Hexter's trades mellowed everyone. In the end we agreed to a five-day liquidation in everything but soybeans, where the sheer size of Hexter's position made an eight-day schedule necessary.

The offices of Hexter Commodities were wrapped in the abandoned silence of the weekend. The warren of cubbyholes that normally teemed with brokers and clerks was empty, the Quotron screens that circled the boardroom were blank. Savage unlocked the door to his office near the trading desks and cleared a chair for me. He pulled two scratched tumblers and a bottle of scotch from a bottom drawer. Without a word he filled them both and handed one to me. "To the dead," he said, raising his glass in a toast. "May they rest in peace." We touched glasses.

I don't usually drink before dinner on a Sunday, especially when I haven't had breakfast, but I knocked mine back in one swallow. It had been that sort of day.

"The police called my house before I left," said Savage, refilling his glass. "They want to come here tomorrow, talk to me and the rest of the employees about

Bart. I guess they're trying to figure out who'd want to kill him."

"That's their job," I answered. "Do you have any ideas?"

"No. The man was a bastard. On any given day I wouldn't have trusted half the people who work here with a gun, myself included. But hell, in this business it doesn't matter if you're an asshole. As a matter of fact it probably helps. The only thing that matters is that you make money, and Bart made plenty of that."

"So everyone says. He put together one of the longest successful runs in the business. What was his secret?"

"Now that's something *I* would have killed for," replied Savage with a rueful grin. "I don't know what it was. Loretta, who heads our clearing operation, had a nickname for him. She called him Savant, as in idiot savant—you know, like in the movie *Rain Man*. A person who's retarded but has this one incredible talent, like being able to play the piano or speak Latin."

"Did she call him that to his face?"

"Loretta? Shit, yeah. Loretta wasn't afraid of Bart. What a frigging genius. The man hadn't read a book since high school, didn't give a fuck if the world was flat or round, couldn't figure out how to use his computer no matter how many times we tried to teach him, but when it came to trading—anything that had to do with numbers—you couldn't touch him.

"You'll see technical traders in the pits, guys who work for the big firms like CRT, studying their multicolored charts. Shit, Hexter used to do calculations like that in his head. He had a photographic memory for numbers. He never had to look up a phone number. If he dialed it once he knew it forever. He could multiply twelve digits in his head faster than you could turn on a calculator. . . ."

"And now that the master trader is dead?" I interjected.

"You're the lawyer. You tell me."

"What will the brokerage customers do when they hear about it?" I countered. The business of Hexter Commodities divided itself neatly into thirds. Thirty-three percent of the firm's business was brokerage—trades made for individuals or companies that traded futures contracts much as some people traded stocks. Another third was an operation that cleared the trades of small traders, known as locals, who made their money gambling on small price movements. Hexter Commodities guaranteed and processed their trades, charging a flat fee for each transaction. The final third of the firm's business consisted of trades made for Bart Hexter's personal account. Once those positions were liquidated, the brokerage and clearing operations would represent the entire value of Hexter Commodities.

"As soon as they hear he's dead," replied Savage, "ninety percent will move their accounts someplace else unless we give them a reason not to."

"What do you suggest?"

"Who owns the company now?"

"My understanding is that everything was left to the children. His son, Barton Jr., is executor."

"Barton Jr.?" Savage helped himself to another finger of scotch. He rolled a little bit in his mouth for a minute while he considered. "Any chance he'll come in and run the company?"

"I have no idea," I said. "Right now he's trying to get used to the idea that his father is dead. The man's a professor of theoretical mathematics, and from what I gather he's a pretty big deal in his field."

"I know. But he's the one person who really could take over for his old man. He'd do it differently, but he'd do it."

"I don't know what his plans are. We're going to have to give him some time."

"Time is money," snapped Savage. "Especially in this business. What happens if the market takes a big jump tomorrow?"

"What if Barton decides he wants to sell the company?"

"You know and I know," replied Savage in his grave, Texas drawl, "that if the customers pull their accounts, there'll be next to nothing left *to* sell."

Reluctant to return to Lake Forest and the grieving Hexter family, I took the scenic route north on Lake Shore Drive to Sheridan Road. The rest of Chicago, it seemed, was out enjoying the first full-blown day of spring. People had broken out their baseball bats and their Frisbees, let their dogs off the leash, all drawn to the emerald band of parks that fringed Lake Michigan. On the bike path, cyclists, as common as bumblebees in the good weather, jockeyed with runners and Rollerbladers. I wondered whether Bart Hexter's assistant, Tim, was among them, ignorantly enjoying the cloudless day, unaware of his uncle's death.

The fact that I'd been there so soon after it happened, had seen his body, made it hard to put Hexter's death in perspective, much less set it aside. I found myself dwelling on it, replaying my encounters with Ruskowski, rolling them out again and again like some inner movie. But the truth was, to me it really shouldn't matter who killed Bart Hexter. As long as there was no connection with Hexter Commodities, no impending losses or trading improprieties, I had to be content with letting the police do their job while I focused my energies on doing mine.

But attorneys are not immune from curiosity—quite the contrary—and it was hard to deny the appeal of the crime. Bart Hexter was a name, a public man who had held himself out as an example of the triumph of discipline, hard work, and family values. The sort of man meant to die in bed, surrounded by his sobbing family. Carl Savage had said that Hexter was an asshole to work for. Even if that were true, people don't, as a rule, get themselves shot for being assholes. If they did, this town would be knee-deep in corpses. There had to be some other reason. Unfortunately, until they found one, the press and the police—I couldn't tell which one was worse—would hound the Hexter family without mercy.

I found the Hexters in the minstrel-galleried great room, huddled around a drinks cart, indulging in an early and awkward cocktail hour. Pamela Hexter sat on the couch, a drink near at hand, working on a piece of needlepoint. By the door, on a hard chair, removed from the rest of the family, sat a large, damp-looking young man in full Tour de France regalia. Tim Hexter, his beefy thighs encased in black cycling shorts, looked remarkably ill at ease in the company of his closest relatives.

Barton Jr., seeming positively relieved at my intrusion, rose hastily to his feet and introduced me to the other members of his family. His wife, Jane, pale and very pregnant, struggled out of her chair to meet me. Krissy, his younger sister, a spoiled blonde in her mid-twenties, acknowledged the introduction with a weary lack of interest. Her husband, Fourey Chilcote offered up a distracted, "Good to know you." The Chilcotes, I knew, lived on the property in the old Manderson house. I wondered why I hadn't seen either of them earlier that day.

I declined Barton's offer of a drink, cast a yearning glance at a bowl of peanuts, and withdrew with Barton to an adjacent sitting room. At a nod from Barton Jr., Tim Hexter shuffled after us. With his uncomprehending, bovine features, he reminded me sharply of a dim but loyal dog who'd recently discovered its master dead.

I spread the printout of Bart Hexter's positions on a low cocktail table, explaining the liquidation schedule I'd negotiated with the exchange.

Most of what I said, I knew, was not sinking in. Both Barton Jr. and his cousin Tim were in a kind of emotional shock, blocking out the world in the hopes of regaining an inner equilibrium.

"So there's nothing here that looks like it's connected with what happened?" asked Barton, finally, like someone straining to see through the fog.

"Nothing. But that doesn't mean something won't turn up later. Carl Savage is over at the Merc right now going through your father's trades on the other exchange."

"Dad had seats everywhere, the Merc, the NYFE, the COMEX, even the smaller exchanges like the Mid-America, but he only traded customer accounts there. When he traded his own account, he preferred to trade what he knew best—wheat, corn and soybeans—always at the CBOT."

"Savage says that the brokerage customers will pull their accounts as soon as they learn of your father's death. He wants you to come in and call the trades."

"Me?" cried Barton Jr. "No way. I'm not a business-man."

"It would be only temporary, until another arrangement could be made."

"I've got my own work to do—classes to teach, my research. I have to give mid-terms next week. I can't just drop everything because of this."

"I'm sorry to be pushing you, especially today of all days. But the markets will open as usual tomorrow morning."

"You sound just like Kurlander," snapped Barton, springing angrily to his feet. "Dumping all of this on me whether I like it or not. If I'd wanted to go into the futures business I would have gone into it. I don't care about the money. I like my life the way it is. I don't want that kind of responsibility."

"So if you won't do it, who should I get to direct the show?" I asked, the way you'd talk to a small child who was insisting on something unreasonable. "Carl Savage says he doesn't want the responsibility either. His job is basically making sure the orders get filled, seeing that there are no slip ups between the brokers, the runners, and the traders." In a deliberate ploy, I turned to Tim. "Do you think you can carry the ball until we find a more permanent solution?" I demanded.

Tim half rose to his feet, blushing and stammering in panic.

"N-n-no. Not me. I'm really just an errand boy. I

tried trading once, a couple of years ago. The only thing I was good at was losing money."

"Everybody else at Hexter Commodities is in sales," I bore on, relentlessly making my point. "They're just brokers—guys who call dentists in Dubuque and convince them there's a fortune to be made trading futures. I'm sorry if I sound like Kurlander, but when you come right down to it—your father left it to you."

"And I don't want it," Barton Jr. bitterly replied.

"Look at this," I said picking up the top page of the Clearinghouse printout. "One hundred and seventy-four contracts to buy eight hundred seventy thousand bushels of January wheat at fifteen thousand dollars a contract. That's a commitment of two million six hundred and ten thousand dollars in just one market. If the price drops by just five cents, that's a four hundred and thirty thousand dollar loss. Now you tell me. Who do you want making these decisions?"

CHAPTER
5

Living in Hyde Park is one of my continuing acts of rebellion against my family. Here, in the neighborhood that surrounds the University of Chicago, Nobel prize winners, students, and scholars from all over the world go about their business alongside bookies, policemen, petty thieves, welfare cheats, and the adherents of resuscitated African religions. Within its boundaries there are quadrangles of medieval splendor, squat and squalid public housing blocks, mansions, and museums. Here complex drugs are developed in high-tech laboratories while junkies ply the rougher end of the pharmaceutical trade in vacant lots.

I share an apartment with Claudia Stein, a friend from college who is a surgical resident at the University of Chicago Hospitals. Like all the buildings on our stretch of Hyde Park Blvd., ours was built in the '20s and meant to be grand. The rooms are huge with twelve-foot ceilings and the kind of architectural detail that makes yuppie rehabbers swoon. The people who come after us, no doubt, will do it justice—put in a new kitchen, strip the woodwork, redo the floors and make them shine. In the meantime, Claudia and I have just plunked down our odd assortment of hand-me-down furniture and called it home.

I let myself in and headed straight for the kitchen, propelled as much by optimism as hunger. I opened the refrigerator door and was repaid by the vision of two bottles of Evian water, a clove of garlic of uncertain provenance (since neither Claudia nor I had ever, to my knowledge, actually cooked) and a half-full bottle of wine. I knew better than to look in the freezer.

I cracked open one of the bottles of water and wandered into the living room to check the answering machine for messages.

"Katharine Anne Prescott Millholland, this is your mother," came the voice after the squeal of the rewinding tape. Mother's voice never carried much affection, but whenever she used all of my names I knew I was in trouble. I sat down in a fat armchair, my spine prickling with reflexive dread. "I just had a telephone conversation with your friend, Stephen Azorini," continued my mother's recorded voice. "Imagine my surprise when I discovered that you hadn't bothered to invite him to dinner this evening. How could you be so thoughtless?"

Her question was rhetorical, but there was an answer. I had called Stephen earlier in the week to invite him—no, beg him—to join me for dinner at my parents', but he'd been in L.A. on business when I called. When he called back I was in Phoenix negotiating an acquisition for Cragar Industries, and when I came back Bart Hexter drove me so crazy canceling meetings that I just forgot. . . .

Stephen's voice came next, after the beep: "Hi, Kate. Looks like I stepped in it with your mother. It seems she's expecting us for dinner. I have a meeting with the head of the hematology research division, but I can pick you up at six forty-five. I hope I didn't get you into too much trouble. See you."

I looked at my watch. It was twenty minutes to six. I stripped off my clothes as I listened to the rest of the day's messages—someone for Claudia trying to sell prepaid burial plots, a reporter from *Knight Ridder* and another from *The Wall Street Journal*, both looking for quotes about Hexter.

I didn't really have time to run, but I plucked a pair of sweatpants and a ratty T-shirt from the pile on the floor of my closet anyway. Then I laced up my shoes and headed out the door at a sprint. I cut across the park to the pedestrian bridge at Fifty-first Street and picked up the bike path that followed the lake. The park was still thick with people, though the retreating sunshine had left the air chilly. I ran south, dodging cyclists around the rocky peninsula known as the Point, and then across the footbridge at the Fifty-seventh Street Beach. There, with a view of weary tourists dragging their exhausted children through the parking lot of the Museum of Science and Industry, I forced myself to do ten sets of stairs as fast as I could. Then, sides heaving, I stretched it out for the six remaining blocks between me and home.

I took a much shorter shower than I would have liked and, out of a sense of deprivation mingled with mounting dread, I poured myself a Chivas on the rocks. Dripping and wrapped in a towel, I picked my way through the war zone of my closet, searching for something to wear. For safety, I chose a pair of black wool trousers and a blouse of white silk. By the time Stephen rang the bell I was dressed, brushed, and after two scotches, halfway resigned to dinner at my parents' house.

I answered the door, and Stephen walked in like he enters every room—as if he owns the place. Stephen always seems to walk in a spotlight. Six feet five, with his dark hair and chiseled profile, he has long grown used to attention. As the president of his own pharmaceutical company, he has learned to use his looks, and the power of his personality, to his advantage.

Stephen and I have been drifting in and out of each other's lives since high school. And there are times when I've felt the impact of his appearance at low ebb. But there is always someone who brings his looks back into focus. Women stare at him in the street. Waitresses stammer inanely in restaurants. Men look at the two of us and I see in their faces what they are thinking—he could do much better than her.

While there is no denying the physical attraction, ours is primarily a relationship of convenience. Both of our lives are filled with work and neither of us has the patience for the vagaries of dating and nascent relationships. We have fallen into this pattern of accommodation, caught in that strange space between friend and lover. His secretary calls my secretary. They pull out our calendars and agree that the Kidney Foundation Benefit is doable on the fifteenth, but I'll be in Brussels on the nineteenth when Stephen is entertaining the Azor lipid chemists and their wives. I often learn of these engagements from the typewritten schedule Cheryl, my secretary, leaves on my desk every morning. While these evenings often end in bed, Cheryl continues to worry about the lack of romance in my life. Recently she has taken to preceding Stephen's name on my appointment sheet with a small red heart.

Stephen stretched his long legs out on the battered sofa and helped himself to a joint from a small box of rose-colored marble that, along with a book on botany that belonged to Claudia, collected dust on the coffee table.

"This is your last one," he announced, wetting it absently and lighting a match. He passed it to me, but I shook my head.

"I'm working on this," I said, indicating my tumbler of scotch.

"You must be the only person who has to get drunk before she goes home to see her mother."

"That," I replied, "is because there is only one Astrid Millholland. It'll just take me two minutes to put on some makeup."

"You don't need makeup," Stephen said, pulling me into his lap. The electricity we generate always catches me by surprise. I don't know from what deep well it springs. But my lack of understanding doesn't temper my appreciation. As the last button of my silk blouse yielded, I had the fleeting hope that Claudia was at the hospital and not on her way home. But by then the bulk of my inhibitions had been dissolved in scotch—the rest battered away by the bizarre stresses of Bart Hexter's death—so I didn't even suggest that we adjourn to the bedroom.

Like the Hexter children, I, too, grew up in a house set well beyond the view of casual passersby. A high stone wall forms the perimeter of the property, and a second barrier of evergreens must be passed before the house, red brick and Georgian, comes into view. My parents' house is an architect's triumph, large, graceful, and filled with beautiful things. In the years since I left it, I have gained the distance to appreciate my mother's eye, her energy, and the skill it takes to acquire the perfect piece—the right painting, a unique item of furniture. From the vantage of an independent life I can understand the accomplishment of creating a setting of such beauty. But my perception is always clouded by the memory of angry words, alcoholic scenes, and furious denials.

My father met us at the door, an ever-present gin and tonic in his hand. He pecked my cheek and took Stephen's hand. Stephen, I knew, tolerated my mother but felt real affection for Dad. Mother, on the other hand, tolerated Stephen only because I had managed to demonstrate to her that I was capable, in her eyes at least, of doing much worse. After all, I'd married a man named Russell Dubrinski, forcing her to stand shoulder to shoulder in a receiving line with an immigrant tailor and his wife.

We followed Dad into the library where he mixed us drinks. I pounced on a platter of cheese and crackers while Stephen and my father flipped through the channels from baseball to hockey to basketball and back again.

"You know that cheese is full of fat," said my mother archly from the door.

"Then why do you serve it?" I countered. I couldn't remember a time when we had been able to speak without sparring.

My mother is a beautiful woman, occupied fully in the job of being Astrid Millholland. She gives tirelessly of herself to philanthropic causes, makes dressing well into an art, and tends the mirror with frightening discipline. After twenty-nine years of marriage she still weighs, to the pound, what she did on her wedding day. Her skin is fine and flawless. Her wide eyes sparkle. Her signature mane of chestnut hair, swept back from her forehead, is still glossy, thick, and infinitely more stylish than mine.

"I know we're just family, but you might have taken the time to put on a little bit of makeup," admonished Mother. "I can't believe you let Stephen see you like that."

"Can we please go into dinner?" I asked, turning toward my father. "I haven't eaten all day."

These family evenings are prone to strange turns, especially since my little sister, Beth, departed for boarding school. It's as if my mother, the polished veteran of a thousand dinner parties, has no notion of how to converse with someone who is not wearing a tuxedo. So we sit among the silver and the Spode, struggling to fill in the gaps between appetizer and dessert.

Through the soup Mother brought us up to date on her latest decorating project—a complete overhaul of the living room, music room, and solarium.

"I know it will shock people," she confided, "but I've decided to try a new decorator. Mimi Ashford is so *done*. One of her rooms is like a shirt with 'Chanel' on the front. I can tell right away when I walk into a room if Mimi's had a hand in it. There are certain signatures, things that she does in every room the same way, like those elaborate swags and tails for draperies we have in the music room now. Besides, she's terribly strict. While we were having lunch together I said that I thought it would be wonderful if we could have someplace in the living room to put a drink down. Mimi just looked me in the eye and said: 'No coffee tables, period.' That's why I'm trying a new decorator—Gordon something or other. Binnie Wadsworth swears by him, and at least he doesn't seem so bossy. Besides, he should find his schedule a lot freer after today. I know he was set to redo the ballroom at the Hexters'. I can't believe that Pamela will be going ahead with that now."

"Have you heard the news?" asked my father, turning to Stephen. "It seems someone's gone and shot Bart Hexter. Killed him dead at the end of his driveway."

"Miriam called me this afternoon and told me the news," replied Mother. "It seems one of her maids has a sister who works for the Hexters—you know, these foreign servants are all related. I think it's scandalous how bold these thieves are becoming. Miriam is talking about getting an electric fence and calling one of those companies that rents attack dogs."

"I don't think he was shot by a burglar," I said.

"What makes you say that?" demanded Mother. "Miriam has it from Sissy Linder that there's been a ring of thieves positively casing this neighborhood for weeks."

"He was a client of mine. I was at his house this morning right after he was shot."

Stephen, who'd heard all about it in the car on the way to my parents, listened politely to my recitation of the day's events.

"He finally cheated the wrong person," pronounced my father when I'd finished, his face flushed with gin.

"Nonsense," replied my mother. "People who invest in futures expect to be cheated."

"Not cheated, Mother," I protested, ever loyal to my client. "People who speculate are prepared to lose money. They know it is a risky investment."

"He was a no-good Irishman who finally got what was coming to him," declared my father.

"What was he like?" Stephen asked.

"Not quite our sort," interjected Mother knowingly. "Flashy. Pamela did her best with him, but everything Bart did had to be the biggest and the most expensive. It really was tiresome. People put up with him of course, for her sake, but he'd never been accepted in the normal way."

"And were they happy together?" I inquired.

"Happy?" echoed Mother as if the word was not familiar to her. "Who can say whether a marriage is happy? They certainly made a great show of affection. But Bart had a terrible temper, too, and I know they fought sometimes. They were at a party at the club Saturday night, and I know they had some sort of argument—at least Gladys and Elmer Cranshaw had to give Pamela a ride home. But I think in general everyone agrees that they got along."

"And it was a lucky thing," piped in my father. "Pamela was always a peculiar girl. Odd. I'm sure no one thought she'd ever marry. Bart might have not been a sahib, but he did a lot to bring her out of herself. The Mandersons have always been strange. Her father, Sterling, was a bully and a prig."

"No matter what anybody thought of Bart, I'm sure this is a terrible thing for Pamela," said Mother. "How embarrassing. I can't imagine anything more vulgar than being shot."

* * *

I arrived home to find my roommate lying on the living room floor. Dressed in her habitual scrubs of surgical green, she had clamped headphones over her ears. The cord that connected them to the stereo snaked across the floor.

"Bad day?" I shouted.

Claudia opened her eyes, got up wearily, and turned down the volume. She was a tiny woman, barely five feet, but with a core of toughness that transcended her size.

"Did you have a rough day?" I asked again.

"It was like Calcutta," replied my roommate with feeling. "No, I don't think Calcutta ever gets that bad. It was like Calcutta on drugs."

"What happened?"

"Oh, the usual shit, only twice as much of it. We had two stabbings—teenage boys trying to settle an argument about a tape player they stole. They tried to eviscerate each other with kitchen knives. One of them had practically bled out by the time they got him in. After they were prepped for surgery, some genius parked them next to each other in pre-op. The next thing you know, one of the kids has hopped off the gurney, bleeding all over the place, and is trying to choke the other one.

"Next, I get a sixty-three-year-old Portuguese woman with a fractured tibia, only the orthopedic resident has mismarked the X ray and the first thing I do is open the wrong leg. I finish with her; then I do an emergency ruptured appendix and assist on a quick-and-dirty patch job on an eighty-two-year-old woman who was hit by a bus and was bleeding inside from every organ. Finally, it looks like there's a break in the action, and who do they bring in but the same Portuguese woman with the broken leg. It seems that while they were shifting some patients around in post-op, the orderly parked her gurney for a minute in the hallway and she got run over by one of those huge nutrition carts, the ones they use to bring up the dinner trays. She fell off and lacerated her forehead and broke her nose and both of her arms. We drew lots for who was going to have to tell her family. I lost."

"Sounds like quite a day."

"And I didn't even tell you about the yellow man."

"Who," I inquired, "is the yellow man?"

"The yellow man is a famous and semipermanent resident of the University of Chicago Hospitals. He's a fifty-eight-year-old white male with cirrhosis of the liver so extreme that it has caused his skin to turn yellow and coincidentally has caused him to be completely insane. I bet you've seen him sleeping under the viaduct at Fifty-fifth Street. He wears a red hockey helmet all the time because he gets seizures and bangs his head. Anyway, they had him up in ICU because he was having some acute esophageal problems. To make a long story short, he managed to work himself free of his restraints and threw himself out a sixth-floor window. Problem is, he fell only a couple of floors onto the roof of the maternity wing."

"So what happened to him?" I demanded.

"He broke every bone in his body, but the football helmet prevented head injuries. We just fixed him up and sent him back up to ICU."

"Calcutta on drugs," I agreed.

"So how was your day?"

"I thought it was really exciting until you told me

about yours," I replied. "I went out to a client's house this morning for a meeting, but when I got there he'd been murdered."

"You're kidding!" exclaimed Claudia. "What happened?"

I told Claudia about Bart Hexter being shot. Practice was turning me into a polished raconteur of these events.

"And there's no chance it was an accident?" Claudia asked when I was done.

"You mean, might he have gotten into his Rolls Royce wearing only his pajamas and driven to the end of his driveway to clean his gun . . . ?"

"I get the picture. So what does the family say? Do they think it was suicide?"

"Right now everyone's being too well-bred to discuss it. But when I spoke to his wife, she insisted that he'd never take his own life. She also said that they didn't find a suicide note."

"Only half of suicides leave notes," replied my roommate. "A medical education is full of all kinds of valuable information."

"I guess that leaves things in the hands of the police," I sighed.

Don't underestimate the cops," counseled my roommate. "We see a lot of homicide detectives in the emergency room. They don't miss much."

"The homicide detective who questioned me this morning might not miss much, but he gave new meaning to the term *abrasive*."

"That's because you're a suspect, you dope. He's not going to waste his time being polite with you."

"Don't be ridiculous. There is no way he can suspect me of anything."

"Don't they teach you anything in law school? You told me yourself that you were the first person on the scene. Hexter was supposed to meet you the morning he was killed. I'm sure that you're on the top of the cops' list right now."

"Stop it," I said. "You're depressing the hell out of me. I'm juggling too many cases as it is. I don't have time to be a murder suspect. Besides, what would your parents say if they found out you had such an elevated opinion of the cops?" Claudia's parents were both professors at NYU, radical Jewish intellectuals and gray-haired rebels against authority.

"All I said was that the homicide cops, as a rule, have their shit together. Policemen are like plumbers, some of them are good and most of them aren't. I spend a fair chunk of time trying to sew up the holes in people that wouldn't be there in the first place if the cops had been doing their job. You know what they say about cops in the emergency room?"

"What's that?"

" 'Call for a cop and call for a pizza and see which one comes first.' "

CHAPTER
6

The Chicago Board of Trade casts its long shadow down the canyon of office buildings that line LaSalle, Chicago's version of Wall Street. From the top of its pyramid-shaped roof a bronze statue of Ceres, the Roman goddess of grain, presides impassively over the daily tumult of the futures markets while satellite dishes hidden behind her skirts beam commodity prices around the world.

Since the early morning I'd been closeted in a smoky conference room off the trading floor with Barton Jr., Carl Savage, and Tim Hexter—who, if anything, seemed even more flustered and at loose ends than he had the day before. We had summoned the Hexter Commodities floor traders in succession in order to orchestrate the liquidation of Bart Hexter's massive positions. Later in the morning a reluctant Barton Jr. would address the employees of Hexter Commodities. He had also agreed to remain at the office the bulk of the trading day, making himself available for trading decisions. It was hoped that his physical presence at the office would send a strong signal of family continuity and commitment to the firm.

Our business with the floor traders concluded, Barton stole a quiet moment to prepare his remarks. I slipped upstairs to the visitors' gallery to watch the opening of the day's trading in the soybean pit. In Chicago the trading pits are often seen as mythic places, but in reality they are quite plain. No matter what commodity is traded there, each pit is the same: eight-sided risers covered with black rubber meant to promote traction, muffle noise, and be easy on the feet.

From my vantage point above the trading floor I could see the green-jacketed out-trade clerks, some who had been at work since four A.M., finishing with the computer printouts arrayed on folding tables adjacent to the bean pit. Every morning they anxiously check for their employers' names on the daily list of out-trades— discrepancies between buyer and seller that represent mistakes made during the previous day's trading that must be reconciled before the market opens. With the approach of the opening, exchange staff members hovered impatiently, waiting to clear the aisles.

The soybean pit was already filled, though mostly with broker's clerks, not much older than teenagers, who are paid to hold a favorite spot for a particular trader. Most days they spend their time doing crossword puzzles or playing hand-held video games, but today most had newspapers open to the business section where the lead article spelled out the story of Bart Hexter's death.

There is a strict dress code in the pits, but it has to do with information rather than aesthetics. Traders wear color-coded jackets, cut along the lines of a soda jerk's, which correspond to the firm through which that trader clears his trades. For example, traders who clear through Merrill Lynch wear dark green; Dellsher, sky blue; and Hexter Commodities, black. Runners all wear gold. These messengers sprint between the phone clerks who receive buy and sell orders from the various trading firms upstairs and the traders in the pits who actually execute the trades.

When the opening bell rang at 8:30 the noise hit me like a wall as the pit ignited into a swirl of motion. Viewed from above it looked like a whirlpool of psychedelic, churning water as the bright-jacketed traders gestured wildly in the air, arms up, voices raised. This morning's opening seemed particularly intense, and I knew that to some extent the frenzy was attributable to Bart Hexter's death.

Doug Wirtman traded soybeans for Hexter Commodities. I spotted him in his customary place on the top step of the pit, a square mica badge emblazoned with his firm's four-letter trading I.D.—BART—hung from the pocket of his black jacket. Wirtman was a handsome ex-jock who'd played two seasons in the World Professional Soccer League before changing over to the more serious competition of the bean pit. Nothing in Wirtman's demeanor hinted of his employer's recent demise. His concentration was absolute as he made his trades, holding both hands over his head, palms outward, signaling his desire to sell.

Physically, the pits are a despicable place to work. The noise is nothing short of amazing, and over time it takes its toll. Old-timers develop a mild form of deafness known as pit hearing, and their voices grow raspy from years of screaming out their trades. The physical contact is grueling as well, close and constant, like a day-long game of basketball. At times the trading becomes so frenetic that the pits themselves actually sway under the heaving momentum of the traders.

The pits are a male place where there is advantage to being strong, large, and loud. The jargon of futures is unabashedly sexual as well. Traders try to "make the market," to "get a leg up," and to "short the wings on a butterfly spread." They try to "pump," "goose," "ride," or "massage" the market. But they all know that if you go up against it, chances are you'll be screwed if you don't pull out fast.

The pits are a stripped-down, single-minded place where traders have no room for niceties. In the mono-maniacal drive for profits there is no time for hand-shakes or thank you's or pardon me's. Traders push, elbow, slap, punch, and step on toes. Screaming, they spray each other with saliva. Angry, they thrust and parry their pencils like sabers.

And yet for some people the pits are more than just the ultimate arena, more than a place where machismo is measured in dollars earned and lost. The pits are the place where men like Bart Hexter come wondering what they are capable of . . . and stay to hear the market tell them what they are worth every minute of every day.

The first thing you noticed when you walked into Bart Hexter's office was the Bengal tiger that faced the door, crouched as if preparing to spring. Hexter had shot the beast on safari and had him stuffed. The message to visitors was clear: If I wasn't afraid of this tiger, do you think I'm going to be afraid of you?

Barton Jr. addressed the assembled employees of Hexter Commodities from behind his father's desk. The reasons for the choice were both symbolic and practical. We wanted to drive home the message that a Hexter was still in charge at Hexter Commodities. Removed from the constant barrage of the price boards and the ringing of the phones, it was also the only place large enough to accommodate everyone.

Barton Jr. looked older today, his face set in grim lines of endurance. With his jet-black hair combed back from his face, he looked so much like his father that I'm sure I wasn't the only one to shiver at the resemblance.

He spoke with the casual assurance of the lecture hall, his voice unhurried and with enough practiced volume to carry to the back of the room so that everyone, including the gold-jacketed runners who stood on tiptoe halfway out the door, was able to hear. He told them what they had already read in the newspaper about his father's death and urged cooperation with the police. He spoke with quiet sincerity about the value of their loyalty and his family's commitment to keeping Hexter Commodities in business.

I stood at Barton's side while he spoke, pleased with the grace with which he tackled a task for which I knew he had little heart. Tim Hexter listened from the front row, looking miserable. He was the only child of Bart's older brother Billy, and he, too, bore the physical imprint of the Hexter family. The men all followed the same basic blueprint—big as bears, with hands like paddles. While Bart, and to a lesser extent, Barton Jr., translated their size into a strong physical presence, Tim had turned his size into a liability—he was big and slow, lumbering, and not too bright.

Futures is a tight-knit, clannish business where fathers and sons, uncles and cousins all trade shoulder to shoulder, tied together by the iron bonds of blood and money. It was viewed as natural that Bart, unable to lure his son into the family business, would choose his nephew, no matter how limited in his abilities, to be his acolyte and keep his secrets.

Beside Tim a plump and tidy older woman sobbed into her handkerchief—Bart Hexter's long-time secretary, Mrs. Titlebaum—crying the first tears I'd seen shed for the dead man.

Once Barton finished the group broke up quickly. After all, the markets were open. While most of the Hexter employees sprinted back to the trading floor and the cacophony of the phones, some of the administrative staff shuffled forward to express their condolences. I hung back quietly, waiting for Barton to finish.

I could not help but notice a young woman standing at the back of the room. Wearing the gold jacket of a runner over a plain black dress, she leaned against the wall, arms wrapped despondently around herself. Framed by dark hair, her face was extraordinary. Her skin was translucent, her cheekbones high, her lips full and perfectly shaped. Her eyes were smoky, fringed with thick lashes and big enough to drown a man.

Another woman—fortyish and tremendously chic with a sleek bob of dark red hair and a daring lavender suit—walked up to her. Their conversation—if you could call it that, seeing as the younger woman never spoke—was brief and conclusive. The older woman said only a few words, but when she turned away her face was alight with malicious triumph. The younger woman stood absolutely still until the older one had passed out of sight. Then her pale face dissolved into tears, and she fled down the corridor.

"You know he always loved this view," said Barton Jr., looking out the broad window opposite his father's desk which faced north up LaSalle Street. "I'm sure he sat here and felt like the lord of the markets."

The dead man's secretary had come and gone, bringing us coffee and returning to her desk, her face streaked with tears.

"It's so ironic. Do you know what my father wanted more than anything in the world?" demanded Barton Jr.

"What?"

"He wanted me to come and work for him. We even fought about it the last time we were together, Friday night when we went out to my parents' house for dinner."

"At least you were all together."

"It was a disaster. Dad was late, and my kids were starved and cranky, but Mother wouldn't let dinner be served until he came home. We were all testy to begin with. Margot was there. She'd brought her friend, Brooke."

"What's wrong with Brooke?" I asked. "You say her name like she's an ax murderer."

"There's nothing wrong with Brooke. I really like her. It's just that at Christmas Margot announced that she had decided, as she put it, 'to explore the lesbian life-style.' Brooke is the person she's exploring it with. Personally, if Margot's happy, I'm happy. But my parents are slightly less open-minded. So Brooke made a rather strained addition to the family dinner.

"When Dad finally walked through the door I could

tell he was just spoiling for a fight. He got like that sometimes. Something would set him off at the office and he'd come home ready to lay into the first person who crossed his path."

"And he layed into Margot?"

"No. You could tell that Margot bringing Brooke was bugging him, but Margot usually gives better than she gets. So Dad picked an easier target—me. He started in on the old lament. All the people whom he had working for him were thieves, they took their paychecks and spent their time thinking of ways to stab him in the back, and on and on. Dad always swore a lot. It was a habit from his days as a trader, but Jane, my wife, hated it, especially in front of the kids. And I agree with her. It's no fun getting a phone call from nursery school saying that little Peter's been using the f-word again. So Jane asked him if he'd watch his language. Well, he went crazy. He started yelling at Jane, shouting that he wasn't going to be lectured at his own dinner table.

"Well, you don't know Jane, but it doesn't work to raise your voice to her. She just stood up and said, 'Very well, then we're leaving.' In two minutes she'd gathered up the boys, put them in their coats, and was out the door. I was on my feet to go with her, but you should have seen the look on my mother's face—practically begging me to stay. . . ."

"I thought your dad told me that you'd worked for him once."

"Once was enough."

"When was that?"

"About ten years ago. I'd just finished the first year of my Ph.D. program, and I was a burnt-out wreck. All I wanted to do was sit on a beach somewhere. But Dad saw my being wrung out as a sign that I wasn't really cut out to be a mathematician. He's never understood what I do. To him the theoretical seems weak and irrelevant. Guys like me are just gutless wimps, sitting around spinning numbers in the air.

"So anyway, Dad never saw an opening without going for it. He told me that a precondition of his paying for my next year's tuition was that I go to work for him over the summer. But Dad was impossible to work for. I don't know how the guys here did it. He was the most controlling man who ever lived. There was only his way. No initiative allowed. And his temper knew no limit. I don't know what inner demons drove him—I know his childhood was less than idyllic—but I think he got a sick thrill out of having every one of his employees terrified of him. I'd had enough of his temper as a child. I had no desire to come back for a second helping as an adult. And it was so frustrating. My whole life I'd been hearing about how much he wanted me to come to work for him, and yet as soon as I arrived it became clear that he didn't know any other way to treat me than he had as a child. Sure he was successful, but I saw so many ways he could be more so. Simple things, like streamlining the record keeping. But Dad hated computers. He tried to keep all his records in his head; he saw writing things down as a weakness.

"He was also incredibly set in his ways. I was already turned on to chaos theory. I was excited about trying to apply it to futures trading, but Dad wouldn't hear of it. He wanted to stick with what he knew—trading the agricultural commodities, running a boiler room where they made cold calls, and terrorizing the brokers. Do you know anything about chaos?"

"Not the kind you're talking about," I replied.

"It's a relatively new area of theoretical mathematics concerned with modeling complex, real-world systems. It was initially developed in an attempt to understand and predict the weather, which has direct applications to price movements of agricultural commodities. But chaos theory also can be used to model any highly unstable, nonlinear system—like futures markets themselves. Face it, most of the guys down there trading in the pits aren't very sophisticated. They trade a tick here, a tick there. They squeeze out a few bucks trading ahead of broker orders. But there are a couple of outfits that have been very successful in applying higher mathematics to futures trading. Just look at CRT. They're a bunch of philosophers and physicists who've developed a sophisticated trading system. Over time they've been a hundred times more successful than Dad."

"But your father wasn't interested."

"Dad didn't want what he couldn't control. He wanted me to come and work for him all right, but when it came right down to it, he wasn't interested in what I had to offer. He wanted another cowering toady like Tim. You know what they called Tim when I worked here? He had this nickname—'Sniff.' "

"Sniff?"

"Because his nose was always up my father's ass. I know that Tim's my cousin and that Dad gave him a job because his father was Dad's brother, but Tim does not have all of the family's best qualities. He's got Dad's temper without Dad's talent for trading. But, as my Dad never tired of pointing out, Tim was as loyal to him as a son."

"So what did your dad do when you quit?"

"He was pissed. But my reaction was much stranger. I didn't have a job. Dad said he wouldn't pay my tuition for the upcoming year. I went to the university's financial-aid office and explained my situation, and they just laughed at me. Poor penniless Barton Hexter. Then I found out the Merc was running a simulated trading contest with a twenty-thousand-dollar grand prize, and I decided to enter."

"You mean one of those competitions where everyone starts out with a certain number of imaginary dollars?"

"And the person with the most money in his account at the end of thirty days wins. I finished with eight hundred ninety thousand dollars more than the second-place finisher. I got a check for twenty thousand and a first-place certificate. I used the money to pay for my tuition. I sent the certificate to my dad. The bastard had it framed. There it is, right over there, next to the picture of him playing golf with Bob Hope."

"And then what happened?"

"Nothing. I went back to school. Halfway through the second semester checks started coming from my dad again. He and Mom came to see me one weekend, and we all acted like nothing had happened."

"It was good of you to forgive him," I remarked, thinking of the perpetually strained state of my relationship with my mother.

"By then I'd met Jane. She really helped me get a sense of perspective when it came to my father. Dad had such a big personality, he always made me feel like I lived at the periphery of his life. Jane helped me see that I could just accept him for what he was and move on."

"You are lucky to have found her."

"I know. Dad could never understand what I saw in her. Did you know that Jane's a resident pianist with the Chicago Symphony?"

"I knew she looked familiar," I exclaimed. "I've heard her play. Last November. She played a Beethoven piano concerto—she was startlingly good. You know how some pianists get out there and just want to dazzle you with their technique? Her performance was so different. It was as if she was possessed by the music. She was wonderful."

Barton beamed, obviously proud of his wife's accomplishments.

"I'd think your dad would have loved to have a famous daughter-in-law," I added.

"He didn't see it that way. Dad thought a woman's job was to be expensively attractive, like my mother and my sister Krissy. He couldn't understand a woman who wasn't a trophy."

"Does your mother like Jane?"

"I don't think Mother dislikes Jane. It's just that she doesn't understand anyone who's not just like her. She's gotten used to Jane, but I think she'd have been much happier if I'd married the daughter of one of her friends."

The door to Bart Hexter's office opened, and the red-headed woman in the lavender suit walked in, surprised to find the office occupied.

"Oh, I—I'm so sorry," she stammered. "I didn't realize anyone was in here."

"Did you need something?" asked Barton Jr.

"Just some account files," she replied, backing out the door. "I'll come back later."

"Who was that?" I asked, once she'd gone.

"That was Loretta Resch. She's in charge of the clearing operation. If you believe my sister Margot's stories, she was once my father's mistress."

CHAPTER
7

Flanking the twin mahogany doors of Callahan Ross are two enormous pillars of polished marble, incongruous on the forty-second floor of a downtown office building. According to legend, they were purchased from a failing bank by Ewald Callahan, the firm's founding partner, who hoped to create an aura of power and respectability for his fledgling practice. Now, of course, the respectability and power flow like wine. With more than 200 lawyers in Chicago and offices in New York, Washington, D.C., L.A., Atlanta, London, Paris, and Brussels, the work of Callahan attorneys is woven inextricably into the fabric of world commerce.

In the churchlike dimness of the reception room hangs a list of the partners, drawn out like a family tree and framed in gold. My name is the most recent addition. In February of this year I became the youngest partner in the august history of the firm.

In moments of unexpressed yearning I had hoped that partnership would bring with it a sense of accomplishment and belonging. Instead I was delivered an insider's knowledge of how the firm is really run, freedom from the dominion of the abusive partner with whom I'd worked most closely as an associate, and, of course, a bigger paycheck. From the attorneys who joined the firm before me, the ones I leap-frogged to partnership, I receive a mixture of deference and bile. Jealousy, it is said, like a bad cough, cannot be hid. By my partners I am greeted with a mixture of cordiality and suspicion. Callahan has only four female partners including myself, and I've heard a fair amount of tut-tutting over both my age and gender.

But there is no denying that with rank come privileges. My new office is a small wonder of space, with a window facing west from which, if you stand on the bookcase, you can see the river. I even have a famous neighbor—Howard Ackerman. Howard is a legendary cuss of a litigator—a viper in wire frames and a bow tie.

Firm legend has it that, once, while defending a large corporation against serious, but highly technical, charges of stock price manipulation, he responded to the prosecutor's lengthy opening remarks by slowly rising to his feet, scratching his head and declaring: "Yeah. But you can't prove it." He then went on to win the case. I hear him sometimes through the thick plaster of the wall that divides us, shouting out arguments and objections to an imaginary judge and jury, wearing out the carpet in front of his desk as he prepares for trial.

Howard's door is, as usual, open as I pass.

"Heard you shot one of your clients, Kate," he called out.

"Never underestimate the power of a woman," I replied.

"I'll keep that in mind next time I think of pissing

you off," he chortled as I rounded the corner to my office.

I tossed my briefcase onto my desk, took my jacket off, and draped it over the back of my chair.

My office is my refuge, the place where the bitterness and sorrows of the past are crowded out by the constant flow of work—the phone calls, files, and dictation that constitute the relentless grind of corporate practice. There are crises and catastrophes, of course, but ultimately they belong to someone else. I deal with them from a delicious distance, billing my time by the tenth of an hour.

As I glanced at my typed agenda and the mail, opened and arrayed in presumed order of importance on my desk, Cheryl, my secretary, appeared with a thick stack of pink message slips and a pot of coffee. I was very lucky to have been assigned Cheryl when I first arrived at Callahan, and I have clung to her ever since with the fierce instincts of survival. She is the youngest of eight children and is the first person in her family to have gone to college. At night she attends Loyola Law School. By day she keeps my professional life from crashing down around my ears.

She plunked herself down in her usual chair, poured out two cups of coffee, and flipped open her steno pad.

"Do you want to tell me your bad news first," she asked, "or do you want to hear mine?"

"Let me guess," I answered. "My mother called."

"Lots of people called," replied my faithful secretary. "Your mother was the nicest one."

"Oh, God. Then you'd better go first."

"Let me see, there've been calls from eleven different reporters. Everyone from *Crain's Chicago Business* to the *Daily Star*. The guy from the *Star* offered me five hundred dollars if I'd get him an interview with you. When I told him that he was a cheapskate, he said he'd talk to his editor and see if they could offer me more."

"I'm so glad you have such high standards."

"Thank you. Ken Kurlander has called no fewer than six times. He absolutely, positively has to speak to you the very moment you arrive."

"So now tell me the bad news," I demanded, knowing that Cheryl inevitably saved the best for last.

"I have here in my hand a subpoena from the Lake County District Attorney's office. Some guy was here to serve you, but I got Skip Tillman to come down and accept service on behalf of the firm."

She handed me the document, and I scanned it quickly. It required me to produce all of the documents in my possession pertaining to Hexter Commodities. I groaned. When Bart Hexter hired me, his old law firm had sent his files over in a truck. It would take weeks to make the copies.

"This is awfully quick," I commented. "He died yesterday morning. See if you can find me the phone number of the D.A. who signed this. I want him to understand the volume of paper this involves. Maybe he'd be willing to narrow his request." Cheryl bent her head over her pad and made a note.

"Isn't this whole thing creepy?" she commented as she wrote. "I was reading about it in the paper. He must have been shot right before your meeting."

"I know. I was practically the first person who found him."

"How awful for you."

"Not as bad as it was for Hexter. The people who are

really suffering in all of this are his relatives. Not only have they lost a family member, but the media circus is only just beginning. All of a sudden Hexter's son, who has no interest in futures, is responsible for Hexter Commodities. Meantime, no one knows who pulled the trigger or why."

"How can you be sure that none of them know?" inquired my secretary.

My phone rang. While I chewed on that one, Cheryl rose to answer it. "Ms. Millholland's office," she purred. She held the receiver to her ear and her elfin face formed itself into a frown. She nodded seriously and then, covering the receiver with her hand, said, "It's someone from your bank. A process server is there with a subpoena for all of your account records, and they want to know what to do."

If there is anything worse than having your client shot it is being suspected of shooting him. There was no other explanation for the rapid flurry of subpoenas. I put a call in to Detective Ruskowski because it was better than doing nothing. I left a message with the desk sergeant. I was still pondering the mess in which I found myself when Ken Kurlander descended upon me.

"I have been calling you all morning," he said, his tone both imperious and accusing.

"I was at Hexter Commodities."

"Pamela Hexter called me this morning. She is very upset. It seems the police were back this morning. That detective fellow told her that there was no doubt Bart was murdered. They had a warrant to search the house, and they asked some very unpleasant questions."

"Murder is an unpleasant business," I replied with

more vehemence than I'd intended. I considered telling Kurlander about the subpoenas but immediately thought better of it. "I was just about to call you," I said. "I need to know the exact disposition of Hexter Commodities in Bart's will."

"I brought you a copy," replied Kurlander, handing me the blue-backed document. He extracted a pair of reading glasses from his pocket while I began flipping through Bart Hexter's last will and testament.

Hexter's estate was large, and the document was, by necessity, a complex one. Besides the house in Lake Forest, I noted that he had had houses in Vail and Palm Beach, as well as undeveloped property in Montana, Texas, and Maine. He owned a number of commercial properties in Chicago and an office building in New York City. According to his will, the real-estate holdings were left to his three children to be divided equally among them. The house in Lake Forest was the exception, being left exclusively to Barton Jr., with the provision that Pamela be allowed to live there rent free until the occasion of her death or remarriage.

"Let me get this straight," I said, looking up. "Who owns the land that the Hexters' house is on? I was always under the assumption that since the property originally belonged to Pamela's family, it must have passed to her when her parents died."

"It did, with the exception of the acre and a half on which her current house rests. That property and the house are titled to Bart Hexter alone and, by the terms of this will, pass to Barton Jr."

"So Pamela doesn't own the house she lives in?"

"Nor the land on which it rests. That is correct."

I was surprised. The property, divided as it was by

the difference in ownership, would be considerably diminished in value. Who would want to buy a large, expensive parcel of real estate when an acre and a half right in the middle of it belonged to somebody else? The Hexters most likely figured that it didn't matter since it was all in the family, but that's why people had attorneys, to keep them from making this kind of mistake. I expected more of Ken. He must have read as much in my expression.

"You have to understand that Bart and Pamela each approached matters of money and property from very different points of view," explained the trusts and estates lawyer. "It was the cause of considerable friction in their marriage. It irked Pamela to no end that her father gave the parcel of land to Bart rather than to the two of them. However, in recent years when I suggested that they title the entire property jointly, Pamela refused outright."

"It does seem odd."

"Pamela is one of my oldest and dearest friends," said Kurlander. "But there is no denying that she has her eccentricities. She has always been very frugal and peculiar about money. Let me tell you a story. A number of years ago Pamela came to see me, very upset. It seems that Bart found himself in trading difficulties—I believe the appropriate technical explanation is that he got caught in a large naked short position. Needless to say, he was unable to meet his margin call, and he turned to Pamela for help. It was a large sum that he needed, in excess of a million dollars, but for someone of Pamela's wealth it was ready money. But Pamela was more than reluctant to give it to her husband—even though her failure to do so would surely cause him financial ruin. It was a very disturbing episode. Finally I convinced her to lend Bart the money, but she insisted that he turn over ten percent of the shares of Hexter Commodities and that a formal loan agreement be drawn up. If I recall correctly, she even charged him a point or two over the current rate of interest on the grounds that in his position, he posed a credit risk and no bank would lend to him."

"That must have made for some interesting discussions at the breakfast table," I remarked.

"As I said, Pamela and Bart approached money from completely different directions. Pamela, who had never earned a penny in her life, found virtue in taking thrift to what appeared to Bart to be ridiculous extremes. Bart, who earned every penny, was a spendthrift in his wife's eyes. And yet, as far as I know, Pamela and Bart were a remarkably contented couple."

"There are some interesting provisions here," I said, turning back to the will. "A number of mortgages forgiven—Janice Titlebaum, 2719 Manor Drive in Skokie; Loretta Resch, 19501 Sherbrooke in Naperville; Tim Hexter, 2349 Lake Road in Wilmette. . . ."

"Over the years Bart made mortgage loans to a number of his employees. If I'm not mistaken, the loan to his secretary, Mrs. Titlebaum, is very nearly paid up. You'll also see there is another loan of one hundred twenty thousand dollars that he made six months ago to his nephew, Tim. That loan is forgiven as well."

"That's quite a sum," I commented. "Do we know what it was for?"

"It was made at the time of Bart's brother's death. I don't know if you read about it in the papers, but it was a terrible tragedy. Billy and his wife, Lillian, were driving home from a party when apparently Billy suffered a heart attack, lost control of the car, and swerved into oncoming traffic. Billy died instantly, and a young woman who was driving the car he hit was also killed. His wife, Tim's mother, was terribly injured. She had two broken legs, a broken hip, and I don't know how many internal injuries. She did not regain consciousness until after Billy's funeral. Finally, she recovered enough to be told what had happened, but within twenty-four hours of learning that her husband was dead, her condition deteriorated, and she died."

"How dreadful."

"That's not all. Billy managed to keep it a secret while he was alive—though I'm sure that Bart knew— but it seems that he had always had something of a gambling problem. He'd owned a hardware store that appeared to have been profitable enough, but as soon as Tim began to wind up the estate, all sorts of things came out."

"What kinds of things?" I asked.

"For example, Billy was six months behind on his rent on the store. He owed three years' worth of back taxes, and was in for more than fifty thousand to some rather rough fellows. Worse, he hadn't made health insurance payments for almost a year. Unfortunately, Lillian incurred tens of thousands of dollars of hospital expenses before her death."

"Poor Tim."

"Poor Tim indeed. He had no choice but to approach Bart, who in turn had no choice but to come to his nephew's rescue, especially since I believe that loan sharks were trying to force Tim to make good on his father's debts. The entire situation was most unpleasant.

Pamela, I'm afraid, did little to improve matters. I know she hectored Bart at every opportunity about throwing good money after bad, though I have no idea what she thought would happen to Tim."

"So where is the section that deals with Hexter Commodities?" I asked, flipping through the will. All this Hexter family history was very interesting, but I was at a stage in my career where I had less time for digression than Ken Kurlander. "Oh here, I found it."

I had to read it through twice before I was sure that I hadn't misunderstood. I knew from the incorporation papers that even though ninety percent of the shares were owned by Bart, Hexter Commodities stock was divided into two classes, common and preferred. The preferred shares represented the entire cash value of the company but carried with them no voting rights. Upon his death, these shares were to be divided equally among the three Hexter children, with thirty percent of the company passing to Barton, Margot, and Krissy each, while Pamela retained her ten percent. The common shares had no cash value but were in some sense more valuable, since they were the voting shares. All of the common shares had been left to Barton Jr. Simply stated, the girls owned two-thirds of Hexter Commodities but had no say in how the company was to be run.

"This is not a terribly enlightened bequest," I protested. "The girls have no control over the company."

"Bart wanted to insure that the company not pass out of family control," explained Kurlander. "He wanted to make it difficult for the girls, who might be influenced by their husbands, to sell their shares."

There was so much wrong with what Kurlander

was telling me—the will rested on so many faulty and insulting premises that I wanted to shake him—but instead I let it pass. I had neither the time nor the energy to drag Ken Kurlander into a more enlightened age.

I went back and flipped through the entire document from the beginning. "That's it? None of the estate passes to Pamela?" I inquired, genuinely surprised. I was certain that Ken would have been sure that Bart understood that property could be passed to his wife tax-free.

"I know," replied Kurlander with a disgusted shake of his head. "I brought it up every year. The only thing I can think of is that there must be some history between them, some personal reason for his wanting to cut out Pamela. Perhaps the loan she made to him still rankled. Maybe it was his way of paying her back for what he perceived as her stinginess. I know that Pamela is careful with a dollar—she watches every penny that passes through her household like it was her last. I know for a fact that she used her position as minority shareholder of Hexter Commodities to do a quarterly review of the company's books. Like I said, in some ways Pamela is a most peculiar woman."

"Have you discussed the terms of the will with the family yet?" I inquired.

"They're coming in tomorrow morning at ten. But there is another matter that I wanted to bring to your attention. I discovered something very disturbing when I arrived at the office this morning."

"Really? What is it?"

"I was out of the office the entire day on Friday, so

I didn't find out about it until I reviewed my calendar this morning. It appears that Bart Hexter called Friday morning and made an appointment with my secretary to see me this morning."

"Did he say what it was about?"

"No. He didn't mention anything to my secretary, but Bart and Pamela Hexter have been my clients for more than thirty years. In that time the only work I've done for Bart has pertained to estate planning. I can only assume that he wanted to see me about making some changes in his will."

Detective Ruskowski caught me with a cup of chili on my desk and some cream cheese on my chin, the remainder of my lunch, courtesy of my kindhearted secretary. I stood up when I saw him, quickly applying a napkin to my lips and whisking the crumbs off my skirt. From the doorway, he managed a quick appraisal of my office.

"Please come in, Detective," I said, minding my corporate manners and extending my hand. He declined to shake it. Instead he wandered over toward the window. I stood awkwardly, behind my desk. Waiting. Finally he turned to me, running his thick fingers through the ginger brush of his hair.

"Why don't you tell me when you first started sleeping with Bart Hexter?"

Disconcerted, it was a few seconds before I could muster a reply. "I have never slept with Bart Hexter," I responded, finally, reminding myself that unpleasant as it may be, this was Ruskowski's job.

"You don't have to be modest," said the detective. "You're an adult. I'm a policeman. There's nothing that you've done that I haven't heard about before." I noticed that he was wearing the same navy suit he'd worn the day before. His eyes were red-rimmed with fatigue, and his freckled skin had taken on a sickly pallor. I would have been surprised if he'd slept since the discovery of Bart Hexter's death.

"I appreciate your delicacy, Detective, but the fact remains that I never had any sort of physical relationship with Bart Hexter. I was his attorney. He was my client. I represent a large number of people, many of whom I know much better than I knew Bart Hexter."

"You mean like Stephen Azorini?"

"Meaning?"

"Isn't Dr. Azorini a client of yours?"

"Not personally. I represent his company, Azor Pharmaceuticals."

"And you sleep with him, don't you?"

"I've had a relationship with Stephen since we were both teenagers."

"I didn't ask when you started fucking Stephen Azorini," retorted Ruskowski, raising his voice to just this side of a shout. "I asked when you started fucking Bart Hexter."

I struggled to resist being baited by this sudden rise in volume and descent in tactics.

"Just because I have a sexual relationship with one of my clients doesn't necessarily mean that I have a sexual relationship with all of them. If that were the case, I'd have a bed in my office instead of a desk, and I'd charge considerably more an hour."

"Are you telling me that you didn't know that Bart Hexter rented an apartment at Lake View Towers without his wife's knowledge?"

"No. I didn't know."

"Then I suppose it would surprise you to hear that the night doorman at Lake View Towers identified you from a photo array as the young woman that Bart met there."

"He must be mistaken," I said, but my answer sounded lame, even to me.

Ruskowski pulled the yellow envelope of photographs I'd found in Hexter's desk from the pocket of his jacket. He began to lay them out on my desk as he spoke, examining each one judiciously before he set it down. "I guess you figured that since your face doesn't show much, we wouldn't know it was you. Or did you think that by giving them to us yourself we would automatically assume it was somebody else? If you don't mind my saying so, you have great tits."

I was trained to believe that an emotional lawyer is a poor lawyer, and that in business it never pays to lose your cool. I walked up to Ruskowski, not stopping until I was too close to him. I pulled myself up to my full height and leaned into his face. I wanted the message to be clear: I was insulted but not afraid.

"Am I under arrest?" I asked.

"Do you want to be?"

"Don't play that bullshit game with me. I'm not some crackhead you caught holding somebody's stereo. If you want to continue this discussion, arrest me and read me my rights. If not, get out of my office."

Ruskowski stood his ground a moment, weighing his options. I glared back, determined not to back down.

The homicide detective's ugly, freckled face split into a grin. He reached deep into the pocket of his jacket and came out with a set of car keys. He flipped them into the air and caught them smartly.

"We'll talk again soon," he said. Then he walked out the door.

CHAPTER

8

"What did *he* want?" inquired Cheryl after Ruskowski left. As a rule I took pride in my ability to go toe-to-toe with the big boys, but I had to confess that my encounters with the homicide detective were having an increasingly unsettling effect on me.

"He thinks I killed Bart Hexter."

"That's ridiculous!"

"I know. But Hexter was supposed to meet me right before he was killed. When the police arrived I was standing next to the body."

"Come on, if you killed him, why would you show up for your meeting? It doesn't make any sense."

"I'd have to go to the meeting. It would be suspicious if I didn't."

"They suspect you anyway. Don't you think you should get a lawyer?" ventured my secretary.

"I don't need a lawyer," I declared. "I didn't kill him."

"In the movies that's what the innocent guy always says right before they put the handcuffs on him and throw him in jail."

"Thanks for sharing that with me." I sighed. Changing subjects, I asked, "Any luck getting a hold of Herman Geiss?" Herman was the CFTC's enforcement chief.

"Nope, he's been in a meeting all morning. I've left two urgent messages."

"Then would you please get Greg Shanahan on the phone for me?"

"Is he a criminal lawyer?"

"No, he's a futures trader—a client. He should be in the rolodex."

"I still think you need to line up a criminal attorney."

"What I need," I replied with mock severity, "is a secretary who will get Greg Shanahan on the phone for me."

"Yes, boss," replied Cheryl with a cockeyed salute.

"I like being called boss," I called out to her retreating back.

"Don't get used to it," came her faint reply.

For the rest of the morning I tried to put thoughts of Bart Hexter's death out of my head and concentrate on getting caught up with the tide of work that had washed up over my desk. If I let myself, I would work myself into a frenzy of paranoia. My flesh crawled at the thought of Ruskowski scrutinizing my bank records. I knew he must also be interviewing my neighbors and showing my picture to cab drivers who worked the neighborhood around Lake View Towers. I thought of his trick with the nude photos, spreading them around my office. It had felt like a kind of assault.

At one o'clock Cheryl buzzed to say that Elliott Abelman was in the office meeting with Daniel Blumenthal and wanted to know if it would be convenient for him to drop in for a minute. Grateful for the distraction, I told her I'd be glad to see him.

Elliott Abelman defied casual categorization. The son of a homicide detective, he'd broken a three-generation family tradition of policework. Instead he'd gone to college, flown a helicopter in Vietnam, been decorated for bravery, and gone to law school. He'd worked for Elkin Caufield, the defense attorney, until the realization slowly dawned that he liked the objectivity of being an investigator more than the murkier rewards of advocacy. From Elkin he went on to work in the D.A.'s office as an investigator before striking out on his own as a P.I.

Elliott is good-looking in a quiet way, with soft brown hair and eyes to match, not much different than a thousand other guys in Brooks Brothers suits. That is, unless you catch a glimpse of the Browning automatic in the shoulder holster under his jacket.

He came into my office with a carafe of coffee in one hand and two empty mugs in the other.

"I told Cheryl I'd do the honors," he said, smiling. It was the best thing that had happened to me all day. When Elliott smiled you practically felt the sunshine on your skin.

"So how's business?" I asked.

"Good," he said with a mischievous grin. "There are too many bad guys and too few cops. It's an equation that's good for trade."

"I've recommended you to a couple of lawyers at Callahan Ross. I'm glad to hear you're getting some work from us."

"Thanks. Looks like you've come up some in the world," said Elliott with a look around my new office. "So how does it feel to be a partner?"

"Like being the only girl at a frat party," I replied with more candor than discretion. "The associates all hate me, and the partners don't know what to do with me. I think the general consensus is that I made partner early because I'm a Millholland and having my name on the letterhead adds prestige to the firm."

"You busted your butt to make partner. Besides, I thought more and more women are getting partnership these days."

"In the legal profession in general I'm sure that's true, but not at Callahan. There are only four of us. Margaret Schwager came in as a partner from Epps & Fenix in New York and brought her clients with her. She and I operate on different planes of existence. She passes down the hall and people practically genuflect. She is so tough and polished. When we're in the same room I just feel myself shrivel up in comparison. It's the same with Elizabeth Seidel. She was number two at the Justice Department during the Bush administration. I think she's just here for a couple of years to build a bank roll until she's called to the bench. Then there's Claire Halpern. She's wonderful, but she's ten years older than me, and she has a family. After bambino number three she disappeared into her office never to be seen around the water cooler again. Don't get me wrong—she works like a maniac when she's in the office, but then she races home. You can hardly blame her, but it doesn't leave much time for mentoring."

"Sounds pretty lonely," commented Elliott.

"It's what I've always wanted," I replied. "I don't mean to whine about it. It's just going to take a little while before everyone gets used to it. Until then, I try to avoid the back shelves of the library lest someone stab me in the back."

"Speaking of murder, how did you get mixed up with this Hexter thing?" asked Elliott. "I talked to my dad this morning, and he said it's all the cops are talking about. I guess that even though they found the gun in the car with him, the medical examiner's definitely ruled it a homicide."

"They found the gun in the car?" I demanded. "That surprises me. I saw his body. He was sitting behind the wheel of his car. I didn't see any gun."

"It was on the ground near his feet," replied Elliott. "You probably didn't see it because you weren't looking for it. I bet your eyes were glued to the body."

"But if they found a gun in the car wouldn't that point to suicide?"

"From what Dad says, the cops think the killer just dropped the gun in the open window of the car after he was done."

"How can they be so sure?"

"For one thing, Hexter was right-handed and he was shot in the left side of his head. People tend to do things in characteristic ways. Right-handed people generally shoot with their right hands." Elliott made his hand into a gun and wrapped his arm across his face, stretching to prove how difficult it would be to shoot himself on the side opposite his gun hand. "Also, there was gunpowder stippling—flecks of gunpowder lodged under the surface of the skin—on his face and on the back of his left hand where he tried to shield his face just before he was shot. That's pretty common with head wounds. The guy sees it coming and instinctively tries to protect himself."

"Pretty gruesome."

"The irony of it is, whoever whacked Hexter didn't need to go to all the trouble. Seems like Bart had some heavy heart trouble. The ME says his ticker was in such bad shape he wouldn't have made it through the summer."

"How do you know all this stuff?"

"Cops talk more than old ladies at the beauty shop. People always assume that police work is so exciting, but ninety-five percent of the time it's deadly dull— routine calls and reports in triplicate. When something like this happens, it's like the Super Bowl; the cops can't resist talking about it. What I want to know is how you got mixed up in this."

"I was there right after he was killed. I represent his company, Hexter Commodities. The CFTC is getting down on them for some trading infractions. I was supposed to have a meeting at his house the morning he was killed. What I find amazing is that on the basis of that coincidence, the police are treating me like a suspect. All my files on Hexter have been subpoenaed; someone from the Lake County DA's office was at my bank this morning going through my financial records, and I just had a charming visit with one Detective Ruskowski of the Lake Forest Police Department, who has it in his head that I was having an affair with Hexter."

"Rusty Ruskowski?" interjected Elliott.

"Do you know him?"

"He used to be in my dad's squad a couple of years ago. Rusty was a boil on Dad's backside the entire time he was under his command."

"Was he incompetent?" I asked with a sinking feeling in my stomach.

"No. He just lacked imagination. You know, had to do everything by the book. The trouble is, you don't catch killers in triplicate. Dad always said that Ruskowski was a terrific detective as long as the solution to the crime was obvious."

"So how did he end up in Lake Forest?"

"Politics. He got chewed up over the Shawana Morton murder. Remember it?"

"You'd have had to have been in a coma to have missed it. Eleven-year-old girl, abducted on her way home from school, found three days later, raped and strangled. It was on the front page for months."

"Ruskowski was the lead detective. To do him credit, by all accounts he worked the case hard, but after a year there was no arrest. The mayor was looking for a fall guy, and Ruskowski seemed the obvious choice. He took it pretty hard. He did some serious drinking. I think his wife split before he got himself cleaned up."

"No wonder he seems like such an angry guy," I remarked unhappily.

"I'm sure that when Lake Forest went looking for a cop with homicide experience, Ruskowski looked like a bargain."

"What I don't understand is why the Lake Forest PD has a homicide detective in the first place. I thought the extent of violent crime up there was guys getting mad and hitting their caddies."

"You probably don't remember the Leslie Fassbinder murder."

"It doesn't ring a bell," I confessed.

"It didn't get much coverage in the Chicago papers.

Leslie Fassbinder was a high school junior who sneaked out of her house one night to meet her boyfriend, a classmate named Peter Wishburn. At about three in the morning a neighbor made a 911 call about a woman screaming. When the police got there they found Wishburn covered with blood, crying over Leslie's body, which had been stabbed a dozen times. So being geniuses, they took one look at the boyfriend and said, 'Eureka! We've got our killer.' They handcuffed the kid, trampled the crime scene, and took him into custody where they tried their best to intimidate him into a confession."

"Did he confess?"

"No. He didn't confess because he didn't do it. He and Leslie had planned to sneak out and meet each other in a little wooded glen near her house, but when he got there she was already dead. It seems there was another boy in her class who'd overheard them making plans, a boy with a history of mental instability who'd been obsessively stalking her. Trouble was, the cops spent so much time running in the wrong direction trying to make Wishburn the killer that by the time they figured out they had the wrong guy, the real killer had disposed of the murder weapon and any other evidence that might have linked him to the murder."

"So what happened?"

"Nothing good. Eventually they released the boyfriend—his parents sued the city. They never managed to get enough evidence to charge the kid who really killed her. He's a junior now at University of Illinois, dating other girls. Afterward, Lake Forest decided that next time a dead body turned up they'd better have somebody on the payroll who'd know what to do about it. So they hired Ruskowski."

"I am in deep trouble," I moaned. "Deep, deep trouble."

"Why?"

"Ruskowski's got it in his head that I killed Bart Hexter."

"Well, did you?" inquired Elliott. His smile took the edge off the question.

"I'm not in the habit of killing my clients, and if I were, there are quite a few I'd kill ahead of Hexter."

"Wow, I'm impressed. You work for bigger assholes than Hexter?"

"Why do you assume Hexter was an asshole?" I asked. "Don't you read the papers? The man was a paragon, a modern day Horatio Alger and upholder of family values."

"I thought being an asshole was a prerequisite of success as a futures trader. The more successful you are, the bigger jerk you must be. All things considered, I just assumed that Bart Hexter wasn't exactly a prince among men."

"So far I've been told that Hexter was controlling, impossible, and had an abusive temper. I know that at least one of his kids hated him."

"That sounds like the personality profile of what percentage of your partners?"

"My partners are all alive and well. There is a real live police detective who thinks I shot Bart Hexter. I am not finding this a pleasant experience."

"I know," replied Elliott kindly. "But try not to let it get to you. Eventually the cops are going to find the right guy. They almost always do."

* * *

I found Greg Shanahan in the back of Butch McGuire's shooting baskets with another trader. The bet was five dollars a throw. Declining an invitation to get in on the action, I went to the bar and ordered myself a scotch and soda. As the bartender poured my Chivas, I watched Greg land an easy one. McGuire's has long been a favorite spot among futures traders, and it was busy even on a Monday night, filled with aspiring Gatsbys and the girls they attract. The faces were so young it might have been a college crowd except for the trading jackets slung over chairs, the glitter of Rolexes, and the fact that the banter was about money, not grades.

Greg, who appeared to have emerged victorious from the free-throw wars, sidled up to me at the bar.

"I didn't mean to keep you waiting," he said. "But I couldn't pass up the opportunity to take some bucks off that chump. Gotta make a living you know." Greg ran his hands through his curly blond hair and ordered a gin and tonic. With his blue-eyed good looks and his tow-colored hair he looked more like a surfing instructor than a rabid capitalist. But I was not fooled. Greg, like all the guys in the pits with him, was single-minded in his pursuit of riches, unabashed in his lust for cash and flash. And yet, in his work-day clothes—Nike's, jeans, a rumpled white shirt, and disreputable tie knotted about two inches below his open collar, he could be just another office boy, stopping in for a quick one on his way home from work.

"How's it going?" I asked, pushing my empty glass across the bar, giving the nod for a refill.

"Hey, I feel lucky today," he replied. "I made ten

grand at the opening on two trades, netted twenty-five hundred in the Bart Hexter murder/suicide pool and," he said as he wrested a wad of bills from his back pocket, spreading the money on the bar, "fifty-five dollars shooting hoops. Not a bad day's work."

"The Bart Hexter murder/suicide pool? That seems pretty cold."

"It was the sickos in the Eurodollar pit that started it," replied Greg defensively. "Fifty dollars a pop on whether Hexter was shot or shot himself and another fifty on the exact time, within five minutes, that the medical examiner's verdict hit the news."

"You're kidding!"

"No way. There are some seriously twisted individuals in the futures game. You should know that."

"So I guess it's safe to assume that all heads are not bowed in grief over Hexter's death?"

"Some guys loved him. More guys hated him. What the fuck, a bet's a bet. Did I ever tell you that Bart Hexter gave me my first job at the Board?"

"I didn't know that."

"Yeah, I got my start as runner for Hexter Commodities. Black Bart himself interviewed me, though I swear I never saw him again in all the time that I worked for him. There was an opening in the deutschemark pit. I didn't know shit about futures except that my buddy told me I'd get off work at two in the afternoon—plenty of time to get to the beach and pick up girls. Anyway, I'm trying to impress him so I say, 'Deutschemarks, that's good, because it just so happens that I speak a little German.' 'That's very interesting,' says Hexter, 'But what I need is someone who can count to ten and get to work on time.' "

We both laughed.

"So what else can you tell me about Hexter?" I asked. "It's obvious whenever something like this happens to a guy who's as big in the markets as he was, a lot of people get nervous that he was doing things he shouldn't have. Have you heard anything?"

"Well, you know what it's like in the pits. There are always rumors. Hell, I heard a story once about a guy who was trading orange juice futures. One morning he's thirsty so he sends a runner to get him a can of orange juice out of the vending machine in the break room. The runner goes, but when the juice comes out it's frozen solid like there was something wrong with the machine. He goes back out onto the trading floor and tells the trader that he didn't get him the orange juice because it's all frozen. Well, someone else in the pits overheard him, but thought he said, 'the oranges are all frozen.' Inside of fifteen minutes the price of orange juice is up the limit."

"So what are the rumors about Hexter?" I asked.

"Just a couple of ugly things floating around about him. Nothing special. Mostly it's jealousy talking. Day in, day out, the man made money. He hated to lose. You'd hear it said that he'd do anything to come out on top of a trade, anything, up to and including busting trades. But that rap's been on him for a long time. Did I ever tell you that I dated his daughter once?"

"Krissy?"

"Noooooo," replied Greg, with a devilish grin. "I had a date with Mad Margot."

"How did this come about?" I inquired.

"Blind date. Her dad fixed me up. I'll tell you one thing, Hexter was a hustler. I didn't know it then, but by the time he got around to me, he'd already conned half the guys at the Board into taking her out to dinner."

"So how long did you guys date?"

"Just once," replied Greg, motioning for a refill. "It was more than enough."

"Why, what happened? Was it awful?"

"No. Not awful," answered Greg, thoughtfully, "just bizarre. One day I get into the elevator with Bart Hexter. Now bear in mind, even though I clear my trades through Hexter Commodities, I have not exchanged a word with the man since he gave me that runner's job. So here we are in the elevator and suddenly he starts asking me about myself, said he'd heard I'd been doing real well in T-bonds—which I was, no thanks to his trader, who never passed any trades my way—and he wants to know what my wife thinks about it. I'm not married, I tell him. Really, he says. Am I seeing anybody special? No. Well, did I like basketball? Sure, I say, wondering where all this is going. Suddenly, he goes all coy on me, hemming and hawing. I'm getting impatient. It's just a couple of minutes away from the T-bond opening. Finally, he asks me if I'd do him a favor. Depends, I answer, thinking that having Bart Hexter owe you a favor is not a bad thing. He tells me that his daughter is a big basketball fan and he's promised to take her to the Bulls game that night. They're playing the Lakers, and he's got half court seats on the floor. Unfortunately, he's got to go to Washington at the last minute to do some lobbying for the exchange. Would I fill in for him?

"Now of course, any idiot would be wondering why this girl has no friends to ask, why Hexter is collaring strangers in the elevator to take his kid to the game, but like I said, I was hot to get into the pit at the opening, and Hexter is—was—one of the most powerful men at the Board. . . ."

"So you took Margot to the Bulls game."

"And lived to tell about it. It turns out she hates basketball. She didn't even know whether it was the Bulls or the Lakers that played for Chicago. Her dad had badgered her into saying that she'd go. Now she's standing at the door of her apartment looking at some guy she doesn't know from Adam. I didn't know what to do. Finally, I think, I stammered out some suggestion that we give the tickets away and just go and have dinner somewhere, but then she says, just like that: 'No, Daddy would be mad if I didn't go.' And she went and got her coat."

"And did you end up having a good time?" I asked.

"From the minute she got into my car to the minute I dropped her off at her apartment she didn't say one word to me. She just sat there with this pained look on her face and ignored me. The next day, when I started telling guys in the break room about it, I found out I was not the only participant in the Margot Hexter dating Olympics. One guy told me that Bart had set him up for a dinner date with Margot, but when he got to the restaurant he found Margot waiting for him in the bar in a long black negligee and a pair of heels. At first, he's too embarrassed to say anything, but finally, she asks him whether he likes what she's wearing. He answers that it's a little unusual. 'Well,' she answers, 'I just figured that since my dad is acting like a pimp, I should at least oblige him by dressing like a whore.' The girl is a fun date.

"The worst part is that after the basketball game,

Hexter kept on calling me to ask when Margot and I were going out again. It was completely bizarre."

The bartender slid the telephone down the bar toward us.

"Kate Millholland?" he asked.

"Yes," I replied.

"Phone call for you." I thanked him and picked up the receiver.

"Kate? Is that you?" asked Claudia, her voice constricted with emotion. "Cheryl said I might catch you."

"What's wrong?" I demanded, instantly panicked.

"I'm at home. The building superintendent called me. The place is swarming with cops. They say they have a search warrant for the apartment."

CHAPTER

9

There were police cars parked two deep in front of my apartment, slowing the normally sluggish Hyde Park traffic to a chaotic trickle. Horns honked. Tempers flared. By the time I was out of my car my emotions were running too high for me to label them. I was angry, aggravated, and afraid. I bounded up the wide stone steps of my building, brushing past the Polish janitor and his friends who had gathered on the stoop to exclaim over the goings-on.

The front door of my apartment stood ajar. I pushed it open and marched in to find Detective Ruskowski and a couple of policemen joking in the front hall. Beyond them, 5′ and blocking all comers, stood my roommate, arms crossed across her chest.

"Detective Ruskowski," I said, sounding less calm than I would have liked, "what an unpleasant surprise. I assume you have a warrant."

"Here's your copy," he replied, his freckled face splitting into something that resembled a grin. "I was pretty sure you'd want to see it." He reached into his pocket and handed it to me.

"You must like playing hardball," I said, taking the

warrant from his hand. "If you'd asked me nicely, I would have gladly submitted to a voluntary search."

"That's pretty easy for you to say now. Besides, I don't know how to ask nicely. But if you think this is hardball, you haven't seen anything yet. This is the velvet-glove treatment that we give to the stuck-up daughters of influential Lake Forest families. I could have come in here and taken the place apart already, but the city is afraid of pissing your folks off. Besides," he nodded in Claudia's direction, "this little vixen threatened all sorts of terrible things if we didn't wait for you. I could have taken her into custody for obstructing the police, not to mention some of the things she said. You'd never guess that such a little bit of a thing could have such a mouth."

"I see that you two haven't been formally introduced. Dr. Claudia Stein, meet Detective Ruskowski." I took a moment and glanced at the subpoena. "It's all in order," I said, clutching my purse under my arm.

"This is going to take a couple of hours. Why don't you go across the street and get yourself a cup of coffee?"

I weighed the alternatives before answering: "I'll just stay and watch if you don't mind. I wouldn't want you to succumb to temptation and plant something. Let them in Claudia."

White-faced, my roommate stepped aside.

"Does this have to do with your client getting shot?" she whispered as Ruskowski divided his men into teams and dispatched them to various parts of the apartment.

"Yes," I replied. "You stay with the ones in the bedroom. I'll keep an eye on them in the kitchen. I don't want them out of our sight for a minute."

"I don't like this," began Claudia. "They're not going to look in the freezer, are they?"

"I'll handle it," I broke in grimly and followed the low rumble of male voices into the kitchen. Ruskowski had taken up a supervisory position, lounging against the kitchen sink as two plainclothesmen went through the cupboards.

"Not much of a cook, are you Katie?" Ruskowski needled. "These cupboards are pretty bare."

"There's something I want to talk to you about," I said.

"Does it have to do with Bart Hexter?" demanded Ruskowski.

"No."

"Then put a sock in it. I've had enough legal bullshit for one day."

"But I think—"

"Button it," snapped the detective.

I considered a third try, but I figured it served him right. Instead, I casually removed my raincoat, draping it over the arm that held my purse, and hoped for the best.

"Holy mother of God will you look at this!" exclaimed one of the policemen, his hand resting on the handle of the freezer door, his face stretched into a caricature of amazement. "What the fuck? Come and look at this, Rusty! Jesus!"

Ruskowski walked over to the freezer and looked. I stood on tiptoes and took a peek over the top of his head and suppressed a chuckle.

"You want to tell me what this is?" demanded the detective angrily.

"What do you think it is? It's an arm."

"A human arm?"

"No," I replied. "It's the arm of a giraffe. Of course it's a human arm."

"So what's it doing in your freezer?"

"My roommate, Dr. Stein, is a surgeon. She rotates between the University of Chicago and Michael Reese Hospitals. Sometimes she gets a dissection specimen at one hospital and she takes it to the other hospital to work on the next day. In the meantime, she stores it in the freezer here overnight. Let me show you."

I took the gruesome parcel from the freezer—a human arm, folded neatly at the elbow, hard as a frozen pot roast and wrapped in plastic. I passed it to the plain-clothesman with a little toss. He caught it, surprised. "You can see it's tagged from Michael Reese." The cop held the bag away from his body as if it might come to life and grab him.

"Put it back, you joker," exclaimed Ruskowski in disgust. Then he turned to me. "No wonder you don't do much cooking," he said.

For the better part of three hours Claudia and I trailed policemen around our apartment while they looked in every cupboard and every drawer, beneath every cushion and under every chair. They took my keys to the basement and turned our storage locker inside out. Out in the alley behind my building, they searched my car and, after some expostulating with the janitor, they went through the contents of the building's garbage dumpster.

Eventually I overcame my indignation and began to formulate a hypothesis based on the pattern of their search. For example, they seemed to have ruled out objects of less than a certain size, because they didn't look in small containers, including the small, stone box on our coffee table. But they did roll up the rug in the living room which caused tornadoes of dust to swirl up around our ankles and precipitated a flurry of cracks about our housekeeping. By far the most intensive scrutiny was reserved for my clothing, which the police examined with microscopic interest. The brand-new pair of Ferragamo pumps I'd worn to Hexter's on Sunday morning were taken as evidence. Inexplicably, they chose to confiscate every single pair of running shoes I owned as well as an old shetland sweater, last worn horseback riding more than a year before, which was stored in the basement. Also a pair of mud-splattered driving gloves that they found shoved in the back of my front hall closet.

Claudia's shoes, like those of all surgeons, were splattered with blood and posed a special problem for the police. Claudia indignantly explained that even though she wore paper covers over her running shoes in the operating room, some blood always got through. I pointed out that Claudia wore a size six and I wore a size ten, but Ruskowski remained unmoved. In the end he took them all into evidence while Claudia steamed.

"What am I supposed to wear to work tomorrow morning?" demanded my roommate while I signed the evidence receipts.

"And what am I supposed to wear to go running?" I asked, handing the slips back to him.

"Buy yourself a new pair," replied Ruskowski. "But I wouldn't spend too much money on them if I were you. They won't let you take them to the Women's Correctional Facility."

"I'll be sure to keep that in mind," I replied as I closed the door after him.

"I don't know about you," announced Claudia, "but I need a drink. Do we have anything?"

"I think there's still a bottle of wine left from that case that Stephen brought over. It's in the fridge."

"Is there any food?" inquired Claudia as I fetched the bottle and struggled with the cork. "Being violated by the police always gives me an appetite."

"You heard the man. The cupboard is bare."

"I could always whip up some roast arm," quipped my roommate.

"I think I'd rather order a pizza."

"Okay. Then maybe you can explain to me what just happened here tonight."

I did as I was bidden, poured myself a glass of wine, and joined my roommate at the kitchen table.

"I told you I was a suspect," I said. "The police have subpoenaed my files and my bank records, and now they've searched my apartment."

"But why? What possible reason could you have had for killing this guy Hexter?"

"This morning Detective Ruskowski paid me a little call at the office and accused me of having had an affair with Hexter. It seems as though I have a twin who's been shacking up with him at an apartment downtown. The cops showed my photo to the doorman of the building and he identified me."

"Great," replied Claudia, "a twin who's a slut. So what are you going to do about it?"

"Nothing. What is there to do?"

"Have you thought about hiring a lawyer?"

"That's what Cheryl wants me to do."

"Sounds like good advice."

"Not yet," I replied. "I don't want to overreact. If I hire a criminal lawyer it'll signal Ruskowski that I'm taking his suspicions seriously."

"They sound pretty serious," answered Claudia, who usually thought that anything not involving the massive loss of blood wasn't much to worry about. "Aren't you worried that the police will be desperate to make an arrest, even if it's the wrong person?"

"Of course I'm worried. But there's nothing I can do about it. I'm hoping that if they have half a brain among them they'll think it's more important for them to bring in a case that'll stand up in court."

"Sounds to me like you're playing with fire."

"Shit yes."

"I almost died when I got home and found the cops here. I have half a bag of dope in the freezer, hidden in an old margarine container."

"They never even looked," I said. "They only got as far as the arm."

"Saved by the dead," said Claudia. We both laughed.

"I'll tell you what really had me worried. From the wording of the subpoena, the cops could have searched both of us. I was terrified they'd ask to look in my purse."

"Why? What do you have in there?"

I picked up my big Dooney & Burke satchel, big enough to qualify as a small suitcase, in which I carried the daily essentials of my life. I unzipped it and turned it over onto the kitchen table. Pens, coins, paper clips, sunglasses, bobby pins, and tubes of lipstick clattered out amid a flurry of dog-eared message slips, rumpled tissues, and candy wrappers. Finally, after a second shake, a Sig Sauer .380-caliber revolver fell on top of the whole mess with a thud.

"You're kidding!" exclaimed Claudia, horrified. "When did you get this?"

"My father gave it to me after I was attacked last year. He meant well. I mean, he worries about me. It was actually sweet. He was almost shy when he gave it to me. I think he was worried that I would take it the wrong way."

"So how did you take it?"

"How else *could* I take it? I said thank you and put it in my purse. At least now he doesn't nag me about moving to the suburbs all the time like my mother. I hardly even think about it. But when Ruskowski handed me that search warrant tonight, my first year criminal law course came back to me. If he'd found it, Ruskowski would have been able to charge me with possession of an unregistered handgun, which is a misdemeanor, and carrying a concealed weapon, which is a felony."

"Can I touch it?" asked Claudia.

"Be careful, it's loaded. Do you want me to take the bullets out?"

"No, that's okay," she said, picking it up carefully and pointing it at the refrigerator. Her face was a picture of solemn concentration. "It's heavy," she remarked finally, laying it back down on the table between us. "You know, I spend a piece of every day repairing the damage done by guns. Everybody has one—the drug dealers, the kids in gangs, the frightened single mothers who don't have enough money to afford a decent place to live and who are trying to keep their kids safe from the drug dealers and the gangs. I see stick-up artists, guys who just want to feel tough, sixteen-year-olds who were at the wrong street corner at the wrong time, and four-year-olds who get shot by their six-year-old brothers by accident. . . . I've got to tell you. I've never seen anything good that's been done by a gun."

"I know," I said. "And yet you have to admit that people come into the emergency room who never would be in the shape they're in if they'd had a gun. People who've been raped, mugged, beaten senseless."

"Yes," agreed Claudia reluctantly.

"I know there aren't very many circumstances when you need a gun," I said slowly, thinking of the night six months before when I'd been jumped on the beach by my parents' house, beaten, and left for dead, "but when you need one, you need one very badly."

Ruskowski and his men disturbed more than the contents of my drawers. All night I wrestled fitfully with sleep, dreaming that I was forced to clean up after Bart Hexter's murder. Pamela Hexter handed me a bucket of soapy water, and I worked on my hands and knees, washing out the splattered white interior of the Rolls Royce until the bucket was filled with red and my arms were slick with soap and blood. Finally, as dawn approached, I fell into a sleep beyond dreaming. When the alarm went off I reached for the button and was wrapped, for one sweet moment, in the certainty that Russell was asleep beside me. I could hear the quiet rhythm of his breathing, feel the familiar warmth of him, but when I reached for him I was shocked into consciousness by the cold and empty sheets beside me.

There was a time when I woke this way every morning, with a cry stuck in my throat and the dizzying downward spiral of loss. Over the years I've done it less frequently, but I always combat it the same way, by forcing my reluctant body out of bed, dragging myself into sweats and going for a run. It wasn't until I was scrabbling through the chaos of my closet floor that I realized my running shoes were bagged and tagged and in the possession of Detective Ruskowski.

I arrived at the office practically growling with bad temper only to be reminded, as Cheryl and I went through the day's schedule, that I was supposed to go to the Arthritis Foundation Benefit that night.

"Damn it," I snapped, disgustedly. "I forgot all about it. I wanted to bring my dress to the office and change here tonight. Now I have to go all the way back to Hyde Park."

"Did it ever occur to you," replied my secretary, "that the reason you always forget this stuff is that you want to? In the four years I've worked for you, you have never once forgotten anything related to work. Not one single thing. But when it comes to parties and the things you do with Stephen, you always have your dress but not your shoes, or you schedule a deposition that you know will take four hours for two hours before you're supposed to leave. . . . Why do you do this stuff when it's so obvious that you hate it?"

"I do it because I have to."

"Be serious," snapped Cheryl. "I'm not going to let you off that easy."

"My mother is very involved in a number of charities. For reasons I don't understand, it's important to her that I go to the events she's involved in. And it's easier to go than to listen to her abuse me for not going. Stephen obliges by being my escort, and I reciprocate by going with him to functions where he'd rather not go alone. And there you have it—no dress, no shoes, no excuses."

"I worry about you, Kate. What do you do for fun? And don't tell me that you run, because I know for a fact that no one in their right mind runs for fun."

I was spared further examination of my social life by a phone call from Herman Geiss, the elusive head of the CFTC's Enforcement Division. Herman was a veteran of many bureaucratic wars. Like all prosecutors, he was convinced that there was no end to scoundrels in this world. He had pledged himself with the fervor of the underpaid and overworked to stamp out abuses in futures markets.

Over the years I'd developed a healthy respect for Herman's intelligence and ribald sense of humor. We had, I thought, always enjoyed as good a relationship as is possible between two professionals who continually find themselves on opposite sides of the fence.

I picked up the phone expecting some off-color ribbing about my client's untimely demise, so Herman's tough-guy act caught me off guard.

"You've had three extensions already, Millholland," growled the CFTC's burly enforcement chief. "Either shit or get off the pot."

"But the defendant is dead," I protested. "I'm not making this up, Herman. It was on the front page of the *Tribune* yesterday."

"Read the Wells Notice, Millholland. Our allegations apply equally to Bart Hexter and Hexter Commodities.

I don't care if he's dead. You'd better have your answer by Friday."

"But Herman," I pleaded, "have a heart. I'm scrambling to keep the company going after what's happened. You're being unreasonable, even by bureaucratic standards."

"Don't 'but Herman' me. Hexter Commodities has been snubbing its nose at the government since you were in diapers. I've been waiting a long time to bring Hexter Commodities down. Stay tuned, Millholland. I'm about to teach you a thing or two about bureaucratic murder."

CHAPTER
10

It was rapidly turning into the kind of morning where I wished my desk chair had come equipped with a seat belt. Besides finding myself in the midst of an intrigue between the CFTC and Hexter Commodities, another matter, long dormant, sprang to life in crisis form. As a result, I was forced to spend the better part of the morning talking on two phones at once, putting out fires.

When Barton Jr. arrived he found me sitting at my desk cursing. I had just received word that an acquisition agreement that I'd painstakingly negotiated over a period of four months had just disintegrated beyond redemption two days before the final papers were to have been signed.

"I wasn't swearing at you," I explained, waiving him into a seat. He was on his way to Kurlander's office for the meeting with his sisters about the will. He looked immeasurably tired, as if the weight of what had happened to his father had lodged somewhere between his shoulders, dragging him down.

"How are you doing?" I inquired.

"It's very hard. My father took charge of everything that touched this family. Now, in some reflexive form of primogeniture, everyone is turning to me to take his place. Kurlander calls and lectures me on responsibility, Krissy cries on my shoulder and begs me to take care of her, and Margot . . . Well, Margot just plain scares me. I never know what she'll say or who she'll say it to. Jane and I were up late last night discussing how crazy you have to be to be really crazy."

"How's your mom?"

"I have to say that during our discussion of craziness her name came up a few times. This—Dad's being killed, all the publicity—has done something to her. Mother's always been a bit peculiar, but now she's gone completely off the deep end. It's as though she's been transformed into the Emily Post of funerals. She called me at four this morning to discuss the funeral service. She has the whole thing planned down to the most minute detail. All day long the phone rings and we have these discussions about what I'm supposed to wear, whether the servants should come in their uniforms or be allowed to wear what they want, what kind of music, and on and on. Jane says that it's just Mother's way of compensating for the unsavory way that Dad died, but I can't help but find it very strange. And she seems to have developed this weird grudge against the exchange."

"In what way?"

"Well, for one thing she's insisting that none of the pallbearers be people whom Dad knew through business. She's asked Buck Farnscroft, whom Dad hardly knew except to play golf with once a year, to be a pallbearer, but she doesn't want Tim because he worked for Dad at the CBOT. Tim was Dad's nephew, for goodness sake."

"Won't Tim's feelings be hurt?"

"Of course, but Tim's used to it by now. Mom's never been overly concerned about his feelings. She's always looked down on Tim because Uncle Billy ran a hardware store and Aunt Lillian came to the house in a polyester dress once. She's never really treated Tim as part of the family. I don't know. This is bringing out all the worst parts of her personality."

"Funerals have a way of doing that," I said.

"Plus she's got it in her head that the proper time for the funeral is ten in the morning. When I pointed out that the market will be open and a lot of people from the Board of Trade won't be able to come, she actually hung up on me. She's also announced that she's closing up the house and moving to Palm Beach as soon as the funeral is over. She's given the staff notice, and when I was over there this morning I found them all packing boxes."

"Why?" I asked, surprised.

"She says she's always hated the house, it takes too many servants and costs a fortune to heat. Now that Dad's dead, she's not going to live there anymore. She says that she's making way for Jane and me, but Jane said she wouldn't live in that house for anything in the world. Who knows what's going to happen? Anyway, I've given them instructions to box up all of my father's business papers and send them here to you."

"Thanks," I said. "I'm very concerned about this CFTC matter. When I spoke to the head of the enforcement section and asked for an extension I was very surprised by his response. Not only did he refuse to grant us more time, but he seemed to take vindictive glee in the whole situation. He flat out told me that he was determined to shut down Hexter Commodities."

"It is weird that the CFTC is coming down so hard," said Barton Jr. "I thought they spent most of their time lobbying Congress over sunset provisions to keep themselves in operation. What's their beef with Dad?"

"A month ago your father received a Wells Notice. That's a copy of a formal communication from the CFTC's enforcement division to the Commissioners that says that, after extensive investigation, they think the agency should bring charges against an individual or a firm. In this case it's both. According to the Wells they're alleging that your father and Hexter Commodities traded two accounts in tandem last March and April in order to exceed position limits in the soybean market. You know that in every market the CFTC sets an upper limit on the number of speculative contracts that can be bought and held for any one account. The Enforcement Division is alleging that by trading his personal account and an account for a company called Deodar Commodities together, your father's limit was exceeded."

"That doesn't sound like that big a deal," protested Barton Jr.

"No, it doesn't. In cases like this you can either fight it or decide up front to negotiate a settlement. Either way the end result's the same—the CFTC levies a fine. That's why I don't understand Geiss's attitude at all. It sounds like he has some sort of vendetta against Hexter Commodities. Does he?"

"I don't know. But one thing's for sure, Dad hated the CFTC. He always said they were a bunch of pencil necks who got their kicks making up irritating rules to impede trading. Dad did a lot of lobbying on behalf of the industry, and I know he made no secret of the fact that he thought the CFTC was ineffective and self-serving. Maybe they're just looking for a chance to finally get even. What do you think?"

"I have no idea. Your father and I never got around to discussing it. I still don't even have copies of the trading records of the two accounts. I don't know who it is who does business as Deodar Commodities. Your father promised he'd have all that material to give me on Sunday morning. That's why I'm surprised that I didn't find anything at the house. Do you know if the police took papers away with them when they searched?"

"I have no idea. I can ask my mother. But I'm sure there are copies of all of that stuff at the office. Why don't you ask Tim?"

"I was planning on doing that this morning until this other matter came up. I think I'm just going to go over there if you don't mind. We're a little pressed for time. Usually the CFTC gives the defendant two weeks to respond to a Wells. We've had three one-week extensions already. From the sound of things I don't think we're going to get a fourth. I'm going to have to get copies of those documents today. Plus, I want to have a look through your dad's files. I want to see whether he was holding any warehouse receipts for physicals, check if any confirmations of trades from other exchanges came in. I want to be sure we're not headed for any unpleasant surprises."

"Speaking of unpleasant surprises," began Barton Jr. reluctantly, "there's something I wanted to talk to you about. I know it's really more in Kurlander's line, but I can't bring myself to talk to him about it. I know it sounds stupid, but he reminds me of Father O'Donnell, one of the parish priests when I was growing up. He frightened us into believing that he could tell what sins we'd committed just by looking at us. Every time I talk to Kurlander I get this pain in my chest. He makes my father's money seem like this enormous cross I'm going to have to cart around the rest of my life."

"I know. Ken is into Duty with a capital D. But there's no denying that this kind of money does tend to develop a life of its own. What did you want to talk to me about?"

"Last night I got a phone call from someone who works for my father. Her name is Torey Lloyd. It was a strange conversation. At first she wasn't very direct. But I think what it boils down to is that she claims to have been having an affair with my father."

"And she wants money," I guessed.

"Yes. Yes, she does. I was wondering if you might be willing to talk to her for me. I honestly don't think I can face it."

My mother caught me just as I was leaving for Hexter Commodities. I was standing behind my desk, snapping the locks closed on my briefcase when Cheryl rushed in, a look of apology on her face. Following close on her heels was my female parent. Mother always fills Cheryl with a kind of terrified awe. She is so perfect, like a photograph from *Vogue* come to life. Everything about her sets her apart from the workaday world—her magnificent hair, the makeup that has taken hours, the elegant line of her skirt, the handmade Italian pumps that all speak of a quiet fortune and a lifetime of leisure.

Mother seldom came to my office, and I did nothing to hide my surprise.

"I was on my way to the Carolina Herrara trunk show at Neiman Marcus, and I thought you might like to join me," she announced, looking around my office as if she'd just gotten off the train only to find herself at the wrong station. "You know I always think Carolina's clothes would be so good for you—elegant and feminine. I might even take you to lunch afterward."

"I'm so sorry, Mother," I said, managing to squeeze some semblance of regret into my voice. "I was just leaving for a meeting. We'll have to have lunch another day."

"I'm sure you could rearrange your schedule if you really wanted to. After all, it's not every day that your mother invites you out to lunch. And besides, you really need to order something to wear when they take your picture for that magazine article."

"What article?" I demanded with a sinking feeling.

"Stephen probably hasn't had time to call you yet. Vera Masterson's daughter, Avery, has some big job at *Chicago Magazine*, and they've decided to do a cover story on the city's power couples—you know, where both the man and the woman do these important things. They're interviewing Marv and Shelly Quinlen—he's head of Quinlen Steel of course, and she's chairwoman of the Art Institute Board this year; and they're using Terry Binstock and his wife, Susan—he's the big heart surgeon at Northwestern, and she owns that gallery on Huron where they charge a fortune for those awful canvases where people just splash paint. And then, of course, they want to put you and Stephen on the cover."

"They what?"

"You and Stephen on the cover. That's why you'll want to wear something inspired for the picture. Your clothes are always so dowdy, and frankly, dear, you and I both know you've never been very photogenic. That's why I had the brainstorm about the trunk show. Now you understand why you should reschedule your meeting. I know that Carolina will do her best, but it'll still be a rush to get whatever you order today in time for the photo shoot. Where do you think they should take the picture? I don't think your office is big enough. What is Stephen's like? Of course you're welcome to come out to the house. I'll just give Avery a call and let her know she has that option."

"Mother," I broke in. "I can't possibly cancel my meeting."

"Whyever not?"

"Because it's important."

"And this isn't?" she demanded with an edge to her voice.

"I didn't say that. But I have to review some documents. I have to respond to a Wells Notice by Friday." My mother looked at me blankly. I might as well have been speaking Chinese. "Mother, this is my job. I have responsibilities. I can't just cancel this meeting." I was trying to sound adult and rational, but in the end I felt like I was blabbering.

"You always manage to make it perfectly clear where your priorities lie," my mother replied as she slipped on her gloves.

"If you'd let me know ahead of time," I implored.

"Next time I'll make an appointment with your secretary," she said. She made it her exit line.

* * *

Before I left for Hexter Commodities I called
Stephen Azorini only to be told he was in a meeting. I
didn't like hearing about the *Chicago Magazine* business from my mother. Frankly, I didn't like the whole
idea of being interviewed for an article about power
couples. Last year Stephen's company had successfully
fought off a hostile takeover, and in its aftermath both
of us had gotten a lot of attention in the press. I had
been surprised to discover that while Stephen had a def-
inite taste for ink, I did not. Plus, how would *Chicago
Magazine* feel about my gracing their cover after I was
arrested for murdering Bart Hexter?

The offices of Hexter Commodities had the bizarre
air of calamity. The waiting room was empty, and
phones rang unanswered while employees huddled
away from their desks, conferring in somber little
groups. Several brokers were in the process of clearing
out their desks. Bart Hexter's body was not yet in the
ground and already his tight ship had turned slack—a
rudderless, engineless vessel, drifting, I feared, toward
disaster.

I walked, unchallenged, across the trading floor.
Through an open door I glimpsed Carl Savage pacing
next to his desk. He was wearing the kind of headset
that phone operators use and was bellowing into it. I decided to bother him later, and changed course toward
Bart Hexter's office. Barton Jr, I knew, would still be
meeting with Kurlander, but the people I was really interested in talking to were the two who worked most
closely with the dead man—his secretary, Mrs.
Titlebaum, and his nephew, Tim Hexter.

Tim was not at his desk, but I found Mrs. Titlebaum
at her post, grimly slitting open her dead boss's mail.

She was a plump woman in her fifties, with well-disciplined gray hair and a no-nonsense air about her.

"May I bother you for a minute?" I asked.

"Of course," she replied, looking up from her work. "Barton Jr. told me you'd want to see me about some papers. I know I should call him Mr. Hexter, but that's what I called his father," she added sadly.

"You worked for him for a long time," I said, easing myself into a chair.

"More than thirty years. He and my Leo started trading at about the same time, but my Leo didn't have the knack. He got himself into trouble and lost all his money—lost all the money his family had given him, too. He couldn't face it, and he killed himself. He left me with nothing but a ten-month-old baby to take care of. Leo's friends took up a collection afterward, but that money didn't last very long. It was Mr. Hexter who didn't forget about me and gave me this job. I've been with him ever since, and he was always there for me. When the neighborhood started changing he helped me with a new house, when Evie needed braces, whatever. We could always count on him."

"Obviously you didn't find him a hard man to work for."

"I wouldn't say that," she exclaimed with a chuckle. "He had the devil's temper, and when he said jump you'd better jump. But he was the boss, and he never meant any of the bad things he said. I just let it roll off me like water off a duck's back."

"Did Mr. Hexter ask you to pull information together for me regarding the most recent CFTC business? I'm looking for copies of documents regarding his trading account and the Deodar Commodities account."

"I pulled the customer file for Deodar Commodities and had accounting print out a trading record for the two account numbers he gave me Thursday morning, if that's what you mean."

"Did he tell you what they were for?"

"I assumed he wanted them for his regular bull session with Tim that afternoon."

"Bull session?" I inquired.

"They called it that as a joke. You know, a bear market is a declining market, and a bull market is a rising one. Every day Mr. Hexter met with Tim for an hour after the close. Once, a couple of years ago, I asked him about what they were doing in there and he answered, 'Catching the bull and taking him by the horns.' The joke stuck, and we started calling their daily meeting the bull session."

"What did they really do during their meeting?"

"They'd go through the day's trades. I don't know if you ever saw Mr. Hexter while the markets were open, but he was something to see. He'd trade thousands of contracts, barking out instructions to Tim to relay to Carl. He kept everything in his head—he joked that he didn't need a computer because he'd been born with one between his ears, and I believed him—but it was hard for everybody else to keep up. Every day at four Tim would go into Mr. Hexter's office and check the written record of the trades against what Mr. Hexter had done that day. When they were done reviewing the contracts, Mr. Hexter would leave, and Tim would stay and make sure that all the mistakes were corrected. Then he'd drop the final version at the Hexters' on his way home at night in case Mr. Hexter wanted to trade

Globex overnight or do something in the European currency markets in the early morning."

"And they did this every day?" I asked, thinking ruefully of the four o'clock meetings that Bart Hexter had made with me, no doubt never intending to keep them.

"Oh yes. Mr. Hexter was very superstitious. He called it his lucky schedule and would get furious if anything or anybody changed it. Every so often it took Tim too long to do the Friday report—on Fridays he not only had to do the daily trades but also the summary for the week—and he'd have to bring it out to the Hexters' on Saturday morning. It would take days for Mr. Hexter to get over it."

"So you delivered the information Mr. Hexter requested on Thursday in time for the regular four o'clock meeting?" I said, pressing on.

"Well, I think I had it ready a few minutes late because when I brought it in they'd already begun reviewing the trades. Poor Tim. There must have been a lot of discrepancies because Mr. Hexter was already screaming at him."

"What was he angry about?"

"I have no idea. He was just like that. Something would set him off—a clerical error or a missed trade—and he'd get into a rage that would take days to end. It really didn't make sense to wonder about why. We all understood that, especially Tim. Working so closely with his uncle, he bore the brunt of his temper. But Mr. Hexter loved him like a son.

"I know for a fact that Mr. Hexter helped him out with the terrible mess when Tim's father died. That was just like Mr. Hexter—all shouting and temper, but when it came right down to it, he was there to help when all the people with their sweet talk and polite ways were long gone."

"Do you have any idea what happened to the material?"

"This morning Barton Jr. told me it was for the CFTC matter you were handling, so I assume Mr. Hexter took it home with him for your Sunday meeting."

"I was at his house right after he died," I told her. "I looked through his things. I didn't find any of the material you mentioned anywhere." I sighed.

"Did you look in his briefcase?" asked the dead man's secretary.

"Yes. It was practically empty. I suppose the police must have taken everything."

"Is that bad?"

"It's inconvenient. Police or no police, I still have to have Hexter Commodities' answer to the CFTC on Friday. Is there any way you could duplicate the material you gave to Mr. Hexter? Are there file copies or any kind of backups?"

"I gave Mr. Hexter the original files," answered Mrs. Titlebaum dubiously. "We don't keep backups of many things. The trading records are on computer disk. I could have a clerk run you off another set."

"I'd appreciate that," I said. "Especially anything you have on Deodar Commodities, like a phone number or a mailing address. Do you have any idea who they are?"

"No. All I know is that it was a discretionary account. You know, Mr. Hexter didn't have to consult anyone about the trades he made. I don't think the customer ever called him. Still, I'll see what I can find."

"One more thing, Mrs. Titlebaum. Do you know what Mr. Hexter wanted to discuss with Ken Kurlander? Ken told me that your boss called his secretary Friday afternoon and made an appointment for Monday morning."

"He did?" replied the secretary, obviously surprised. "Well, this is the first I've heard about it."

I found Tim Hexter in a tiny office wedged between Bart Hexter's and Carl Savage's. I suspected that it had once been a storage closet but that Bart, wanting his assistant within earshot at all times, had had it converted into an office. What was surprising was not its size—though the contrast with Tim's bulk made it almost comical—but that its occupant had, for all intents and purposes, turned it into a shrine to the Chicago Cubs.

Every conceivable inch of space was filled with Cubs memorabilia, lovingly displayed. Wrigley's finest were all represented: photos of Ferguson Jenkins on the mound, Andre Dawson at the plate, even autographed pictures of famed Cubs announcers Harry Carey and Jack Brickhouse. On the wall behind the desk, extending from the ceiling to the floor, were game bats hung on racks, autographed by players like Ryne Sandberg, Mark Grace, even hall-of-famer Hank Wilson, whose bat smoked for the Cubs in the '30s. The ceiling was ringed with Cubs hats, signed on the bill by the players who had worn them. On his desk was an Ernie Banks autographed ball, entombed in Lucite.

The overall effect was extraordinary, and I said as much to Tim as I took a few minutes to take it all in. Tim pointed out the highlights of his collection and for a few minutes the usual dimness of his countenance was lit up by his love of baseball.

I found myself wondering what it must be like to love something as impersonal, something as intangible, as a baseball team. What great vistas of inner emptiness such an avocation could fill. It was, I realized, the perfect counterpoint to Bart Hexter—his obsession with the markets and his rages—another way for Tim to escape his exacting and temperamental master. If he wasn't physically unreachable on his bicycle, he could at least build a comforting cocoon of baseball memorabilia— physical reminders of the sport, and the team, that existed in a world completely untouched by the markets.

I wondered what would become of Tim now that his uncle was dead. In his brief stab at trading, Tim had crashed and burned in spectacular fashion. He had spent the last ten years as Bart Hexter's whipping boy. With Bart gone, I could imagine few skills he could parlay into another job—short of his ability to absorb abuse. Perhaps Barton Jr. would keep him on out of family loyalty. Either way it was clear that Tim was yet another innocent casualty of Hexter's murder.

When I was done admiring Tim's collection I squeezed into the chair reserved for visitors and got down to business.

"Do you know anything about some documents that Bart had pulled together for the meeting he was supposed to have had with me Sunday morning? They were account files and trading records for his personal soybean account and for a client called Deodar Commodities."

"What about them?" Tim's voice was deep, but contained an empty ring, a slowness, that immediately made you realize he must be short quite a bit of candle power.

"Do you know where they are?"

"Nope. Did you ask Mrs. Titlebaum?"

"She said she gave them to Bart Thursday before your afternoon meeting."

"Bart never showed them to me, if that's what you mean," he replied defensively. "We just did the usual stuff, you know, reconciling the trades."

"Are you familiar with Deodar Commodities?" I inquired.

"Sure. It's one of our accounts."

"Do you know how I could get in touch with them?"

"What do you mean?"

"I mean, do you have an address for them or a phone number?"

"Why would I?"

"If you don't have that information, do you know where I could find it?"

"It would be in the account file I guess," he replied, scratching his head.

"Which no one can find." I groaned. "Did you know that the CFTC has been investigating Hexter Commodities?" I asked, trying another tack.

"Bart was pretty mad about it," Tim confided. "He said that the bastards were really out to get him this time. He thought they were trying to get back at him because of the surveillance camera thing."

"What was that?"

"Oh, a couple of years ago the government wanted to put cameras on the trading floor at the board—you know—like they have in banks to catch hold-up men. They have them at the Merc, but Bart kept them out of the Board. He told me on Friday that the CFTC was just trying to get even.

"He said the charges against him were bullshit," Tim added in no uncertain terms. "He said that the CFTC was just looking for an excuse to come after him. They manufactured the whole thing."

"Would you happen to know why Mr. Hexter might have made an appointment to see Ken Kurlander Monday morning?"

"Ken Kurlander the lawyer?" Tim asked. "I have no idea."

Mrs. Titlebaum appeared at the doorway, her face clouded with concern.

"I don't know how to explain this," she said. "But I've been through all the files, and I've just been with Rita in Accounting. There's not one scrap of paper about Deodar Commodities, and all of the computer files have been erased."

CHAPTER

11

"Where the hell is that fucking Barton?" demanded Savage. The day's trading was clearly taking its toll. There were tiny beads of sweat on his forehead and his custom-made shirt was dark-ringed with perspiration. "He said he was going to come in and call the trades. He shows up yesterday, reads the screen, makes some suggestions, and then he's out of here. Today there's no sign of him. Fuck him. There are no sick days in this business."

"He had to meet with the attorney for his father's estate," I offered.

"He should do that kind of shit when the market is closed. This isn't college, for Christ sake. It's war out there. I've got a half a dozen clients who say they're pulling their accounts if they don't hear from Barton personally. There's something going on with the Krauts and D-mark prices are all over the place. We're going to get killed."

"I know where I can reach him."

Savage pushed the telephone across the desk toward me. "Tell him to get his ass over here," he said.

I got Barton on the phone and explained the situation.

"He's on his way," I reported, hanging up the receiver.

"It's about fucking time," declared Savage.

"I need to ask you about something," I said. "I've been trying to track down some files that Bart was supposed to give me on Sunday. They've disappeared. It's the Deodar Commodities account. It's regarding the CFTC's investigation."

"The CFTC is a pain in the ass."

"They've alleged that Bart was trading soybeans in conjunction with the Deodar in order to exceed position limits."

"That's bullshit. Why would Bart want to exceed position limits in soybeans? What a crock."

"All the computer records of the accounts have been erased."

"What?"

"That's what Mrs. Titlebaum says."

"It must be some kind of mistake. Why would anybody want to erase account files? Those babes in accounting, they've got only one brain among the four of them."

"Would the files be easy to erase?" I asked.

"I don't know. I don't do anything with the computer except read the Quotron screen. You should ask Loretta. She'd be able to tell you."

"Loretta Resch?"

"Yeah. She's in charge of the clearing operation. She understands all that computer shit."

"I'll talk to her," I said. "Maybe she'll be able to recover the files. But if she can't, is there any way that we can piece together the information that's been destroyed?"

"You can ask for a printout from the clearinghouse. They keep track of all the trades. We keep all the trading tickets in storage. What time are we talking about?"

"Last February through April."

"Then they should still be in the building. Tim would be able to get them for you."

The division of Hexter Commodities that serviced local traders and cleared their transactions through the exchange was in a separate but adjoining set of offices. Here, with no retail customers to impress, the decor was sparse and functional. Instead of a stately reception desk and oak paneling, the clearing side of Hexter Commodities boasted a large conversation pit couch, a pinball machine, and an arcade video game. One wall was covered with small wooden pigeonholes for messages, each labeled with the name of a trader who cleared through Hexter. Next to it was a large corkboard on which was posted that day's out-trades. A soft drink machine hummed quietly in one corner.

By necessity, futures traders carry their offices in the pockets of their trading jackets. The thick 'deck' of their order cards bound in a lucky rubber band, a fist full of pencils, a battered calculator, and a bottle of antacid tablets was about all any trader needed or indeed had room for in the crowded arena of the trading pit. Money spent on anything more—a desk, a phone, a place to lock up a wallet—was just money wasted. A clearing firm that could handle transactions efficiently, wasn't overly strict when it came to capital reserves, and could provide some of the amenities, like a shower and phone messages, would find itself with plenty of business.

Different clearing firms had different personalities. Like corporate cultures they drew in their own kind. I'd heard stories about Hexter Commodities' clearing operation that made me think that either Bart Hexter himself, or the reputation he had cultivated in his years on the trading floor, had some sort of trickle-down effect. Hexter Commodities was where the wild men cleared their trades, where aggressive scalpers streaked like shooting stars across the dark orbit of the markets. It was the place where they played liar's poker and where the high-stakes card games materialized after the close. As I walked through the lounge I saw a group of clerks playing a game of spoof. Each reached into his pocket and pulled out his closed fist, in which was concealed either one, two, or three coins. The person who guessed correctly the number and value of the coins in his opponent's hand was the winner.

I found Loretta Resch in a modest office behind two rows of computer clerks. She rose and extended her hand in a flash of crimson manicure. She was an attractive woman in her forties. Her hair was a luxurious, if improbable, shade of dark red, cut with deceptive simplicity in a straight line at her chin. Perfect eyebrows arched in symmetry above eyes brought to an alarming shade of emerald by contact lenses. The jacket of her suit was bright yellow and draped across the back of her chair. She conducted business in a black silk blouse with a plunging neckline. I knew that her look was deliberately sexy. I wondered whether men found her so. I introduced myself and told her that I needed her help, explaining what Mrs. Titlebaum had just reported about the computer files being erased.

"I know. Rita—she's one of my data-entry clerks—was just in here telling me about it. She was very upset. I can't understand it. We have a backup system that makes it almost impossible to erase anything by accident." She turned to the computer terminal on her desk and set to work on the keyboard. "Let me see what I can come up with." She talked as she worked. "I heard you were there the morning he died. I know it seems ghoulish to be so curious, but I can't help it. Do they know who killed him?"

"I don't know. There hasn't been anything in the papers. The police haven't said anything. You must have some ideas."

"No, I don't. That's what's got me so bugged. I've known Bart for ages, and yet I feel completely in the dark. I realize Bart wasn't exactly a lovable guy all the time. Nobody could have the kind of temper he had and not make enemies—but someone who'd be mad enough to shoot him?"

"He wasn't involved with organized crime, was he?"

"Bart? You've got to be kidding. I know there are guys on the floor who're supposed to trade with mob money. But there are all sorts of rumors in the pits. Bart didn't have anything to do with the Mafia. Why would he have to? He was very successful."

"Maybe someone was jealous? Maybe someone was angry that Bart had made money at his expense?"

"Lots of traders get jealous. Lots more get angry. There's a fistfight a day down there, probably more. But the beauty of this business is that there's always another day's trading. All you have to do is hang in there and you'll have a chance to do to the other guy what he just did to you. I just can't see this being a trading thing. This has to be something personal."

"The police asked me whether Bart was happily married. Do you think he was?"

"Marriage doesn't make you happy," replied Loretta, turning away from the screen for an instant as she spoke. "I should know that better than anybody. But I do know that there were three things that Bart loved: risk, money, and Pamela. I think of the three, Pamela was the thing he was most afraid of losing. I know that sounds strange, coming from me," she turned back to her computer. "It's no secret that Bart and I had a thing once. It didn't last very long. Mostly because there was no chance that he'd leave his wife. Bart was too used to her; she was like a habit to him. He didn't have to pretend with Pamela. He could be his petty, evil-tempered self. I know for a fact that Bart was terrified of losing her. It took me awhile to figure it all out, but once I did I broke it off."

"Why was he afraid of losing Pamela?" I inquired, genuinely perplexed.

"Because she had more money than he did."

"But he had plenty of his own money. He didn't need his wife's."

"But his money was different, wasn't it? With his kind of money he could buy a Rolls Royce and build a big house. But it takes Pamela's kind of money to get into all those snotty clubs and get invited to all those parties he loved to hate. He used to say that Pamela's friends' horses were better-looking and twice as smart as their owners. He used to say that if you put any one of the pantywaists he played golf with into the trading pits with a wad of their own money they'd wet their pants. He loved feeling superior to them, but he also knew that if it wasn't for Pamela, they'd never even let him in the front door. That's not to say he was afraid to have Pamela mad at him, but he was always careful that she didn't get too mad, if you get what I'm saying."

"You said he loved risk. Do you think he could be in any kind of big-time gambling trouble?"

"Bart wasn't like his brother Billy. They both loved to gamble, but unlike Billy, Bart never bet more than he could stand to lose. He was too calculating to get into trouble."

"Everyone I talk to says the same thing. Hexter made his share of enemies, but nothing out of the ordinary, nobody who'd be angry enough to kill him."

"Except that we're all wrong," said Loretta, frowning at the screen.

"Wrong how?"

"Well obviously because someone did kill him," she answered distractedly. I sat and watched her while she punched in more numbers and stared at the computer display with a troubled look. Finally she turned to me.

"I can't understand it," she said. "Rita's right. All the files have been erased and the backups too. It's all just gone."

"Do you think Bart might have erased the files himself?" I asked, dismayed.

"No. Bart didn't know enough to even switch on his computer. Besides, according to this, the files were erased Monday morning at 8:46. Bart was already dead."

It had taken some bullying—both on my part and Barton Jr.'s—to convince Tim to extract the original trading tickets I needed from the bowels of basement storage. I still couldn't decide whether Tim was dumb, lazy, or just paralyzed into immobility by his uncle's death, but after a while I didn't care. He had wasted a lot of time making lame excuses for why it would be hard to find the records that I'd asked for, and said that they wouldn't be any use to me anyway. I suspected that he just didn't want to be bothered with digging them up. It wasn't until I'd made it very clear that I wouldn't leave without getting what I'd come for that he finally dragged himself into storage for them, but not until after I'd concluded that if Tim Hexter were my assistant, I'd spend a fair amount of time yelling at him, too. But then, unlike Bart, I'd never have someone as dim as Tim working for me.

Before I finished at the Board I also made a stop at the office of the Clearing Corporation to request copies of the relevant trading records and wait for them to be printed off.

Back at my office I looked at my watch and called Stephen. He was in a meeting so I left a message with his secretary saying that I would probably be a little late for the Arthritis Foundation benefit and would meet him there.

I wolfed down the Italian beef sandwich I'd picked up at a greasy little stand on my way back from the CBOT. Then I told Cheryl to call Sherman Whitehead and tell him I wanted to see him. Sherman was a first-year associate and my own personal favorite when it came to scut work. While he'd graduated first in his law school class, Sherman's obvious lack of social skills made him less popular among the partners. With his dork haircut and crumpled suit he might have been cut from the same cloth as Tim Hexter, but unlike Tim, Sherman's intellect made up for his other shortcomings.

Sherman appeared in a few minutes. On his face was the same look of resignation and dread with which all associates greet late-afternoon summonses to a partner's office. I told him that computer printouts and trading tickets were due to be delivered any minute from Hexter Commodities. I explained that I needed the two sets of documents to be spot-checked against each other by morning. To Sherman's credit he accepted the assignment with some grace and promised to report to me first thing the next day.

I was just about to pick up the telephone to try Detective Ruskowski again when Lillian, the receptionist, called to say that there was a woman in the waiting room who wanted to see me. I could tell from her wary tone that my visitor did not fit the button-downed profile of the corporate clients who usually passed her desk. Also that she was standing close enough to Lillian that the receptionist couldn't speak freely. At least it's not a visit from the police, I thought to myself.

The woman who came to my office was my age but from a world away. Thin and dark-haired, she had a pretty face, but it was marred by an expression of deep-seated dissatisfaction. She wore a churchy dress made of cheap, flowered fabric and painfully pointed patent leather shoes with high, high heels. I knew I'd seen her before, and recently, but out of context it took me longer than it should have to recognize the Hexter's sullen-faced maid.

"Hello, Elena," I said, pulling her name out of the air

at the last second. "Why don't you have a seat and tell me what I can do for you."

She took the offered chair and considered me with suspicion.

"I come to find out what money Meester Hexter leave for me in his will." Her voice was at once soft and defiant. From her accent, I guessed she was Latin American.

"I am afraid that I'm the wrong person for you to ask," I replied. "You'll need to speak to Mr. Kurlander. He's in charge of Mr. Hexter's estate. I can call down to his office, and you can make an appointment with his secretary to see him."

"I cannot speak to Meester Kurlander," declared Elena with feeling.

"Why not? If you were mentioned in Mr. Hexter's will I'm sure Mr. Kurlander will be sending you a letter in the next few days."

"I cannot speak to him," she replied again. "He is a friend of that woman." At this Elena made a sort of spitting sound that was distinctly foreign.

"What woman?"

"The Meessus Hexter."

"I am surprised that you feel that way about your employer."

"She eez not my employer," Elena snapped. "She fire Elena. No give me notice. No give me severance. Nothing."

"I understand she's let the entire staff go. She is planning to move to Florida."

"She not fire me because of Florida. She fire me because she say I too slow answering bell. She say I always watching her with my cow eyes. She not give me severance. She just say—'Go, Elena. Pack your bags and get out.' She throw Elena out into street."

"Mrs. Hexter's husband has just been murdered," I said. "Sometimes people who have suffered a tragedy act unlike themselves. Sometimes they do thoughtless, hurtful things."

"You tell me about hurt? I lose my job. I have no money, no food, no place to live. What does that woman know about hurt in her big house? What is tragedy is that Elena lose job because of what I know. Because of what the Meesus want to hide."

"You must be very careful about what you say, Elena," I replied, sharply.

"Is not Elena who needs to be careful," the maid sneered. "Is the Meesus who needs to be careful. She thinks if I have no job I must go back to Guatamala, no tell anybody about gun."

"What gun?" I demanded.

"Meester Hexter's gun. The one he keep in the money drawer in his desk. Meesus Hexter, she so mean with money. When I go to her for job she say she pay me two hundred per week. Two hundred a week, I say, that too little money. Must be crazy work for two hundred a week in big house in Lake Forest America. My sister, she work for Meesus Franklin. She make four hundred and twenty-five dollars a week plus she get three weeks' vacation—go back to my country. I go home from interviewing thinking Meesus Hexter crazy, cheap lady. That night, the job agency call me, say every week Meesus Hexter, she give me check for two hundred and Meester Hexter, he give me one hundred fifty a week, cash money. But I no tell Meesus Hexter that Meester pay me money."

"What does this have to do with a gun?" I asked.

"Meester Hexter always keep gun in drawer where he keep the money. I see it Friday when he pay me."

"Last Friday? What time?"

"Friday morning."

"What kind of gun?"

"What kind of gun?" parroted Elena as if she found the idea that there could be more than one kind completely fantastic. "Black gun," she answered finally.

"After Mr. Hexter was killed, didn't you talk to the police?"

"Sure. The police, they come. They ask me questions. Just like TV."

"Did you tell them about the gun?"

"No, they no ask me about no gun. They ask me about the Meesus and the Meester. Are they happy? Do they fight? Do they make love?"

"But you didn't tell them about the gun?"

"They no ask. They ask about fighting. I tell them the Meester and the Meesus, they fight all the time. They fight in the morning. They fight at night. Friday night the children come for dinner, they all fight. Sunday morning, before we leave for church, they still fighting. Policeman ask what fighting about. I tell them—'You listen to rich people fighting it make you crazy. I no listen.' "

"Elena," I said slowly, taking time to think. "If you would like, I will speak to Barton Jr. about getting you your severance pay."

"Meester Barton very nice. Very funny. Please, you talk to him."

"Is there someplace I can call you after I talk to him? Where are you living now?"

"I stay with my seester at Meesus Franklin's. She nice lady. I do ironing. I give you phone number."

Repeating my promise to see what I could do about getting her severance pay, I ushered Elena out of my office. When I returned, I picked up the phone and placed yet another call to Detective Ruskowski.

CHAPTER
12

I didn't really have the time, but curiosity prompted me to pay a quick call on Ken Kurlander. I found him in his corner office preparing to leave for the day.

"Do you have a minute?" I asked. "I wanted to know how your meeting with the Hexter children went this morning."

"About as I expected. These situations are often difficult, especially with an individual like Margot. After his sisters had gone, I spoke privately with Barton Jr. about whether or not Margot is truly competent to have control of the money that is coming to her."

"Competent or legally competent?" I ventured.

"Legally competent," replied Kurlander dryly.

"That's a very rough row to hoe. Very rough."

"It's a very large sum of money that will likely be taken from her by the first crank cause or charlatan that attracts her affections."

"It's her money," I said, though I knew it wouldn't earn me any points with Kurlander. "I'd be surprised if Barton felt differently."

"You and Barton seem to be aligned on any number of issues," replied Kurlander tartly. "But who do you think Margot will turn to for support when she's squandered the money her father left her? Barton might not have the stomach to institute guardianship proceedings for his sister, but either way the end result will be the same. Margot is, to put it in its most favorable light, unstable. Whether Barton likes it or not, he will have to be his sister's keeper. If he bites the bullet now and institutes legal proceedings, he will at least insure that he has the funds with which to provide for her."

"Certainly Margot's father was aware of his daughter's shortcomings. He could have chosen to leave her portion of the estate in trust if he'd wanted to."

"He and I discussed it many times," sighed Kurlander. "But Bart was eternally optimistic that Margot would eventually marry and straighten her life out."

"Do you think that Hexter might have changed his mind about Margot?" I asked. "Maybe that's why he made an appointment to see you." If Hexter had really counted on Margot finding a husband to straighten her out, her announced intention to try a lesbian life-style might have finally convinced him that he should put the money outside of her control.

"I'm afraid we'll never know what Bart intended," confessed Kurlander.

"Have you told the police yet that he made an appointment to see you?"

"No, I have not."

"Do you intend to?"

"I don't see what bearing it has on the case."

"Don't you think that's for the police to decide?"

"I see no reason to fruitlessly divert their attention."

"Ken," I countered. "This is not some parlor game. A man was murdered. It is your duty as an officer of the court to pass along any information that might aid the police in their investigation."

"Please, Kate. That makes a very fine speech, straight out of your legal ethics class, no doubt. But you are speaking of principles, and I am speaking of reality. Detective Ruskowski may be a competent and experienced homicide detective, but he is the sort of man who would look for an apple in an orchard by first chopping down all the trees. I see no reason to turn his attention toward the family on the basis of what? The fact that Bart Hexter made an appointment to speak to me about something that has gone with him to his grave?"

I knew that on some level Kurlander was right. But perhaps it was because the mere coincidence of my appointment with Hexter the morning he was killed had caused the spotlight of police suspicion to be turned upon me—or maybe my legal ethics class was recent enough to have left an impression—but when I got back to my office, I called Ruskowski and left yet another, more urgent message.

No one who had their shit together would be on the phone an hour and fifteen minutes before the Arthritis Foundation Benefit while a saleswoman at Neiman Marcus described all the evening gowns she had in size ten. Leon, one of the mail clerks, had already been dispatched in a taxi with my credit card and instructions to pick up my selection, knowing that there was no way I would be able to get to Hyde Park, change, and get to the party in time. I was beginning to think Cheryl might have a point.

I tended to other business until Leon appeared with two dresses, each in a plastic shroud, and a small shopping bag with a pair of Stewart Weitzman black satin pumps. I locked the door behind him, pulled the shades and, with a glance at the time, began to shed my suit.

The dresses were pretty, though definitely more glamorous than I usually wore. One was emerald green, with long sleeves and a gored skirt, but the back plunged too low. The other one was midnight blue and seemed more promising. I slipped it on. It was a slim, fitted gown with a sweetheart neck, from which a tiny shower of translucent beads flowed into rivulets down the body of the dress. I examined my reflection in the dim and narrow mirror that hung inside the door of my office closet and saw at once what always greeted my mother's disappointed eye.

The dress was lovely, but it was worn by a slightly frazzled corporate attorney—a woman who'd had too little sleep and was wearing too little makeup. With a sigh of resignation I pulled the hairpins out of my French twist, bent at the waist like my nanny taught me, and gave my hair a hard brushing. Then I pinned it back up, rummaged in my desk for mascara and lipstick. Not finding any, I raided Cheryl's drawer and found her makeup bag. Then, with cosmetic first-aid accomplished, I stuck my tongue out at myself in the mirror and headed out the door, only twenty minutes late.

Running up the wide stone steps of the Field Museum of Natural History I felt a little bit like Cinderella—out of place and late for the ball to boot. The museum was a favorite venue for charity functions, and I'd eaten cool canapés and drunk warm wine on innumerable occasions in the shadow of the great woolly mammoth in its marble rotunda. I gave my name at the reception table, took my placecard and silent auction number, and went off in search of Stephen.

I found him standing in front of the diorama of penguins, dead and long-stuffed, that had decorated the same frozen, arctic scene since before I was born. He looked sleek and in his element. The front of his shirt and the flash of his smile were the whitest things in the room. He slipped his arm around my waist briefly in greeting.

"You made it, Kate," he said. "You know Ed and Happy Lassar."

I extended my hand to the real-estate developer and expressed myself pleased to see the most recent Mrs. Lassar. A waiter passed with a tray filled with champagne glasses, and Stephen procured one for me.

"I was just telling Stephen that we're all a little surprised to see Krissy Chilcote here tonight," Happy whispered confidingly. I looked over the socialite's shoulder and, sure enough, there was Barton Jr.'s sister, looking palely pretty in a gown of black point d'esprit lace surrounded by a gaggle of sympathetic friends. "I know she's one of the co-chairmen, but still, I don't even think they've had the funeral yet."

"My impression is that Krissy has always done exactly what she's wanted from the time she was a little girl," remarked her husband kindly. "I don't think her father would expect her to do any differently now."

"I don't know," replied his wife. "From what I hear about her, it seems more likely that she couldn't stand the thought of the party going on without her."

"You know, I haven't had a chance to look at the silent auction items," I interjected, feeling awkward gossiping about the Hexters. Stephen made a graceful excuse, and we proceeded to the geology wing, where long tables covered with donated items were arranged. Beside each item was a sheet of paper for bidders to write the dollar amount of their offer.

"You look very pretty in that dress," remarked Stephen as we browsed through the various displays—tickets to the symphony, dinners at restaurants, trips, jewelry, and art objects—all donated to raise money for arthritis research. "Is it new?"

"Very," I replied. "I'm sorry I was late. This Hexter business is taking all of my time."

"At least you seem to have freed Krissy up."

"You really are offended that she's here," I commented.

"It certainly doesn't look very good. Her father was just murdered, and she's out at a party. Do they know who shot him yet?"

"No. I've tried to reach the detective in charge of the case a couple of times today, but he's always out, so he still must be investigating something." It didn't seem right somehow, standing in my evening gown, to tell him that that something was probably me.

"I really feel for the family," said Stephen. Stephen's niece had died recently—under the worst of circumstances—and his face was momentarily clouded over in remembrance. Then something caught his eye, and he bent over the auction table. "This bracelet is very nice," he said, picking it up. "Here, give me your hand." I extended it as instructed and Stephen fastened the bracelet around my wrist. It was a series of oval sapphires in a platinum setting. In between each stone was an x of smaller diamonds. "I like the design," continued Stephen admiringly.

"It's called hugs and kisses," I replied, feeling strangely self-conscious. "You see, x's and o's. My mother has one like it."

"What do you think of it?" he asked.

"It's very pretty."

"Then let me buy it for you."

"No, Stephen. That's very sweet of you. But the only jewelry I ever wear is my wedding ring."

"But this suits you. Let me at least put a bid on it. After all," he added apologetically, "it's for a good cause."

Unable to give words to my internal discomfort— first Mother's revelation about *Chicago Magazine*, now this—I said nothing. Stephen wrote down his bid, and we moved on.

We spent the rest of the cocktail hour making the rounds of the arthritis specialists who'd turned out for the fund-raiser. Stephen's company, Azor Pharmaceuticals, had just released a new anti-inflammatory drug called Fizac, which had shown itself to be dramatically effective in cases of juvenile arthritis. Stephen's attendance at the Arthritis Foundation Gala fit into his company's public relations agenda. I followed along from rheumatologist to rheumatologist, hopefully looking decorative, listening to Stephen charm the doctors.

At a certain level Chicago is a very small town, the faces all familiar. How many people are there, after all, who are willing to put on a tuxedo or an evening gown (on a Wednesday night no less) and plunk down four hundred dollars for the dubious pleasure of eating mediocre food in a chilly museum? And yet there was something about it all that I found fundamentally disturbing.

When I came back to Chicago to practice law I assumed that everyone who'd gone away to school had changed like I had—developed their own values and gained the distance to see through or at least evaluate their parents' choices. It has never stopped surprising me that so many of the people I grew up with seem to have rushed back home, eager to take up exactly where their parents left off.

Many of them were there tonight, still nodding acquaintances, the women dressed by de la Renta and dieted down to emaciation, discussing their horses, their divorces, and their nanny problems. The choices I'd made as an adult had turned me into an outsider. My relationship with Stephen only widened the breech. Half of my girlhood friends wondered what someone as handsome and available as Stephen Azorini could possibly see in me, while the other half wondered how I could possibly allow myself to be so blatantly used for my position. I looked at them, their hair sprayed into perfection, their jewelry glittering in the candlelight, smiling, gossiping, already planning for their cosmetic surgeries, and wondered whether I wasn't a fool for choosing my worries over theirs.

I thought of Detective Ruskowski and squirmed inside. There were too many unconnected pieces. Elena had seen a gun in Hexter's drawer on Friday morning that hadn't been there when I'd looked on Sunday. Bart Hexter had made an appointment to see Ken Kurlander. A young woman named Torey Lloyd claimed that she had been having an affair with Bart Hexter and wanted money. Someone had erased the files relevant to the CFTC's case against Hexter Commodities. Black Bart had kept nude photos of a mystery woman in his drawer. The CFTC's enforcement chief was straining at the leash, panting to come after us. And then there was the small matter that someone had gotten up Sunday morning, put a gun in their pocket, and waited for Bart Hexter at the end of his driveway.

Stephen tapped me on the shoulder. I started and looked around me. All but a handful of the partygoers had already gone in to dinner. I wondered how long I'd been standing there, staring off into space.

Instead of taking me home, I asked Stephen to take me back to my office so that I could pick up my purse, my briefcase, and my car. The new sapphire and diamond bracelet hung, glittering and unfamiliar, on my wrist.

"My mother came to my office today," I said, as we turned onto LaSalle Street.

"That must mean it's time to string fresh garlic around the doors. The old stuff must be wearing out."

I laughed.

"She told me that you and I are going to be on the cover of *Chicago Magazine*."

"Damn her!" exclaimed Stephen. "I hadn't even made up my mind whether to ask you about it. What did she tell you?"

"That *Chicago Magazine* is planning an article on couples in the city where both the man and the woman have high-profile jobs. She named some of the other people whom they're planning to interview, but I've forgotten who they are."

"How on earth did she find out?"

"One of her friends has a daughter who works at the magazine. You have to understand that my mother is part of a gossip network where information is passed at the speed of light."

"Jody Synnenberg, our public relations director, approached me with the idea just this morning. She thinks it would be nice exposure for Azor. I said I'd talk to you about it."

"I would have thought you guys would have had all the press coverage you could handle for the next five years," I remarked.

"Jody said it would reach a more general audience than the business press."

"So you want to do it?"

"Obviously it depends on how you feel about it," said Stephen, pulling up in front of my office. He shifted into park and turned toward me. "I know how much you hate this kind of thing," he said, quietly. "I don't want to push you into the light if it makes you uncomfortable."

After beating back a corporate raider last year, Stephen's classic profile graced the pages of every business periodical. Even I hadn't been spared. I had been visited by a witty young woman from *BusinessWeek* who was putting together a story on Azor's legal defense. Which is how I found myself lying on the floor of my office one Wednesday afternoon while a bedraggled photographer and his assistant of dubious gender arranged tombstones on the carpet around my head.

In my world, tombstones are announcements of completed transactions, printed with black borders on the business pages, in a sparse style reminiscent of headstones. At the end of a deal, small copies are often made, encased in Lucite cubes and distributed to the participants. The photographer, no doubt confronted with an endless parade of lawyers posing with their briefcases, thought that the stunt with the tombstones would make an interesting shot. It did, but I still can't see the photo (Stepehen has a copy in his office) without remembering how ridiculous I felt lying on my own office floor.

I hate the "light," as Stephen so eloquently put it, but what was making me more uncomfortable were all the assumptions that would be made explicit if I agreed to do the magazine article. But, as ever, I found it impossible to give speech to my emotions. If you can't ask, How do you feel about me?, the question of whether or not you are actually a couple becomes equally unbroachable. For Stephen and me there had always been these unspoken chasms. We had been through so much together—through Russell's illness, the assault on his company, his niece's death. And yet saying things, simple things, like 'I feel lonely' or 'Will you come home with me tonight?' seemed surrounded by layers of insurmountable silence.

"I have to run it by the firm's management committee, see if they think it'll be good coverage for the firm," I said finally. "Why don't I let you know in a day or two?"

"Good enough," said Stephen, patting my hand in farewell. "Thanks for coming tonight. I know you're swamped with this Hexter thing."

"Good night," I said, "and thanks for the bracelet."

I knew from my gut that I didn't want to do the *Chicago Magazine* interview. But was it because I didn't want to answer questions that assumed an intimacy that did not exist between us? Or because I was afraid of developing that intimacy? Did Stephen want to do the article because it would be good publicity for Azor or because he thought that publicly declaring ourselves to be a couple would help to make us one? I had no idea. I had been Stephen's friend for more than a decade and still knew little more about him than what was readily displayed on the surface.

I was glad to find my roommate home when I finally got there.

"Great dress," Claudia said as I walked in. "But you sure don't look like you had a good time."

"Stephen bought me a diamond and sapphire bracelet at the silent auction," I said, holding it out to show her.

"Oh, well, that explains it. Whenever someone I'm seeing gives me an expensive piece of jewelry it ruins my evening, too."

I dropped into my favorite armchair and kicked off my shoes. "But what does it mean?" I asked.

"You're just a little slow," replied Claudia, whose day had probably gone no better than mine. "In fifth grade, when the boy punched you it meant that he liked you, remember? But now that the boys are older, they do things like give you jewelry."

"You know that it's not like that with Stephen and me. At least I think it's not."

"Oh gee, you could have fooled me," quipped Claudia. 'This morning I lost a contact lens, and when I got down on my hands and knees to look for it, I found a pair of Stephen's underwear underneath the chair you're sitting on. However did it get there? Were you discussing each other's bottom line?"

"Enough, enough!" I cried. "I've just been in a bad

mood since Hexter's been shot. Murdered clients always do that to me."

"So, are you still suspect de jour?"

"I don't know. Am I? I think the suspect's always the last to know."

"Gwen, a friend of mine who's doing a fellowship in plastic surgery, got her hands on a head—you know—a head from a cadaver, for practice. I thought maybe she'd lend it to us for a while. We could keep it in our freezer in case the police come back."

The doorbell rang, and we both looked at each other.

"Expecting company?" asked Claudia.

"No. You?"

"No."

I got up and pushed the button on the intercom. In Hyde Park, unexpected late-night visitors are not to be treated lightly. "Who is it?" I demanded.

"Detective Ruskowski," growled a familiar voice.

"Come on up," I bellowed into the intercom, squaring my shoulders and preparing for the worst.

CHAPTER
13

"Come on in, Detective," I said, opening the door. "Make yourself at home. You remember where everything is."

The policeman followed me into the empty living room. Claudia must have beaten a hasty retreat. Even with my unsympathetic eye I could see that Detective Ruskowski was looking unwell. In the three days since Hexter's murder, Ruskowski's suit, the same one he wore on Sunday, did not seem to have had time to rest.

"Going someplace?" he asked as his eyes raked over me in my evening gown.

"No, I've just come home. What can I do for you?"

"You called me three times today," replied Ruskowski. "I sort of figured you wanted to talk to me."

"Yes. But it wasn't necessary to see you in person. I hope you didn't make a special trip."

"I was in the neighborhood. What do you want?"

"When the police searched Bart Hexter's house on Sunday," I inquired, "did they take any business papers away with them?"

"Why do you ask?"

"Hexter had promised to turn over some documents to me that morning pertaining to a CFTC investigation. When I looked for them at his house on Sunday I didn't find them. Since then I've checked his office and they still haven't turned up. Naturally I've been wondering whether the police might have them."

"We didn't take any of his business papers."

"Then who did?" I asked.

"How can you be sure he had them in the first place?" countered the detective. "According to his secretary, he'd canceled your meeting four times before Sunday. Sounds like he was avoiding you."

"Either that or he didn't put the CFTC investigation high on his list. But doesn't it strike you as odd that the files would just vanish? Not only that, but the backup computer files have been erased at Hexter Commodities. Someone came in and dumped them on Monday morning. It's quite a coincidence. Hexter is murdered, and the records vanish. Sounds like there could be a motive in there somewhere."

"You lawyers are all alike. Something's easy and you've got to make it hard. Hexter pissed somebody off, and that somebody decided to get even. This isn't 'Murder She Wrote.' This is the real thing. You know how cops solve murders? Physical evidence, witnesses, confessions. You tell me how it was done, find me somebody who saw something, heard something, and I'll show you who did it. I don't give a fuck about motive. On the Orient Express motive might count for something, but not in Chicago. Fuck the why. Find out the how, and nine times out of ten it'll give you who."

"So I guess you might be interested if I told you that Hexter used to keep a gun in the drawer of his desk at home. One of the maids saw it on Friday morning, but when I looked through his desk on Sunday it was gone."

"You took your fucking time telling me," snarled Ruskowski.

"I just found out today. A woman named Elena Olarte came to see me."

"The maid," declared Ruskowski.

"Yes. She wanted to know whether she'd been left anything in Hexter's will. She claims that Pamela fired her because she knew that Hexter kept a gun in the house. She may just be a disgruntled employee trying to stir up trouble. I don't know. But I can give you the phone number of the place where she's staying." I fetched the piece of paper from my briefcase.

"She's probably lying," said the detective as I handed it to him.

"What makes you say that?"

"Because if there is anything that you learn on this job, one God-given truth," replied Ruskowski wearily, "it's that everyone lies." He looked at me hard. "And I mean everyone."

I know that my secretary loves me because when Elliott Ableman asked her if there was someplace near the courthouse he could meet me for breakfast, she immediately suggested Lou Mitchell's. You can have your freshly made brioche and your twelve-dollar grapefruit sections at your see-and-be-seen power breakfast restaurants like La Tour. Give me battered formica tables set into long rows so that you eat like loggers, elbow to elbow. Give me shoe salesmen, futures traders, bookies, and bail bondsmen. Give me the best breakfast that Chicago has to offer.

As usual, Lou greeted me at the door, offering a warm doughnut hole as he ushered me to the booth where Elliott waited, freshly pressed and brushed for his day in court, wearing a white shirt and fine blue suit. I slid across from him and gratefully accepted a cup of coffee from the waitress.

Today Elliott was scheduled to testify in the Ernest Folkman trial. Folkman had been a running back for the Bears who'd gone to medical school after retiring from football, returning to his old neighborhood to practice after graduation. On every level Folkman appeared to be a success story until it turned out that he'd been ripping Medicaid off for a cool million a year by charging for services not performed on patients that never existed.

Folkman managed to keep the whole scheme going by keeping two mistresses, each in a different section of the Medicaid office. The scam might have continued undetected if one of his girlfriends hadn't caught him cheating on the examining table with one of his nurses and decided to drop a dime to the district attorney. Elliott, who had been an investigator in the DA's office at the time, spent the better part of three years unraveling Folkman's long skein of fraud.

"Big day in court today," I said. "Are you nervous? I hear Pete DeGrandis is trying the case personally. Rumor has it he wants to move out of the DA's office and into the governor's mansion."

"I don't know if the governor's mansion is big enough. If he wins the election, they might have to build an addition for his ego." We both laughed. "I confess I'm not exactly looking forward to the cross. You know, Morry Greenblatt's defending Folkman. From what I hear, the trial is going to be one long game of 'how low can you go?' "

The waitress came, and we ordered omelets. Western for Elliott, spinach and feta cheese for me.

"How long do you anticipate being on the stand?" I asked once the waitress had gone.

"Just today. Why?"

"I was wondering if you'd have time to look into something for me."

"Sure."

"One of the employees at Hexter Commodities phoned Barton Jr.. She claims to have been having an affair with Black Bart and wants money. The son wants to know whether she's telling the truth and asked me to talk to her. I thought maybe you could check her out for me before I pay her a visit. Everybody's nervous she might go to the newspapers with her story."

"There are laws against that kind of blackmail, you know."

"You spent too many years with the D.A.'s office," I replied. "All Barton cares about is protecting his mother and keeping it out of the papers. The publicity is killing the family as it is."

"I bet the wife already knows or at least she won't be surprised. There isn't a futures trader born who can keep his pants on."

I looked around the restaurant, which was filled with bright-jacketed traders fueling up for a day in the pits.

"I'm glad you're here to protect me," I said with a smile.

"I wouldn't feel too safe if I were you," answered

Elliott with a wolfish grin. "But seriously, let me give you some free advice. Pay her off, and all she'll do is come back for a second bite."

"I still want you to check her out. I'm especially curious if she might have ever posed for nude photos. I found a set in the drawer of Hexter's desk."

"Can I see them?"

"I gave them to the police. I'm assuming your interest is purely professional."

"That depends on what she looks like."

"I don't know. I'm not sure I've seen her. But if she's who I think she is, she's gorgeous. Her name is Victoria Lloyd, and she works for Hexter Commodities as a runner."

"Do you think you could get me a copy of her personnel file?"

"I'll have it messengered to your office this afternoon. When do you think you might be able to have something for me?"

"If you can wait until the weekend to talk to her, I should have something for you by late Friday. Have you told Ruskowski about her? If she was really having an affair with Hexter she could be a suspect."

"If she was having an affair with him I'm sure they know about her already. Besides, I've already had more contact with the cops than is good for me."

"You're a regular magnet for trouble, Millholland," remarked Elliott as our breakfasts came. "You know, I've been hanging around with the cops who've been testifying against Folkman. They're all pissed that Hexter didn't get croaked while he was at his office. The Chicago cops say they've been robbed. Seems that some of the guys in Lake Forest have been letting on that this one's a dunker."

"What's a dunker?"

"From a homicide detective's point of view, there are only two categories of murder: whodunits and dunkers. Whodunits are genuine mysteries. Dunkers are easy shots. Word on the street is that they're close to an arrest."

I pushed my plate away as cement fingers wrapped themselves around my stomach.

"I hope," I said in a small voice, "the person they end up arresting isn't me."

When I got into the office I found Sherman waiting for me, obviously distressed.

"I was here until midnight last night," he complained. "I've been trying to do the comparison between the trading record from the Clearinghouse and the original trading tickets, but the tickets they delivered are a mess."

"What do you mean they're a mess?" I demanded.

"They're a mess! They're not sorted by date or commodity, and they're turned back to front and every which way. It'll take days to sort them out."

Sherman led me down to the small conference room where he'd been working. I could see that he'd tried sorting the sheets, each not much bigger than a playing card. There were hundreds laid in piles according to date on the polished mahogany table. I could also see that there were literally thousands more still to be sorted. The little he had done had taken all night. As Sherman talked, it took a few minutes before the obvious struck me. The trading tickets had been deliberately shuffled.

I returned to my office cold with fury at a dead man. His motives may have been a mystery, and there were games being played with the CFTC that I had yet to understand, but one thing seemed abundantly clear. Even dead, Bart Hexter was still jerking me around.

I didn't need to look at the calendar to know that it was already Wednesday, two days before Hexter Commodities' answer was due at the CFTC. My first instinct was to go back to Herman Geiss, on my hands and knees if necessary, explain the situation, and beg for another continuance. But when I thought about it I realized that if Geiss was looking for a way to bring Hexter Commodities down, I would just be telling him that it was time to close in for the kill.

The real power of a firm like Callahan Ross lies not in the intelligence and experience of its attorneys, but rather in the interlocking web of associations and favors that it has woven around itself like a mantle. I sent Cheryl to the library for biographical information on the CFTC commissioners. Then I trawled my partners for anyone who might have an inside track on the Commission. I worked the phones until lunchtime, pleading my case with those to whom Geiss would have no choice but to listen. It wasn't until after twelve that I remembered my promise to Elliott to have Torey Lloyd's personnel file messengered over to him.

I picked up the phone and called Hexter Commodities. I waited on hold for a minute before Barton Jr. himself picked up the line.

"Kate?" he demanded. I almost didn't recognize his voice it was so thick with rage. "I was just about to call you. I have a bit of a situation here. Can you come to the office?"

"Now?" I asked, taken aback.

"I'd hurry if I were you."

When I arrived at Hexter Commodities I didn't have to ask where to find Barton. I just followed the shouting. The door to Carl Savage's office was closed, but the rumble of his deep bass and the more strident tones of Barton's tenor could be clearly heard. The words were unintelligible, but there was no mistaking the angry nature of their duet. The Hexter employees stood in silent little groups, clustered together like children outside the room where their parents are fighting.

I felt the stares of everyone on the trading floor burning through my back. I knocked on the door, but there was no response. No doubt they hadn't heard me over their own shouting. I just took a deep breath, turned the handle, and waded in.

Both men were on their feet, squared off, while the phone rang hysterically, unanswered. Savage, the veins in his bull-neck throbbing, was screaming at Barton Jr.: "Screw you. I have a contract that runs through January. I'll sue your ass. You'll be bleeding legal fees for years!"

"Go right ahead," snapped Barton Jr. He looked every bit as angry as the chief of trading operations, but more in control of himself. "Go right ahead, but just go."

"You'll be sorry if I do. The only reason you're still in business today is because I'm here now. If I walk, all the customers will come with me. This place will be shut down in a week."

"I don't think so," growled Barton Jr.

"Oh no? Who the fuck do you think is going to make the trades? Who's going to decide when to buy and when to sell? Do you think any of those bozos out there have what it takes? Or do you want to take a shot at it yourself, Mr. Wizard? This isn't some computer simulation. This is a real game played with real money, and you don't even have the balls to try it."

"I'm only interested in the opinions of my employees," said Barton. "And you are fired."

"Bullshit!" shrieked Savage.

"Fired. Terminated. You have three minutes to remove yourself from the premises before I call the security guards and have you thrown out."

"No fucking way!" Savage yelled. Barton Jr. looked at his watch.

"Two minutes and forty seconds," he said.

"Take forty of these, you white-faced, pansy-ass motherfucker!" Savage spat as he threw himself at Barton Jr.

Instinctively I stepped in between them, bracing myself for impact. "Hit him," I hissed, "and I'll see to it that you are arrested for felonious assault so fast that your head will still be spinning by the time they throw you in the county lockup."

Savage's reply was a growling sound that came from deep in his throat. But it was Barton Jr. he wanted to hit, and I presented enough of an obstacle that he reconsidered.

"Just walk out now," I commanded. "Come to my office on Friday morning, and we'll formally wrap up your employment." I reached into my pocket and handed him a business card.

"Cunt," he said simply.

"You can call me whatever you like," I replied
sweetly. "But you have nothing to gain by continuing
this confrontation. I'd advise you to leave now."

"You'll be sorry," Savage countered, wavering in the
doorway for one taut minute. Then he stalked out of the
office.

"What was that all about?" I asked, my heart pounding. Barton Jr. was sitting in Savage's chair, looking
spent.

"About an hour ago Carl said he had something to
talk to me about. He said he'd received an offer from
one of our competitors and if I wanted him to stay at
Hexter I was going to have to double his salary and
give him ten percent of the company."

"Really."

"He knows better than anybody what a vulnerable
position we're in. He sure didn't waste any time trying
to take advantage of it. Dad's not even buried yet, and
he's asking for more money. I told him that I expected
loyalty, not avarice, from our employees. He said that
was easy for me to say since I'd just become an overnight millionaire. I told him that I wouldn't even consider granting his demands. By the time you called it
was getting ugly and personal. I'm glad you came when
you did. If you hadn't surprised him, he'd have decked
me for sure."

"Carl's a bully," I remarked. "One of the few things
that bullies respect is someone doing it right back to
them."

"That's a theory that requires a certain amount of
nerve to put into practice," commented Barton apprecia-

tively. "I'm glad it worked. It wouldn't have done much for my standing with the employees if he'd given me a black eye before he left."

"This is a tough time to be losing a key employee like Carl," I ventured.

"I know. I feel like I just sawed off the branch I was sitting on."

"So who's going to be making the trading decisions?" I asked as someone began knocking furiously at the door.

"Come in," called Barton.

A young man in a rumpled jacket charged in, frantic, his tie askew. "I have all these fill orders that need to be called down to the floor," he blurted. "There are a bunch for July beans at thirty or below, and Doug just sent word up that July's are at twenty-seven and moving up fast. Carl practically knocked me down on his way out," he continued uncertainly. "When I asked him what to do, he said I'd better ask you."

"Give me those," demanded Barton Jr., taking off his jacket and grabbing the order slips from the clerk's hand. "What's the number for the phone clerk in the bean pit?" Bart Hexter's son put the phone to his ear, looked up at me, and nodded his farewell.

When I got back to the office Cheryl told me that I'd received an urgent summons from Herman Geiss. Herman usually worked out of the CFTC's main office in Washington, but today he was in town, waiting to see me at the Commission's Chicago office. I called to say that I was on my way, hopped a cab, and soon found myself at the Commission's cramped Chicago offices.

Herman was waiting for me in a small windowless

conference room. It was furnished with a scarred conference table ringed by a disreputable assortment of battered chairs. The room smelled of other crises, acrid and sour reminders of distress.

Around the table Herman had arrayed the first team: Gary Sanders, also from the Washington office, and Darlene McDonald, the Commission's hot new acquisition from Treasury who was due to replace Herman when, at the end of the year, he left government for the payoff of private practice. As soon as I was seated, Herman locked the door. In one corner there was a small table set up for a stenographer, but none was present. My guess was that he wanted no record of what he was about to say.

Herman had thinning hair, a spreading waist, and an air of perpetual irritation about him. He took up his place across the table from me, slapping his hands down on its scarred surface for effect. He leaned his pudgy, bespectacled face into mine like a gospel tent preacher trying to see into my soul.

"What the fuck are you trying to pull, Millholland?" he demanded, his face close enough to mine that I could smell his lunch on his breath.

"In what regard, Herman?" I inquired.

"Don't pull that innocent shit with me," he screamed. "Is there a senator you haven't called today?"

"I might have missed one or two. You didn't give me much choice. You made it very clear when we spoke on the phone that you weren't prepared to be reasonable, despite the fact that I was dealing with an extraordinary set of circumstances. Whatever happened today you brought on yourself."

"What happened today was the worst kind of underhanded, smug, corporate influence peddling. I didn't think you sunk to that shit, Millholland."

"Wait until you're on the other side," I answered, knowing that Herman felt ambivalently about leaving government. "My job is to do whatever it takes to further my client's interests. That's what I get paid for. It's the difference between being an advocate and being a crusader."

One look at Herman's face and I feared that I'd gone too far. The others watched us warily from around the table, their glances flicking from Herman's face to mine and back again.

"You may call yourself an advocate, Kate. But what you really are is a whore. It makes me sick to see you subvert the process for a man like Hexter."

"Hexter is dead, Herman," I said. "Save your hate for the living."

"Don't tell me what to do. The powers that be saw fit to give you a five-day extension. But just so that we understand each other. This one came out of my hide. In five days, I plan on taking it out of yours."

CHAPTER

14

On my way back to the office I made a couple of stops. First at the newsstand for a bag of M&Ms and then at Starbucks to pick up a double espresso. To say that it had been a rough day would be an understatement. Within the space of two hours I'd come within an inch of being decked by Hexter Commodities' ex-chief trader and been informed by the head of enforcement at the CFTC that a week from Friday he planned to burn me and my client at the stake.

Cheryl took one look at the coffee and M&Ms and said: "That bad?"

"I should have worn my fireproof suit," I replied. I walked into my office, kicked off my shoes, and took off my jacket. There was a lavender chiffon dress on my chair. "Cheryl?" I called. "What's this?"

"Sorry, Kate," she replied, scooping up the offending garment. "I picked it up at lunch and tried it on in your office. It's my bridesmaid's dress. I'm in my friend Camille's wedding this weekend." She held it up to show me. "Isn't it hideous?"

"There isn't a bridesmaid's dress made that isn't," I

replied. "Do you know what the three great lies of all time are?"

"No, tell me."

"Number one—'I was just about to call you.' Number two—'The check is in the mail.' Number three—'You'll be able to wear the dress again.' "

"You're right. I wouldn't want to be buried in this dress. I can't wait to see Camille's sister in it. She's five-two and weighs two hundred pounds. You've got to see the shoes." She darted out to her desk and came back with a pair of open-toe pumps with three inch heels dyed lavender to match the dress.

"Lovely," I said. "You'll definitely get a lot of wear out of those."

"Oh, sure, every woman has a place in her wardrobe for a pair of lavender FMPs."

"What, pray tell, are FMPs?"

"Didn't your mother teach you anything? FMP—fuck me pumps."

I was still laughing when the phone rang. Cheryl answered it and handed it to me. "It's Barton Jr.," she whispered, her hand covering the mouthpiece. "I assume you want to talk to him."

"Can we get together?" he asked when I took the phone. "I think I did saw my branch off today."

"Sure, when's good for you?"

"Actually, I was hoping you might be able to come out to the house tonight. I promised Jane I'd be home for dinner. Wednesday is our au pair's day off, and by six Jane's just beat. Maybe you could come and have pot luck with us."

"Oh, no. I don't want to impose. Why don't I come out after you're done eating?"

"No, really. Dinner's best. To be perfectly honest, I'm a little nervous about telling Jane what happened today. I wouldn't mind having you around."

"You mean in case she tries to deck you?"

"Something like that."

Barton and Jane Hexter lived in a pleasantly restored Victorian house on a quiet, tree-lined street in Evanston. Theirs was a comfortable, family neighborhood, with tricycles on the front walks and wooden swing sets out back. Prosperous and serene, it was remarkable only when viewed from the vantage of the house in which Barton Jr. had grown up.

Jane met me at the door holding a kicking two-year-old high up over the crescent of her belly. She wore a flowered jumper in a dull shade of dark red that only accentuated the paleness of her thin skin and the fine lines that pregnancy, fatigue, and the hideous stress of the past few days had etched there.

"Welcome to the monkey house," she said, managing a smile. "This little monkey is named Peter."

"Eeee, eeee, eeee," obliged Peter happily with monkey noises.

"Now run upstairs and find that other little monkey," she said, releasing him and giving him a good-natured pat on the bottom. "Come on in. Barton's in the dining room. He says he's trying to get some exams graded, but he's really hiding from me. Did he tell you that he fired Carl Savage today?"

"I was there. I hope that doesn't mean I get arsenic in my soup."

"You'll get soup. I'll think about the arsenic. Let's go chase him out of there."

Jane led the way through the house, which was decorated in the manner of university professors the world over: comfortable, vaguely modern furniture in neutral tones, polished wood floors, and books jammed into every conceivable space. A Steinway concert grand piano dominated the living room. A harp graced the bay window. Toys were strewn everywhere in between.

At the sound of our voices Barton ducked out of the dining room, tucking his shirt into his jeans. "Oh, hi, Kate. Gosh, is it already dinnertime? Can I get you something to drink? Beer? Wine?"

"Wine would be lovely," I ventured.

"Done," said Jane. "I'll get it. Why don't you two have a seat. I've got to check on dinner anyway."

"Are you sure I can't help?" I asked.

"No. I've got it under control."

Barton and I made ourselves comfortable. Above us I could hear the sound of little running feet and shrieks of what I hoped was laughter.

"I see you came clean with Jane," I said.

"She took it surprisingly well. I think the worst she called me was idiot."

"So how did the day's trading go?"

"Okay. I'm not like Dad. I can't keep a running total in my head, which means I'm going to have to come up with some sort of record-keeping system. Tim doesn't seem too happy about it. He and Dad used to meet at the end of every trading day to go through the trades, but I think it took them twenty minutes. We were at it for better than an hour today, and we only got through two commodities. When I told him he'd have to come in at six tomorrow morning so that we could finish up, he didn't seem too pleased."

"Are you going to fire *him* next?" inquired Jane, appearing with my drink. "In a university you don't get to fire anybody, not even your secretary. I think the power's gone to his head. Did you tell Kate about Margot?"

Barton covered his face with his hands. "Is there any hideous family secret that won't be revealed?" he cried in mock horror.

"Well this one won't be a secret for long," replied Jane. She turned to me. "Margot called me this afternoon. She's terribly excited. It seems that she's pregnant."

"So much for the lesbian life-style," I remarked.

"Oh, no. You don't get it. This *is* part of the lesbian life-style. Brooke, that's Margot's girlfriend, excuse me, 'life partner,' artificially inseminated her. I guess they got a gay male friend to make a contribution. Margot was not shy about sharing the details. It seems they used a turkey baster. They plan on raising the baby together—Mommy Margot, Mommy Brooke, and Uncle Daddy whatever his name is."

"Has she told your mother?" I asked.

"Yes," said Barton. "All mother could say was she was thankful that Dad wasn't alive to hear it. She also says that she's glad she's moving. I guess she leaves for Palm Beach Friday morning. I don't know. It seems like the whole family is experiencing a meltdown. You see it in chaos theory. A complex, rapidly changing system develops its own, unique kind of equilibrium. Then, one exogenous event sends the whole thing careening out of control."

"What a happy thought," said Jane. "You're losing your sense of proportion. What happened to your father is terrible, true. But nothing has changed when it comes to Margot. She was nuts before he was killed, and she's still nuts now."

"What about mother moving to Palm Beach? Don't you think that's a little sudden? Plus, there's something going on between Krissy and her husband. When I was with them yesterday, something was not right."

"Oh, bother. I'm sure it's just that Krissy thinks that she's not getting enough attention. There's nothing new in that."

"I was a little surprised to see Krissy at the Arthritis Benefit last night," I interjected. "I know that she worked very hard on the event, but there was a lot of whispering going on."

"Mother was just furious," admitted Barton. "It was good for not one, but two four A.M. phone calls."

"She just wants to be sure that she gets her fair share of sympathetic adoration," added Jane. "I'm sure she's milking your father's death for all it's worth, while Fourey's out exercising his horses. Not that I blame him. If I were married to your sister, I would *live* in the barn."

"This is hard on Krissy," countered her husband. "Of all of us, Krissy was closest to my father."

"She had him wrapped around her little finger, is what you mean. I've always felt sorry for Fourey. Your dad was a hard act to follow. We talked about it when they got married. Bart always treated Krissy like a princess. Fourey is a nice guy, but he's not a prince. In the end this will probably be good for Krissy. She's twenty-six years old, and this is her first encounter with reality."

"I think Krissy is immune to reality," Barton muttered.

"Were you invited to Krissy's wedding?" Jane asked me.

"No, I don't think so."

"No offense, but you were probably the only English speaker in this town who wasn't. It's really too bad you missed it."

"It was a bit much," conceded Barton. "But it was all my dad's doing. As I recall, Mother fought him every inch of the way."

"Bart planned the entire wedding as a surprise for Krissy," continued Jane. "He arranged for the decorations, the color scheme, the food. If Fourey hadn't shown up I don't think anyone would have noticed until it was time to say 'I do.' Bart even took her to Tiffany's blindfolded, to pick out a diamond necklace and tiara for her to wear during the ceremony. She had two wedding dresses, one for the ceremony and one for the reception. He flew Stuart White and his fifty-nine-piece band in from New York for the reception. She and Fourey departed for their honeymoon in a helicopter."

"A helicopter?" I echoed.

"Like I said," answered Jane, wryly. "Bart Hexter is a tough act to follow."

Dinner was casual and delicious, the kind of home cooking that seldom passed across my plate—roast chicken, baked potatoes, peas, and salad. I had thirds. The Hexters' two little boys, Peter—the two-year-old I met at the front door—and his three-and-a-half-year-old brother, James, turned the meal into a small scale riot. Milk spilled, food flew through the air, a burping contest was begun and quickly put to a stop. When Jane was in the kitchen and Barton was engaged in mopping up yet another spill, Peter succeeded in stuffing a pea up his nose before I could stop him and had to be taken from the table for its extraction.

"So are you ready to take a vow of childlessness?" inquired Jane after we had abandoned the table. Barton had taken the boys upstairs for their bath. I was helping Jane with the dishes.

"Not at all," I replied truthfully. "By comparison my life seems unexciting."

"I'm not sure that exciting is a great way to describe it. When I walk out onto the stage and the orchestra stands up and all the faces in the audience are turned toward me—that's exciting. This is just chaos."

"But I bet you wouldn't trade places with me for all the money in the world," I replied.

"I'd do it for the weekend," answered Jane with a smile. "Especially if we could swap bodies. Mine seems to be getting rather full of somebody else right now."

"Do you know what you're having?"

"No. I'm hopelessly low-tech about everything. Even though everyone says they're safe, I'd rather not have an ultrasound if I don't have to. Besides, it's nice to be surprised."

"Are you hoping for a girl?"

"A girl would be nice." Jane sighed. "Otherwise, can you imagine what it will be like? I'll be living the rest of my life in a locker room. Still, as long as the baby is healthy, I'll be thrilled whether it's a boy or a girl. The more experience I have at parenthood, the more I appreciate what a miracle a normal child is."

"No matter what you're in for a busy time," I said, with the wildness at dinner still ringing in my ears.

"You better believe it," answered Jane with a laugh.

"With three children three and under, my martyrdom is practically assured."

"I don't think my dad believed that he was ever going to die," said Barton Jr. as Jane poured the coffee. The boys were upstairs in their pajamas watching their daily quota of television. "You know Dad had a massive heart attack two years ago. He was clinically dead when they brought him into the emergency room. Even after that, I still don't think he believed his life would ever be over. He just figured if he wanted it enough, if he was stubborn enough about it, he'd get what he wanted and live forever."

"Talk about stubborn," said Jane. "Remember what we went through last year with the defibrillator? After the heart attack Bart developed a condition called ventricular tachycardia," Jane explained to me. "It's an intermittent, grossly irregular heart rhythm that originates in the ventricle of the heart. His doctors insisted that he have a defibrillator implanted in his chest, but he wouldn't have it."

"What's a defibrillator?" I asked. "Is it like a pacemaker?"

"No," replied Bart. "It's bigger than a pacemaker and you have to have a fair-sized battery, about five inches square, implanted in your abdomen to power it. It's sort of an automatic jumpstarter for your heart. It monitors the heart rhythm so that whenever you have an episode of ventricular tachycardia—they call it VT—the defibrillator sends electricity through your heart and jolts it back into normal rhythm."

"Doesn't sound very pleasant."

"It's not," said Jane. "But the family thought that it

was a preferable alternative to death. Bart said he wasn't going to have them cut him open and put some machine into his chest. He said he was a gambler and he'd take his chances. Pamela was sick about it. The doctors told us that if he went into VT again it would almost certainly be fatal."

"Thankfully, then, last year a new drug came on the market for regulating VT," interjected Barton Jr. "But until he started taking it we were all nervous wrecks."

"I don't think your father lost a single night's sleep over it," said Jane. "I think Barton is right. His father thought he was immortal."

"I was talking to a friend of mine who's in law enforcement," I said. "He claims that the police are hinting that they're close to an arrest."

"That's great," said Jane. "The sooner they catch the guy who did it, the better. I just want this whole thing to be over."

"It's not going to be over for us," replied Barton glumly. "Before you came, Jane and I discussed it, and I think I'm going to go to the dean and ask for a leave of absence until September. It's not what I want, what either of us wants, but I've been through the options over and over, and I don't see how Hexter Commodities is going to survive the next couple of months without someone committed to running it full-time."

"Barton is convinced that he's the only one who can do it," said Jane in a resigned voice.

"Even if we decide to sell the company, or liquidate its assets," continued Barton, as if trying to convince himself, "we have to prove it's a viable company without my father. If I don't step in, it'll all have been a waste."

"There are worse things to waste," said his wife.

"He worked his whole life to build it, Jane. No matter what you or I thought about him, I just can't let it go down the drain."

I arrived home exhausted, confused, and vaguely depressed. I found that I liked Jane and Barton so much. I envied them their life together, their casual intimacy, their clever banter, and their two little boys, for all the noise and the spilled milk. I found also that I was angry at Bart Hexter for having gotten himself killed. Even though I had not the slightest notion who had killed him or why, I was convinced that Hexter himself had contributed in some way to the circumstances of his death. This was not the case of some lunatic creeping out of the woods to commit a senseless act of violence. Bart Hexter had been shot for a reason. But no matter the motive, the people who were really paying the price were Barton and his wife Jane.

I looked at my watch. It wasn't even ten o'clock. My briefcase was full of work to be done. The light on my answering machine blinked, indicating calls to be answered.

I threw the mail down on the coffee table unread, took off my clothes, and crawled into bed.

CHAPTER
15

I got up early and was at the office before eight. By next Friday I was going to have to come up with something pretty convincing to say to the CFTC. The time had come to stop worrying about who had shot Bart Hexter and start worrying about how I was going to avoid having Herman Geiss mount my head on his wall.

I pulled Sherman Whitehead out of the morass of trading tickets in the conference room after he assured me that he had two paralegals who would finish the job by the weekend. I set him to work in the library hunting down cases that involved the subject of a government investigation dying before charges could be brought. There couldn't be very many, but there was a slim chance that he'd unearth some sort of favorable precedent. To Cheryl I gave the task of tracking down Deodar Commodities.

That done, I had the file room bring up the boxes upon boxes of files that I'd inherited from the law firm that had represented Hexter Commodities before me. In response to the subpoena for my Hexter Commodities files I'd been able to send copies only of recent documents. Most of the material that was now heaped in my office, I'd never before had occasion to consult. It made for interesting reading.

If I was looking for clues to the source of the CFTC enforcement chief's vendetta, I found them peppered throughout the documents before me. Herman Geiss's name cropped up like a recurring infection.

Geiss, I knew, was of the opinion that when it comes to futures traders, big is bad. But I'd never understood the extent to which he applied the resources of the agency to keep tabs on traders like Hexter. With monotonous regularity Geiss had investigated Hexter traders, questioned the speed and integrity with which Hexter cleared trades for others, and generally kept the agency's hand in Hexter's pocket. While most of the actions had been dropped or settled for relatively small fines, I could imagine that the overall effect on someone of Hexter's temperament must have been like a continual tapping on the same spot.

Not that Hexter hadn't taken his shots when the opportunity came his way. During the years he'd been chairman of the CBOT he'd done his best to thwart Geiss and his team of government regulators at every turn. When I came to a correspondence file dated from four years before, I came across an exchange of letters that made it clear that Hexter had gone so far as to try to have Geiss fired. My stomach churned. I was, I concluded, in deeper shit than I'd thought.

I was still reading when Ken Kurlander appeared at my door with his black top coat over his arm and his black gloves in his hand. It seems he'd taken the train in from Kennilworth that morning, assuming that I would give him a ride to Bart Hexter's funeral. I began to tell him that I hadn't planned on going—I had to prepare Hexter's answer to the CFTC—but Kurlander's icy stare of disapproval stopped me in my tracks. With a sigh, I fetched my coat.

Kurlander sat primly in the passenger seat of my aged Volvo station wagon, as if to minimize physical contact between himself and my dirty upholstery. To make conversation, he talked about Pamela Hexter. It seems that the police had made another, more thorough search of her house that morning, this time going so far as to even dismantle the garbage disposal. From the loop through Wilmette, Kurlander maintained an indignant monologue about the brutality of the police.

The funeral was held at St. Stephen's Church. When we arrived it occurred to me that the parking lot would have made a car thieves' Eden. It was teeming with Lambourghinis, Testa Rosas and the other heavy metal favored by futures traders mingled with the BMWs and Mercedes of Pamela Hexter's old-moneyed friends.

The media was out in full force. A broadcast minivan complete with rooftop radar dish was parked askew on the sidewalk in front of the open oak doors of the church like a dead whale washed up on the beach. Reporters worked the crowd as if it were a prizefight, wielding microphones like truncheons.

Unhappily, in the church, I found myself seated with my mother on one side and Ken Kurlander on the other. The two of them played 'who do you know?' across my lap, pointing out late arrivals, bringing each other up to date on divorce, detox, and disgrace. After the service Kurlander, predictably, accepted Mother's offer of a ride to the cemetery, thus trading up from my dented Volvo to a Lincoln with a driver.

The mourners filtered slowly to the graveside. I positioned myself a safe distance from Kurlander and my mother and watched the crowd. Pamela Hexter was as elegant as a Kennedy widow, dry-eyed in a suit of dull black silk. Barton Jr. was at his mother's side, her arm linked through his, her black-gloved hand grasped protectively by her son. I heard the shutters of the reporters' cameras and knew that this would be the picture that the newspapers would run next day.

The Hexter daughters flanked the two of them. Krissy, her pretty face ruined by the scarlet of her spoiled mouth, stood beside her mother fretting with her jewelry. Her husband, Fourey, stood a half a step behind, his head bent in conversation with Jane. Margot, looking bored, had taken up the place beside her brother. She wore a dress that looked like it had been made out of a tattered black tablecloth. She had her arm around a tall, thin young woman who was wearing, of all things, a yellow raincoat.

Barton Jr. had ordered Hexter Commodities closed for the funeral, and I spotted all the employees off to one side, clustered around Loretta Resch as if for protection. Mrs. Titlebaum was at her side, sobbing quietly into her handkerchief, while Tim, looking lost and miserable, shifted his weight uncomfortably from foot to foot like an oversized little boy trying to keep still at church. He wore a shapeless black raincoat. The sleeves were too short, and his ham hands hung out, awkward and exposed. As the nephew of the deceased he should have been included in the group with the immediate family. I wondered if he'd chosen to stay with his co-

workers out of loyalty, or if Pamela's snub—not select-
ing him as a pallbearer—extended to exclusion from
riding in the limousines reserved for the family.

When the throng had finally assembled, the last
prayers for the commodity trader were said and Black
Bart Hexter was lowered into the ground. Pamela
watched the casket's descent, poker straight and dry-
eyed. Krissy sobbed. Margot stared off into space. Beyond the fringes of the crowd, my eye picked out a man
who had partially concealed himself behind a tombstone
topped by an elaborately carved statue of an angel. He
was using a videocamera to photograph those who had
come to pay their last respects to Bart Hexter. With a
shudder I realized that he was one of Ruskowski's men.

Since Pamela planned to leave for Palm Beach the
following morning, those wishing to express their condolences had no choice but to proceed to the house directly from the funeral. The crush of people quickly
divided itself into two groups. In the living room the
wing-tipped WASPs and their tasteful spouses sipped
coffee and shook their heads over Bart Hexter's passing. In the trophy room, where a bar had been set up,
the traders and their big-haired wives drank and in-
dulged in noisy reminiscences of the glory days of Bart
Hexter.

"Kate," said Barton Jr., taking my arm as I waited for
my coffee cup to be refilled, "I'm glad you're here.
Mother says that all of my father's papers are boxed up
for you in his study. Unfortunately, she hasn't done anything about having them delivered to you. Do you think
you could possibly make the arrangements?"

"Sure. How many boxes are there?"

"I don't know. If you want, you can go and take a look."

"I'll do that. Is there anything else I can do for you?"

"It's only another hour. Mother's throwing everybody out at seven, if you can believe it. Her plane leaves at eight tomorrow morning. I never thought I'd say it, but I think her leaving is a good idea. Otherwise all of this would just drag on and on." An elderly couple appeared behind him, waiting their turn to offer their condolences.

"I'm going to check on those boxes," I said. "Do you think you could spare a minute later on? You'll remember that I told Carl Savage to come to my office tomorrow morning. You and I need to talk about formally terminating his employment."

Barton Jr. groaned.

"We'll talk about it later. For now, just point me in the direction of the study."

"It's down that hall. Take a right, and then it's the third, no maybe the fourth door on the left."

I set out optimistically, but the fourth door turned out to be not the study but the billiard room. However, it was not the majestical expanse of green baize that first caught my eye, but rather the couple exerting themselves on top of it. The woman was perched on the edge of the pool table with her legs wrapped around the waist of a dark-haired man who appeared to be busy trying to unbutton her blouse with his teeth.

At the sound of the door the woman looked up. Krissy Hexter Chilcote stared wide-eyed at me.

"Excuse me," I stammered in retreat. I closed the door after me and let out a soft, involuntary whistle. I had just seen Fourey Chilcote talking to Ken Kurlander in the living room. Besides, Krissy's husband's hair was blond.

It was definitely my day for walking in on people. I finally located Bart's study only to find Jane Hexter sitting in the soft glow of a single lamp, crying.

"I didn't mean to disturb you," I said. "I'll come back later."

"No, that's okay. I have to be getting back to everyone, anyway." She took a deep breath and dabbed at her eyes. "I guess the advantage of a funeral is you don't have to feel embarrassed to be caught crying."

"You're definitely allowed," I replied soothingly.

"Being pregnant makes it worse. All day long I haven't been able to stop crying."

"You've had some pretty good reasons."

"That's the worst part," said Jane, suddenly back at the brink of tears. "I am so ashamed of myself. I'm not crying for good reasons. All my reasons are so ... twisted. Do you know how I felt when I found out that my father-in-law was dead? I was relieved. It's not that I hated him. There were many things about him that I admired, but when he died I felt set free. It's hard to explain, but Bart was such a dominant personality. It was as if he'd lashed his children to him with his will—he controlled the water even as they tried to swim away."

"But you and Barton Jr. lived your own life. You didn't do what Bart wanted, didn't live the way he wanted you to live," I protested.

"No, at least we made a show of independence, not like Krissy. But whenever we made a decision we measured it against what Bart would have thought, like some inner metric. When he died I thought that it would be over, we'd be free. But now the man is dead and damn him, he's gotten everything he ever wanted. We're sucked into his life." Jane raised her arms and dropped them in a gesture of despair. "We're saddled with this monstrosity of a house, and Barton is going to work every day trading futures. Reporters are following my children to school, trying to take their pictures. And every time I turn around there's Ken Kurlander whispering in Barton's ear about his responsibilities until my poor husband can't sleep at night. Damn it, Barton and I already have a life. We don't need to take on his father's."

"Things are at their most intense now," I said. "It will get better as time goes by. And if nothing else, there'll be the new baby to be happy about."

"The thought of starting with a new baby when I'm so drained . . ." she shivered. "It's hard. I have to be strong for so many people. I need to listen to Barton and be supportive. After all, he's just lost his father under horrible circumstances. I have to be reassuring and matter-of-fact for the kids. Some hateful child at nursery school told James that bad guys had shot his grandfather in the head—bang, bang. So naturally, James is having nightmares. I know it sounds awful, but I'm furious at Bart for dying, let alone getting himself murdered. It's awful to say, but it's not like some burglar shot him. I'm sure it was someone whom he wronged in some way. He did something awful, and now we're the ones getting slimed. . . . Oh God, I can't believe I said that. You must just think I'm a witch."

"I think you're a nice person who deserves better than what's been handed to you recently," I replied honestly. "I think you feel it's unfair because it is."

"And yet I feel guilty about that, too. How can I expect anyone to understand it? That's the irony. We've inherited millions of dollars, and I'm crying because it's unfair. But I don't want the money. I hate it. I wish it had died with him."

Barton Jr. was standing by the front door saying good-bye to the last of the visitors. Pamela was relaxing in a wing-back chair, her head bent in conversation with an old friend who was preparing to take her leave. Margot hovered nearby with Brooke in tow, hopping impatiently from one foot to another waiting to catch her mother's eye. Krissy, composed but shooting wary looks at me whenever I passed, was in the dining room supervising the cleanup by the staff.

Barton closed the door and leaned against it for a moment, his shoulders slack, his cheeks hollow. Framed against the black timbers of the door he was the very picture of exhaustion. Slowly he loosened his tie and ran his fingers through his hair.

"I can't talk about Savage tonight, Kate," he said. "I'm dead. I've got to just find Jane and go home. I'll call you when I get up."

"That's okay," I answered. "We can do it over the phone. Jane's already gone. She was exhausted. I told her that I'd give you a ride home."

"Are you sure?"

"Absolutely."

"I'll just get my coat."

Margot, I noticed, had finally gained an audience with her mother. Brooke was raising her hand in an awkward farewell. Margot bent to kiss her mother, who quickly turned her head away. Margot grabbed her coat from a nearby chair, pulled Brooke by the hand, and walked past me without saying a word. She opened the door and let her friend pass through before her. Then she turned, flipped her mother the finger, and wordlessly stepped out into the night.

Recently, I'd been getting flack from Cheryl and Stephen (I suspected a conspiracy) about getting myself a new car. True, the Volvo had seen better days. But it was the car that Russell and I had bought together our last semester of law school, planning for the day when we'd fill it with children. And while I finally had gotten myself to the point where it didn't seem a wrench to replace it, I found the matter of choosing a new car much more difficult than I anticipated.

I loved driving Stephen's BMW but balked at the rigamarole of keeping an expensive car in a neighborhood inhabited by car thieves. Stephen's building had a doorman and an attended underground garage. Parked in the alley behind my apartment, an expensive German car would have a half-life of less than a week.

For a while I toyed with Cheryl's suggestion that I celebrate my ascension to partnership with a sleek Miata roadster. But when I took one out for a test drive, the number of lewd offers I received from male pedestrians surprised me. One aspiring stud in a tank top and tight jeans even suggested, at the corner of Grand and Ohio, that if I gave him a ride in my Miata he'd give me a ride on his mustache. It took me the seven blocks to Michigan Avenue to figure out what he meant.

Whatever it said about me, the Volvo, I decided, suited me best. Tonight, driving Barton back to Evanston, I was grateful for its comfortable familiarity. Barton sat beside me in the passenger seat, sunk into the dark folds of his overcoat like someone very old or very ill. The night was clear and cold, and dark clouds blew fast across the night sky.

When I pulled into the driveway of his house, Jane was there waiting for us. She was standing in the pool of light from the open garage dressed in a nightgown. She had a woolen shawl thrown around her shoulders. Her eyes were enormous, her face white with shock.

Barton vaulted out of the car. I leapt out after him.

"Jane!" he demanded, "are you all right? What's happened? Is it the baby?"

"No, no. That's not it," she replied, obviously struggling for words "No, it's your mother. Krissy just called. The police came to the house a few minutes ago. Your mother's been arrested for murder."

CHAPTER
16

For a moment all three of us stood there, absorbing the enormity of it. Barton Jr.'s face was ashen. He took a small step toward his wife that was like a stagger and grasped her hands.

"What time did Krissy call?" I demanded sharply. I felt like the only doctor at the scene of an accident.

"Less than ten minutes ago," said Jane, picking up the strained cadence of emergency.

"Were the police still at the house when she phoned?"

"No. They had just left. Krissy said it was all over in a minute. That detective was there—the one with the red hair whom nobody likes. I can't remember his name. He marched in and announced to Pamela that she was under arrest. Krissy said they put her in handcuffs."

"How is Krissy doing?" I asked.

"She's really upset. She was crying so hard on the phone I had a tough time understanding her."

"There has to be some mistake," whispered Barton Jr. "Where did they take her? Is she in jail?"

"Krissy said they were taking her to the Lake Forest Police Station," answered Jane.

"Jane," I ordered. "You go back into the house and

call Krissy. Tell her to stay in the house and not to talk to anybody, especially any reporters who call. Call Margot and tell her the same thing. Tell Krissy I'm going to send out the same security people who were there on Sunday. I'm going to have them send a few men here as well."

"Do you really think we'll need them?" asked Jane.

"Unless China falls into the ocean overnight, this is going to be the biggest news story in the country tomorrow morning," I replied grimly. "Reporters will be going through your garbage. I'd keep the boys home from school tomorrow."

"I have a rehearsal with the full orchestra," protested Jane.

"Then one of the security guys will drive you. Don't worry, this too will pass, but for the next few days you're going to have to brace yourselves." Jane nodded seriously. I looked at Barton. He looked like he was going to be sick.

"I have to go to the police station," he said.

"I'll drive you," I said.

"That's okay. I can drive myself."

"You're in no condition to drive," interjected Jane sensibly. "Let Kate take you."

"We can make some calls on the way," I said, opening the car door for him. "I'd like to get there before the reporters do. But the first thing we have to do is get your mother a good attorney. Do you know who your mother would like to have represent her?"

"Ken Kurlander handles all her legal affairs," replied Barton Jr. doubtfully.

"He can't handle this," I said. "Let me see if Elkin Caufield is available. If your mother doesn't like him,

she can make a change. But right now she needs someone to be with her when she's interrogated and someone
to arrange bail." Ironically, in a fleeting moment of
panic the night before I'd decided that if the police
came to arrest me, it was Caufield who I'd ask to represent me.

Barton took both his wife's hands and kissed her
quickly on the cheek.

"Will you be okay?" he asked her.

"I'll be fine," she assured him. "Just hurry and go
take care of your mother."

Barton plunged into the car and pulled the door shut
behind him. As I backed out of the driveway, Jane stood
and watched us go.

Barton Jr. huddled miserably in the front seat, twisting his hands in despair. While I drove I talked on the
car phone, first to Caufield's answering service and
then, a few moments later, to Elkin himself, whom they
connected from his home. He agreed to meet us at the
police station in twenty minutes. Next I called Elliott
Abelman's office expecting another answering service.
Instead, the phone rang seven or eight times. Just as I
was about to hang up, Elliott himself came on the line.

"Hey Elliott, it's Kate. You're working late. I need
another favor."

"What's the trouble?"

"Pamela Hexter's just been arrested. I need you to
send some more men to the Hexter house in Lake Forest, to Margot Hexter's apartment in Hyde Park, and to
Barton Jr.'s house in Evanston." I gave him the ad-
dresses.

"So they arrested the wife," commented Elliott. "Better her than you. Do you think she did it?"

"I have no idea," I replied. "I'm on my way to the police station with her son. The funeral was this afternoon."

"Pretty gruesome for the family," remarked Elliott.

"You can say that again."

When we arrived at the Lake Forest Municipal Center, the modest parking lot nearest to the police station was already filled with cars including broadcast vans from all three networks. Video technicians swarmed over the steps laying cable. The harsh glare of TV lights illumined the night like flashes of mortar fire. So much for wanting to get there before the press. No doubt Ruskowski had tipped them off.

I fished in my purse for the card that Ruskowski had given me the day of Bart Hexter's murder. I dialed the number and explained to the sergeant who answered the phone that I was in the car with Mrs. Hexter's son and we wanted to get into the building without being torn to shreds by the mob in the parking lot. Would it be possible for someone to come to the other side of the building and let us in through the community center doors? No way, was his succinct reply. But he would be sure that a uniformed policeman met us at the doors of the police department to be sure no reporters followed us into the building. I hung up on him.

I parked the car at the farthest corner of the parking lot and turned to Barton.

"Listen," I said. "I think we'll be less conspicuous on foot. It'll be awhile before they figure out we're not reporters ourselves. But as soon as they do, they'll be all over us. This is how we're going to do it. Walk quickly. Don't make eye contact with anybody, but don't cover your face or you'll be on the news looking like a Mafioso. No matter what anybody says to you, don't answer. Until Elkin gets here you should conduct yourself as if the police have just made a terrible mistake."

"But they have," protested Barton Jr.

"Remember," I said as we got out of the car and linked elbows. "Don't talk to anybody and don't stop for anything."

Chet Ellway, the reporter from Channel Eight, spotted us first and let out the alarm. The media rushed us as a group, running with their microphones in the false daylight of the TV lights, cameramen lumbering under their heavy cameras, bringing up the rear. I felt the stutter in Barton's stride as he saw them coming, and I pulled at his arm to keep him from slowing down. They shouted questions, hands grabbed at my sleeve as reporters jostled each other for position and jostled us in return. Barton, over his initial hesitation, turned his shoulder to the task, and together we pushed our way through the crowd.

Two uniformed officers met us at the door, nightsticks at the ready. After the frenzy in the parking lot, the police station, neon lit and half-deserted for the night, seemed incongruous—almost sleepy. The desk sergeant informed us that Mrs. Hexter was in interrogation and pointed to a bench where we could wait. With an eloquent shrug he seemed to indicate that we might as well make ourselves comfortable for the night.

"What happens now?" asked Barton Jr., too restless to sit.

"We wait for Elkin Caufield to get here. Then they'll let him go and talk to your mother."

"They're going to let her go, aren't they? They can't make her spend the night in jail, can they?"

"Elkin will do his best," I assured him. Two semesters of criminal law, I reflected ruefully, were no preparation for real-life encounters with the criminal justice system. I had no idea how long they would keep Pamela Hexter before arranging a bail hearing. I looked at my watch and hoped that Elkin would arrive soon. "You're going to have to talk to Ken about getting things together for your mother. If the judge does agree to grant bail, you can be sure it's not going to be an insignificant sum. Why don't you sit down. I see a coffee machine around the corner. Let me get you a cup. It's going to be a long night."

Waiting for the cup to fill, I turned to look at Barton Jr. sitting on the hard wooden bench. He seemed to have shrunk since morning. His jacket hung on him like a man's suit on a little boy. His pallor, the claw marks of fatigue under his eyes, the thought of Jane, pale and pregnant, all made my heart turn over. Innocent or guilty, Pamela Hexter's arrest was a hideous assault on their lives. For the Hexter children the alternatives were equally painful. Either their mother had been falsely accused of a capital crime or she was, indeed, a murderer. Either way, the ugly ordeal of her arrest and trial would be a punishment for the innocent as well as the guilty.

It was best not to judge Elkin Caufield too quickly. His manner was disarming—upbeat and reassuring, as if all unpleasantness must dissolve in the face of his particular blend of energy and good sense. But with Elkin only a fool would let his guard down. I had seen his good nature change in a heartbeat into thundering wrath or sarcasm as quick and sharp as a surgeon's knife.

Short, and with the whippet build of a marathoner, in the relative stillness of the police station he was not much of a physical presence. His black hair was cut short in military style, which did nothing to soften his face, pitted long ago by acne. His eyes were dark and piercing, fringed by improbably long lashes. But many a jury member had started out trying to figure out the inherent contradictions in that face, only to find themselves mesmerized by the force of the intellect behind it.

He gave me a distracted wave as he made his way to the desk sergeant where he presented himself as Mrs. Hexter's attorney and carried out a brief conversation. That part of his business concluded, he came to see us, all charm and reassurance, shaking my hand warmly and accepting my introduction of Barton Jr.

"Any trouble making it through the reporters?" I asked as he shrugged off his Burberry, revealing an expensive custom-made suit.

"Nah," he said. "Those guys are all my buddies. I did kick Dick Preston in the shins. He should know by now that when I say 'no comment,' nothing he says about my wife will change my mind. What a schmuck. Barton, young man, the desk sergeant informs me that they are still processing your mother, so it will be a few moments before I am permitted to see her. I'm going to ask you to take a little walk with me so that I'm sure we understand each other."

The two men strolled down the corridor, the criminal attorney's hand on the mathematician's much higher shoulder, while they conferred in whispers about representation and fees and what was likely to happen over the next few hours and days. For Barton Jr. the day's events were like a step into the abyss, but Elkin had been at the receiving end of many panicked phone calls from the homicide lockup. He had taken this walk down the corridor with the family of the accused many times. When the two of them returned to the bench, Barton Jr. looked noticeably reassured.

"Okay, Kate, my dear," said Elkin. "Now it's your turn to step into my office."

I got to my feet with a smile and accompanied Elkin down the hall. He slipped his arm absently around my shoulder as I walked. I knew that in some circles Elkin had a reputation as a grabber, but in my experience he was just one of those people who touches everybody, man or woman.

"Thank you for calling me," said Elkin. "This has every appearance of being an interesting case. Tell me how you came to be a part of this. Are you, perhaps, involved with young Barton? He seems a charming young man."

"No," I replied. "He's married to Jane Barber, the pianist. They have two little boys and a baby on the way. I became a part of this, as you so aptly put it, because Bart Hexter was shot an hour before a meeting with me."

"So you represented the father."

"No, his company, Hexter Commodities. This evening I gave Barton a ride home from his mother's house. His wife was waiting for us with the news of Pamela's arrest."

"What is Mrs. Hexter like?" asked Elkin, of the client he had not yet met.

"I don't know. She's like my mother's friends. You know, beautiful manners, beautiful clothes. She and Bart were married for thirty-six years. By all accounts it was a marriage that worked. They have three grown children. They worked together to raise money for a number of worthy causes. I guess I really don't know her at all."

"I, too, have been aware of them as a public couple. This is one of those cases that will try itself in the press ten times before we ever see the inside of a courtroom. Image will be very important. Does Mrs. Hexter have any history of alcoholism or mental instability?"

"Not that I know of."

"Good. And the family is supportive? They are behind their mother?"

"I've talked only to Barton. He thinks there must be a terrible mistake. He can't believe that his mother is guilty."

"Of course," said Elkin, for whom issues of guilt or innocence were by necessity of less importance than those of conviction and acquittal. "Now, I believe, it is time for me to meet my client."

The next morning my own face stared at me from the front page of the *Tribune* as I walked past the newsstand in the lobby of my office building.

"So his old lady shot him," remarked the man behind the counter as I passed him a quarter for my copy. "Too bad they didn't get your good side."

I unfolded the paper. It was a full quarter-page shot of Barton Jr. and me looking stricken and harassed.

They must have snapped it while we were fighting our way through the pack on the way to the police station the night before. Mother, I thought silently to myself, is going to really love this.

The real abuse, of course, began as soon as I walked through the doors at Callahan Ross.

"I see you're making headlines," remarked Lillian, the receptionist, wryly, as she handed me the messages that had come through the switchboard for me. Stopping to fill my coffee cup, I saw that some wit had already cut out my picture and put it up on the wall above the photocopier. It was displayed next to a photo of Cindy Crawford with the hand-lettered caption: American Lawyer Beauty Makeover. Cindy Crawford's picture was labeled "before." My picture was "after."

"Morning, Kate," called Howard Ackerman, my office neighbor, lounging in his doorway. "Now that you're a partner, do you think you'll be able to afford to buy up all the copies of today's *Trib* and destroy them?"

"I'm going to my desk to count my pennies right now," I replied.

I turned the corner into my office to find Cheryl lying in wait and looking grave.

"Skip Tillman has been down here looking for you twice, and he didn't look happy," she said. "You're supposed to go to see him as soon as you get in."

"Wonderful," I said. "I just love starting the day with a trip to the woodshed with the managing partner of the firm."

"I'll be waiting here for you with coffee and bandages," replied my faithful secretary.

Skip's secretary ushered me into the great man's office like a nurse escorting a patient for whom she knows the prognosis is not good. Skip looked up at me from the file he was reading, peering over the top of his half glasses. His white hair was thinning on top, and with the passing years his face had regained a babylike pinkness. Skip was an old friend of my family's. His wife, Bitsy, played bridge with my mother. Ever since I'd joined the firm he'd treated me alternatively as a beloved niece or a wayward daughter. I couldn't help but feel affection toward Skip, but that didn't change the fact that he was such a big WASP he probably had a stinger on his ass.

"You wanted to see me?" I asked, trying to push down the unpleasant sensation of being called into the headmaster's office.

"I take it you've had an opportunity to see this morning's newspaper?" he demanded.

"It was rather hard to miss," I confessed.

"Did you also catch yourself on the news?"

"No," I replied, wincing inwardly. "I never watch TV."

"I have it on good authority that you made all three networks. Both the eleven o'clock news and the morning broadcasts."

"You know what Andy Warhol said—everyone is famous for fifteen minutes," I ventured.

"And you know very well the policy of this firm regarding this kind of publicity. It is an axiom of this partnership that we do not appear in sordid, criminal matters. I don't think we've had a partner associated with the crime of murder in the entire history of Callahan Ross. I hope I don't need to remind you that as this firm's most recent partner you have a very special responsibility."

"And I'm sure I don't need to remind you that the day that I was accepted into partnership you called me into this very room to lecture me on service to the client and a partner's obligation to bring new business into the firm. Well, I brought in Hexter Commodities, and it is my intention to help the company and the Hexter family through this difficult time of transition. If you read the *Tribune* article you know that Elkin Caufield is representing Mrs. Hexter. All I did was give her son a ride to the police station."

"You are in a special position, Kate," warned Tillman. "As one of this firm's first female partners, you must do better than avoid wrongdoing. Like Caesar's wife, you must avoid the appearance of wrongdoing as well. Unfair as it may seem, it falls to you to set an important precedent."

"I am confident that none of the male partners of this firm would have allowed concerns about appearances to prevent them from serving a client."

"This has been a friendly warning, Kate. Not all of your partners would have been this reasonable."

"You don't have to tell me that," I replied, rising to go. "When you come to work for this firm, one of the first lessons you learn is just what the partners are capable of."

CHAPTER
17

"Tourniquet?" inquired my secretary politely as I stormed back to my office from Skip Tillman's.

"It's only a flesh wound," I answered. "I wouldn't mind a fresh cup of coffee, though."

Cheryl appeared a few minutes later with the coffee and her steno pad. "While you were down the hall getting chewed out, Elkin Caufield's office called. Mrs. Hexter's bail hearing is set for eleven o'clock. They said they'd keep you informed, whatever that means. Do you think she killed him?"

"I don't know what to think," I replied honestly. "For her children's sake, I hope she didn't. Imagine if your mother were arrested for murder. Besides, this is going to be the made-for-TV movie scandal of the year. It's only a matter of time before the Hexters' butler is on 'Oprah,' along with some psychologist who's just spent three weeks writing a book on murder among the rich."

"That's not an answer," pressed Cheryl. "You've met her. Do you think she murdered him?"

"There is no limit to what people are capable of," I ventured cautiously. "Who knows what goes on inside of a marriage? Pamela Hexter doesn't seem like someone capable of murder. She's a kinder, gentler version of my mother—you know, a fiftyish woman in a Chanel suit who plays bridge, goes to parties, and shops. I saw her the morning after the murder. She was methodically making a list of people to be invited to the house after the funeral."

"That sounds awfully cold for someone who's just found her husband shot to death."

"I know," I countered. "But if she'd just shot him, don't you think she'd have made a better stab at playing the grieving widow?"

Carl Savage sauntered into my office, making no attempt to hide the fact that he found the Hexter family troubles vastly amusing. I explained that under the circumstances I'd had no chance to discuss a severance package with Barton Jr. Instead, I suggested that Carl give me a proposal that I would relay back to his former employer.

"You can tell him to shove it up his ass," said Carl, leaning back in the armchair that faced my desk. "I start work at McKenzie on Monday. In the meantime I'm going to hire a lawyer and sue."

"It doesn't have to be this way," I said. "You'll end up paying your lawyer more than you'll win in settlement."

"It's not the money," Savage snorted. "I've got plenty of money. It's the principle. Baby Barton would have to pay me a shit load of money before it would make even a dent in the pile he's got. I want him to feel it."

"You worked for his dad for how many years? Nine?"

"It would have been ten years next January."

"I'd think that under the circumstances you might want to cut his son a break just out of common decency. It doesn't look very good, you coming after him over this when his mother's just been arrested."

"Aah, they're gonna let her go. There's no way that Pamela killed him."

"Why do you say that?" I asked, interested.

"I know Pamela. She'd never shoot him. Too messy. The woman was a neat freak. You'd go over to the house for a drink, and she'd be ringing for the maid to come and pick the crumbs out of the carpet while you were still sitting there. Besides, why would she have to kill him? The lady was loaded. If she was sick of Bart, all she had to do was pack up and split. With Bart's temper I'm surprised she hadn't hit the road years ago. But then there's no accounting for taste."

"Speaking of taste, you must know a Hexter employee named Victoria Lloyd."

"Sure, I know Torey," Savage answered cautiously. "She's a runner. Worked at Hexter about two years."

"Do you know if she and Hexter were having an affair?" I asked.

"Yeah," replied Savage, his face clouding. "They were doin' the old horizontal hula. You see stuff like that all the time. An old guy like Hexter discovers he can still get it up, and pretty soon he's believing that this young babe wants him for his wonderful self, not his money. What a sap."

"So if you don't think his wife killed him, who did?" I asked.

"I don't know. Maybe it was his crackpot daughter—you know, Mad Margot. She hasn't been playing with a full deck for a long time. Maybe it was just some poor schmuck dentist from Dubuque who lost his life's savings in the markets. Who knows?"

"So you don't think it's whoever is behind Deodar Commodities?" I ventured.

"Deodar Commodities?" demanded Carl Savage incredulously. "Oh, come on, Deodar Commodities is just a front account for Hexter. You bill how much an hour and you still haven't figured that out yet? Jeez, what do they pay you for?"

"Let me see if I get this straight," I said to Carl Savage after he'd already explained it once. "Deodar Commodities is just a shell company that Hexter traded through in order to disguise his presence in the markets. Why was he trying to systematically exceed position limits?"

"You don't get it, do you? That's why this CFTC thing is all bullshit. Hexter didn't want to do *anything* to attract attention to Deodar."

"So then what's the point? What was he trying to hide from the CFTC?"

"Bart wasn't trying to fool the CFTC with Deodar, he was trying to fool Pamela."

"Pamela?" I demanded. "Why would he try to fool Pamela?"

"Because Pamela was born wearing a green eyeshade, that's why. That broad kept track of every penny. She was the kind of cheap you get when you're either incredibly poor or very rich. Pamela used to send the maid to the grocery store with coupons. Bart came in one day just seething. It seems the little woman had decided to save some money and start using generic toilet paper. Jesus, was Bart steamed." Savage smiled at the recollection. "Bart was just the other way. He'd tip his caddy a hundred bucks. He loved it. It was like the Rolls Royce. He wanted the whole fucking world to know that he'd made it and had it to spread it around. Deodar Commodities was how Pamela and Bart could live together. Pamela used to go through the company books, for God's sake. Deodar was how Bart got his poker money. That's what I'm saying. Why would Pamela want to kill him? She already had him by the balls. If anything, you'd think it would be the other way around. If anybody shot anybody, you'd think it would be Pamela who got it between the eyes."

"While you were in with Mr. Savage your mother called," reported Cheryl. "Since you were unavailable, she yelled at me instead. It seems she's very upset that Pamela Hexter has been arrested, and she wants to know what you're going to do about it. She'd like you to call her."

"Thanks. If you'll take all my calls from her I'll double your salary."

"No thanks."

"Did anybody else call?"

"Nobody who can't wait." Cheryl handed me the other message slips. "These don't include the reporters who called. Seems you're famous. That guy from the *Star* called me again. He's now offering me five grand if I can get him some good dirt on Hexter. I told him no, but I hinted that I might be able to get you to pose nude for less. He wasn't interested."

"Mother's right, I'm not very photogenic."

"Oh, and Stephen called. He said something about wanting to know about *Chicago Magazine*."

"Call him and tell him I'll do it. Ask him not to set anything up until after next Friday. I'd rather keep my calendar clear until after I've finished the answer to the CFTC. Do me one more favor while you're at it. Call over to Hexter Commodities and talk to someone named Victoria Lloyd. She's a runner, so you might have to try her later in the afternoon after the market closes. Tell her I want to see her this weekend. I'll go to her place. She'll know what it's about."

"Will do."

"Tell me, am I doing anything with Stephen this weekend?"

"Saturday night," replied Cheryl, grabbing my calendar off my desk. "You've got an eight o'clock dinner at Charlie Canter's with a Swedish chemist and his wife. I write all this stuff down for you. You should try reading it sometimes."

Ken Kurlander came to see me in the middle of the afternoon, looking distressed.

"What can I do for you, Ken?" I inquired, motioning him into a chair. "I heard they allowed Mrs. Hexter's bail. Is she home yet?"

"Just outrageous!" he said, shaking his head. "Nearly two million dollars. I never thought I'd see such injustice." It took an effort of will to keep from asking whether he was referring to the amount of money or the arrest. "When Barton and I were at the bank making arrangements this morning, we took the opportunity to empty Bart's safe-deposit boxes. We came across something I was rather hoping you'd be able to shed some light on."

"I didn't think you'd be able to get into the box," I remarked. "Not until you'd begun the probate process."

"At my suggestion, Bart didn't maintain any safe-deposit boxes in his own name," replied Kurlander. "I've seen too many occasions when, once the appropriate papers have been filed, and the time comes to inventory the contents of the boxes for the estate, some greedy family members with access to the key have already helped themselves to articles of value. Bart kept his box in the name of the family corporation with Barton Jr. and myself as co-signators."

"How prudent," I remarked, thinking about the underbelly of human nature that Ken Kurlander must have been exposed to over the years of his practice. "What is it that you wanted to show me?"

"It's a real-estate contract for a condominium." Ken handed me the document. It was for the new River North development that was going up near South Water Street. It must have been some apartment, since the full purchase price was in excess of a million dollars. According to the papers, a payment of one hundred thousand dollars in earnest money had been paid six weeks previously. A further payment of five hundred thousand was due on April fifteenth, three days from now, with another five hundred thousand due on July fifteenth.

"This is all news to me," I said honestly. "I assume, since you're asking me, Pamela doesn't know about this."

"I spoke to both Barton and Krissy. Neither of them has heard their mother speak of it. When I called the developer just now to see if I could get some additional information, he said that it was his understanding that Bart was buying the condominium for a young lady."

"Any chance it's for Margot?"

"When I suggested that it might be for one of his daughters, he laughed most unpleasantly. I think we can assume we are dealing with a very different relationship. Unfortunately, unless the five hundred thousand is paid, the earnest money will be forfeited. I hesitate to trouble Barton Jr. at such a difficult time, but it is not an inconsiderable sum. Unfortunately, the developer is not prepared to be flexible. He says he has a waiting list of people interested in units."

"And, of course, it wouldn't hurt to just take the hundred grand and turn around and sell the condo to someone else," I ventured.

"You understand. Since it appears that you and Barton have become quite close recently, I thought you might be willing to discuss the matter with him."

"Of course, I'll talk to him."

After he'd gone, I buzzed Cheryl and asked her when she had scheduled me to meet with Torey Lloyd.

I had dinner with Elliott Abelman at Scoozi's, a noisy Italian restaurant on Huron in the heart of the gallery district. Formerly a warehouse, the restaurant looked more like the set of a Fellini movie than a place where they make their own mozzarella and roast garlic in wood-burning ovens. But I had learned from experience never to question Elliott's judgment, especially when it came to food.

I found him standing at the jammed bar holding two glasses of red wine.

"Salut," he said, handing me one. "Thanks for

meeting me here. I've been in a meeting at Elkin Caufield's office since ten o'clock. We didn't even take a break for lunch, and I'm just starved." He loosened his tie with one hand as he spoke.

"Are you working on the Hexter case?" I asked. Elliott took me by the elbow and led me to the far corner of the bar, where two stools had opened up.

"I confess, after you called me last night, I took the initiative and offered my services to Caufield. I've done quite a bit of work for him in the past, but when you're in business for yourself, you can't let these opportunities slip by."

"So what's the lowdown?" I asked.

"Ten-second summary? The cops think she cooled her old man in a fit of jealous rage. She says she didn't do it."

"What kind of case do the cops have?"

"Circumstantial, but strong. It seems that all of the Hexters' servants who live in are Guatemalan and go to eight o'clock mass at a church downtown. They always leave at the same time, six-thirty Sunday morning. Pamela and Bart were home alone. None of the servants saw either Mrs. or Mr. Hexter that morning, but the cook said that she heard the two of them arguing around five-thirty when she went into the kitchen to turn on the coffee."

"Did she hear what they were arguing about?"

"No. Just angry voices. The newspaper is usually delivered around six-forty-five, so Hexter had to get it himself on Sundays. The morning of his death his wife says she isn't sure of the exact time he left. Anyway, Hexter got in his Rolls and went out to get the paper and didn't come back.

"According to some of the cops I've talked to, the police have two witnesses who heard the shot—a woman walking her dog on Parkland Road, and the guy who lives two doors down who was out jogging. Both of them said they heard a shot a few minutes before seven. The runner said he saw a cyclist on Parkland Road who might have heard it, too, but I don't think the cops are looking too hard for him since both the jogger and the dog lady agree on the time.

"Anyway, Pamela said that she came into the kitchen, poured herself a cup of coffee, and waited for her husband to come back with the newspaper, which they were in the habit of reading together. She said that after fifteen or twenty minutes, she became alarmed. She went into her bedroom and changed into a warm-up suit. When he still hadn't returned she got into her golf cart and went out looking for him. Do all rich people ride around their property on golf carts?" Elliott asked.

"It is the accepted mode of transportation in Lake Forest," I replied. "I'm surprised that Hexter didn't use it."

"According to his wife he never did. It made him feel like a pansy—best thing I've heard about him so far. Also, if he took the car, he didn't have to get dressed. Anyway, Pamela said she was worried because her husband had a history of heart trouble. I guess he had a major heart attack two years ago that left him with a condition that screwed up his heart rhythm. As a result, he'd occasionally suffer blackouts. So she went out looking for him. She said when she saw the car in the ditch she immediately assumed that her husband had suffered a heart attack. She says she opened the car and grabbed him before she realized what had really happened. She says that once she saw that he was dead, she went into shock. She claims to have sat in the golf cart for some time before finally going back to the house. When she got inside she realized that she had gotten blood on her. She took off the sweat suit and rinsed off in the shower. She said that all during this time it was as if she was in a daze. Once she was clean and changed into dry clothes she called an old friend named Ken Kurlander, who I gather is a partner at your firm. Kurlander told her to call 911. The call was logged in at seven-fifty-three.

"In terms of the physical evidence there's not much. The only fingerprints in the car were Hexter's and Pamela's. There were some footprints near the car that the cops took casts of, some were identified as belonging to you and some to Pamela. There were a couple others that they took casts of near the top of the driveway, but it turned out they came from a cyclist or a jogger. He was definitely shot with his own gun, but it had been wiped clean."

"And why do the cops say she did it?"

"From what Elkin pieced together from their questions, the cops say that she and Barton had been fighting off and on all weekend. There'd been some sort of disagreement when they had their children and grandchildren to dinner Friday night. Saturday they had a golf outing, but Saturday night they went to a party at their country club and several people reported seeing them argue. I gather Hexter stormed out and Pamela had to get a ride home with friends.

"Mostly the cops think it's fishy that she waited for almost an hour before she reported the murder. They don't like it that she called her lawyer first, or that she met them at the door dressed in a suit with not a hair out of place, just like she'd invited them to tea. They didn't like the fact that they found her bloodstained jogging suit at the bottom of the trash can."

"I saw her that morning. She was so calm it was scary."

"Then, of course, there's the whole issue of the gun. I guess Mrs. Hexter told the cops the morning of the murder that her husband didn't own a gun. Turns out he did. He kept it in a desk drawer in his study. He'd had it for seven years—registered to him and everything. Mrs. Hexter claims she never knew he had it, and she never went into his study.

"It's easy to see the story the cops are writing. Barton and Pamela have been fighting. Sunday morning when Barton stormed out to the car to get the paper, Pamela grabbed the gun, hopped in her little golf cart and went out after him. She pulled up next to him. He stopped the car and rolled down the window to say something, and she shot him. His car drifted into the ditch, and she went after him to make sure he was dead. She wipes the gun, drops it in the car. In the process, she gets blood on herself. She gets back to the house, takes off the bloodstained clothes, takes a shower, and calls her lawyer. Slam dunk."

"So what does Elkin have you working on?"

"The case is circumstantial. We're trying to find out where it's weak. My first instinct is to go after the gun. Elkin says that one of the maids saw it in the drawer on Friday. According to the police, no one but the family and the servants had access to it after that, and all the servants have an alibi."

Over the loudspeaker our table was called, and Elliott

and I waded back into the restaurant and ordered more wine.

"It's going to be interesting," Elliott continued, talking to me over the top of the menu. "I met Pamela Hexter at Elkin's office this afternoon. She's not going to do herself any good on the witness stand. She is one cool customer. She just keeps saying that they can't convict her if she didn't do it, but you'd think from her attitude that she'd been accused of farting in public, not murder."

"I think she's shielding someone. You said that the only people who had access to the gun were the family. She's not dumb. She's got to know if she didn't do it it has to be one of her children. Do any of them have alibis?"

"I don't know, but you can bet I'm going to find out. Do any of them seem like good suspect material?"

"His daughter, Margot, is a king-sized flake, and she sure didn't much like her dad."

Our waitress came and took our order—scalopine with woodland mushrooms for Elliott, cioppino for me.

"You have to admit it's a juicy case," remarked Elliott, happily tearing into a loaf of hot bread that had materialized on the table.

"I can't see it that way. I'm too close. I've spent a lot of time with Hexter's son this week. This is so painful for him. Besides, there were a couple of times this week I thought the handcuffs were going to be for me."

"You were really worried?"

"Ruskowski accused me of having an affair with the dead man. My files and my personal bank records were subpoenaed. They came and searched my apartment. There's nothing like having a bunch of policemen pawing through your underwear to bring home the possibility that your life can be changed by a murder investigation."

"Your partners would have loved that," remarked Elliott.

"They were in a collective swoon that my picture was in the paper this morning. If I'd been arrested there'd have been wholesale strokes. No, I take that back. Strokes or no strokes, I guarantee that by the time I made bail all of my things would have been in boxes, and my indefinite leave of absence arranged."

"I thought partners stuck together."

"They do, but I think there's a bit more cohesion once you've been at the firm twenty years or so. I've been a partner less than four months, and there are still old guys who are having the bends about my being a woman and so young."

"Oh, come on. The way you talk about Callahan, you make it sound like it's all old men. There have to be some young guys."

"Being an old man is a state of mind," I replied.

"With that attitude it's no wonder you're unpopular at your place of employment."

"It's not like I'm a pariah or anything," I protested. "I mean, they don't throw things at me when I come in in the morning. I do get asked to lunch sometimes. But when you get right down to it, a big law firm is a lot like high school, and frankly, I wasn't very popular in high school. What I want to know," I demanded, "is how do you always manage to get me talking about things like this?"

"It's because I find you really interesting," replied Elliott with disarming frankness. "Maybe they're all like you where you come from, but I can't figure you out."

"I've never considered myself much of a cipher," I said.

"Not many people do," answered Elliott just as our food arrived.

It was a nice night so we opted out of a cab. Elliott told me about Torey Lloyd as we walked toward the loop back to my office.

"Victoria Lloyd," said Elliott Abelman as we headed north on Wells, "born Pinkerton, Illinois. Youngest of four children. Father a farmer, mother died when she was four."

"Where, pray tell, is Pinkerton, Illinois?"

"Bottom of the state, population twenty-five hundred. The guy I sent down there says they still have an A & W drive-in. You know, you sit in your car and the waitress clips a tray to your window."

"Fascinating."

"Pinkerton is a small town, religious sort of place. By the time Torey was sixteen, it was clear that she was a big-town sort of girl. The day she graduated from high school she got on a Greyhound bus and headed for Chicago. She did some modeling, waited on some tables, went to night school. She lived with a guy for six months, but it didn't last. She tried to get a job as a stewardess, but they were laying people off and there were no openings. The night she turned twenty-one she met a man named Carl Savage in a bar on Rush Street."

"The same Carl Savage who worked for Hexter Commodities?"

"Yep. They lived together for almost a year before Carl got her a job as a runner at Hexter."

"So when did she trade up to Black Bart?" I asked.

"I'm still not exactly sure, so I ran a credit profile on her. Within three months of starting at Hexter Commodities, all of her bills were paid off, she had a new car—a Lexus, no less—and she opened accounts at Neiman Marcus, Saks, and Bloomies. She's been charging right around ten grand a month at the department stores, paying in full every month. You'll never guess which address the bills go to?"

"Hexter's?" I ventured.

"No. Lake View Towers. Hexter was paying the rent."

"I guess I should feel flattered. According to Ruskowski, the night doorman picked me out of a photo array. Said I was the girl Hexter was keeping there."

"I talked to that doorman yesterday," reported Elliott. "He's got glaucoma."

"Oh, that makes me feel so much better."

We picked up the river as it wound past the Merchandise Mart, hulking and dark across the water. The night was surprisingly warm, and the air was blessed with an undercurrent of lilacs, a whispered promise of the summer to come.

"I know you didn't ask me for surveillance, but I stopped over at Lake View Towers this morning to see if I could catch a glimpse of her. I got a peek when she left for work. Wow. No wonder Hexter went after her."

"You realize, of course," I said, after I'd taken a minute to consider, "that Torey Lloyd is nothing less than a motive on the hoof for Pamela Hexter. When he came to the police station last night, Elkin told me that this was the kind of case that would try itself in the press before it ever got to court." I told Elliott about the sales contract for River North Condominiums that turned up in Hexter's safe-deposit box. "You've got to admit that it won't look good for Pamela once the police find out."

"Pamela doesn't look good for Pamela," countered Elliott. "There's something very unnatural in the woman's composure. No wonder the cops think she did it." We crossed the street and walked in silence for a ways.

Finally I said: "When I was ten, my older brother, Teddy, committed suicide. He hanged himself in the garage so that my parents would find him when they came home from a party. I came downstairs when I heard my mother screaming. She was in the kitchen trying to get herself a glass of water, but her hand was shaking so badly she couldn't keep the glass under the tap. Fifteen minutes later, when the police arrived, she was completely composed. Afterward, I remembered all my parents' friends admiring her stoicism. It made no sense to me. I remembered thinking that if I had been the one who died, I would have wanted them to cry."

"And what about you, Kate? You talk about the people you come from as if you're not a part of them. Do you cry in front of other people, or do you keep a stiff upper lip?"

"When my husband died, I cried," I said quietly. "It was very late at night, and I was sitting with him in the hospital. He had been in a coma for three days, and we knew he was near the end. I was holding his hand when he died. I called the nurse and told her. She came and took off his wedding ring. She handed it to me and closed his eyes. I don't remember when I started crying, but I cried all the tears in the world that night. I don't think anyone saw me cry after that. Not at the funeral, not afterward, not ever. My grief was too private to share. So I guess I'm not so different from the people I come from."

"I'm sorry," whispered Elliott. "I didn't mean to bring up painful memories."

"It's been three years. For a long time I couldn't even talk about it. I couldn't say his name out loud. I guess it's true what they say about time." We walked in silence for a while. "This is my building," I said. The street was deserted, bathed in the pale light from the office windows high above us. The walking and the wine, and talking about Russell, had all brought things very close to the surface for me.

"When are you meeting Torey Lloyd?"

"Sunday afternoon."

"Do you want me to come with you?"

"No. I think she'll feel safer if it's just me."

He was standing very close to me. I could feel the quiet rhythm of his breathing, and I realized, too late, what line had been crossed.

"It's a mistake to feel safe with you," he said, drawing me to him without touching. My hands brushed the rough wool of his jacket as he kissed me. I felt the softness of his skin against my face, and desire welled up inside of me. He did not reach out for me, and still it took all of my strength to pull away.

CHAPTER
18

Once I was inside the building, I came crashing down on myself. For a long time I had assumed that I was immune from the more obvious kinds of foolishness. I clung to my well-ordered life, so it frightened me that I could come so close to abandoning it on the strength of a spring night and an attractive man.

My office seemed too bright and strangely unfamiliar. On my desk lay files in ramparts: stacked, unopened, mutely rebuking me for matters unattended. I found myself flitting from surface to surface, picking up and replacing the Lucite tombstones—the memorabilia of the dozen or so deals that I'd done since becoming a lawyer.

When the phone rang, I jumped. I felt guilty and reassured to hear Stephen's familiar voice at the other end of the line. He had just finished up at the office. Did I want a ride home?

Did I want a ride home? Whatever for? My car was parked in the garage below me. Stephen knew that quite well. Why couldn't we say what we really meant? Why these other words, this strange reluctance? Do you want me to come home with you? Do I want to go? For us there always seemed to be these bridges we could not cross.

"Are you coming back downtown in the morning?" I asked.

"I have a meeting at ten with Lars Berggren. We're having dinner with him and his wife tomorrow night," replied Stephen. He was calling from his car. I heard the faint honking of horns in the background. "I'll take you back downtown whenever you want."

"I'll meet you downstairs."

That night I made love with Stephen, and felt so lost that he might have been anyone.

When the alarm went off at eight, I woke to the sound of coffee beans being ground in the kitchen. I groaned and covered my head with a pillow. A few minutes later Stephen came in and presented me with a cup of coffee and the *Tribune*.

"Front page of the Metro section—Elkin Caufield expressing outrage at his client's arrest," related Stephen. "Otherwise there's nothing new."

Every morning Stephen rolled out of bed, did twenty minutes of calisthenics followed by twenty minutes on the rowing machine and another twenty on the stair climber. He had an extra bedroom filled with exercise equipment and he put in his hour in it every morning as automatically as brushing his teeth. He stood next to the bed dressed only in sneakers and a pair of black bicycle shorts, his bare chest glistening. Maybe there should be a charity calendar, I thought—Hunks of the Fortune 500.

"Lots of work today?" he inquired as I skimmed the

lead article on the Hexter murder. In the photo that they ran with the story, Elkin Caufield positively glowed.

"Yeah, I've got to figure out what to do about the CFTC. According to one of Hexter's former employees, the whole thing was just a way for Hexter to hide money from his wife."

"So he didn't trade the two accounts in order to exceed position limits?"

"Obviously he exceeded position limits," I replied absently. "But according to Savage you'd have thought he'd have been careful not to. The whole thing doesn't make any sense."

Stephen put two fingers to the side of his neck, checking his heart rate after he'd cooled down from exercise.

"Do you know anything about a heart condition called ventricular tachycardia?" I asked.

"Ventricular tachycardia is a very fast heart rhythm that originates in an abnormal site in the heart—usually one of the ventricles," replied Stephen. "Why do you ask?"

"Bart Hexter developed it after a massive heart attack. The medical examiner said that his heart was badly damaged and that he wouldn't have lived that much longer if he hadn't been shot. His wife said that sometimes he had blackouts."

"Episodes are usually associated with syncope— blackouts," confirmed Stephen. "It's a very serious condition in someone who's had a severe heart attack. Until last year the only truly effective way to treat it was to implant a defibrillator in the patient's chest."

"Barton Jr. said that Hexter was taking some new drug instead."

"It's one of ours. We've developed a new generation of amiodarone—that's the medication that they used to use for VT patients. It's called Ventrinome, and it's very effective."

"Sounds better than having something implanted in your chest that sends out electrical shocks."

"Did you say that Hexter and his wife lived together?"

"Of course they lived together," I replied. "Why do you ask?"

"Well, one of the drawbacks of Ventrinome is that the body becomes totally dependent on it. If you don't take it, even for one day, there's a chance that you'll go into VT. For someone with Hexter's history, that would almost certainly be fatal. I'm sure his cardiologist sat them both down and explained it."

"What are you getting at?"

"Azor Pharmaceuticals has the patent on Ventrinome—there are no competing brands, so we don't spend anything extra on making it look unique. It's just a round white pill—like an aspirin or any number of vitamins that are sold over the counter."

"So?"

"So why would Pamela Hexter shoot her husband when all she had to do was switch his heart medication with aspirin and wait for him to die of natural causes?"

I like Callahan Ross the best on the weekends. The place is younger on Saturdays and Sundays. The dead wood partners are on the golf course or at their clubs or wherever they disappear to at the end of the week. The phones are quiet. Free from pretense and office politics, weekends are a time for real work to get done.

As soon as I got in, I called Detective Ruskowski and left a message. Then I set to work on Bart Hexter's legacy to me, the boxed paper trail that had been delivered to my office over the course of the last week. Besides the trading tickets that were finally ordered and sorted in the conference room, there were still yards of documents in the Hexter file I had yet to peruse. In addition, the boxes of personal records that I'd had sent to me from Pamela's house had arrived late Friday afternoon.

I began in the conference room where the trading tickets were laid out in neat piles, bound together in individual stacks, each one representing a single day's trading. Sherman had made up a key listing the name of the trading account and the corresponding account number. With the clearinghouse's computer list of trades in one hand, I picked up the first stack of tickets and began to flip through them. My heart sank.

Whatever was I going to discover in this flurry of paper? The chain of communication in futures is stripped down for speed. At Hexter Commodities, like other retail futures firms, brokers placed orders on behalf of a client by writing them down on an order ticket, which was then passed to a phone clerk who called it down to the floor of the exchange. From there, another phone clerk wrote out another order form and handed it to a runner, whose job it was to carry it as quickly as possible to the floor broker, who then executed the trade.

Savage's assertion that the Deodar account actually belonged to Hexter didn't sit right with me. I believed that Bart might have wanted the funds free from his wife's scrutiny. But why would he risk embarrassing exposure by flaunting CFTC regulations, especially with someone like Herman Geiss dogging his every transaction? Besides, if it was indeed Hexter behind both accounts, who had taken the account records and dumped the computer files? And more importantly, why?

Yet, as the hours of the morning slipped by, the order tickets seemed to bear out Savage's story. The CFTC required that no order be placed without an account number. This regulation was designed to prevent trade allocation—an illegal practice—whereby profitable trades are systematically assigned to one account and losers passed off on another. But as I examined the tickets, it became apparent that the account numbers for trades made for Hexter's own account and Deodar had been written in after the fact. Sometimes the order was written in ink and the account number in pencil. Frequently it looked as though the account number had been added by a different hand entirely.

And yet, when I forced myself to meticulously chart the trades from the tickets, no particular pattern of allocation appeared—profitable and unprofitable trades appeared randomly distributed throughout both accounts. The only explanation that made sense was the one that Savage had offered.

Clearly Hexter was guilty of exceeding position limits. Entering trades without account numbers was also a technical violation of the law, though I couldn't see how the CFTC would get very far with that one since it did not appear that anyone profited or lost by the practice. It was also apparent that trade allocation between Hexter and Deodar could not have been accomplished by Hexter alone—Savage, the phone clerk, and floor trader must all have been aware of it. Could one of them have been responsible for destroying the account information? Certainly they'd have had the opportunity, but where was the motive?

When I looked at my watch it was four o'clock. If anything, I was more confused than when I'd started.

I spent the rest of the day in my underwear with Jeannette. Jeannette is my good mother. She is a fashionable, no-nonsense woman in her fifties who launched her personal shopping service when her youngest daughter went off to college. A particularly well-turned-out employee benefits attorney I once met at a Bar Association luncheon gave me her name. In time, I've learned that Jeannette is any number of professional women's little secret.

I arrived at Jeannette's—a well-lit loft on Oak Street that was just far enough west of Michigan for the rent to be reasonable—and, as always, I was seized by the inevitable sensation of having unexpectedly arrived in a foreign country. There was a low coffee table with a plate of fruit on it, and I knew there was other furniture in there somewhere, but all of it was buried under an avalanche of clothes. There were mountains of jackets, piles of blouses, box after box of pantyhose. There were bras and panties, nightgowns and bathrobes, and a blizzard of little jewelry boxes. Two long racks, completely filled, were set up on either side of the three-way mirror, to which had been taped my list of what I told Jeannette I needed for the summer. Next to it was a much longer inventory, generated by Jeannette's computer, indicating what I already owned.

I genuinely liked Jeannette, even while I resisted her persistent attempts to open me up to the world of fashion. I knew that clothes meant different things for different women. For my mother and her friends they were the building blocks of an obsessive quest for perfection. Absolutely thin, perfectly groomed, debagged and desagged, they scrutinized each other's clothes like adversaries searching for a weakness. For other women, clothes were fun, or the fabric of dreams, or the means to an end—attraction, seduction, or acceptance.

And for me? For me they are a part of the business of being Kate Millholland. My job demands that I dress a certain way. Being a Millholland, I am expected to do it better than most. I like conservative clothes that don't gather much attention—my mother already has the franchise as the family fashion plate. But if I don't dress well it jars people, takes their attention away from where I want it to be.

We started with evening clothes which, like bad tasting medicine, Jeannette knew were best to get over with first. From there we worked our way through a number of suits, casual clothes, shoes, a new raincoat, and even a cocktail dress of black silk that Jeannette insisted I take home and wear that night.

By six I had made a substantial dent in my assets and acquired a young headache. I lay down on the couch while Jeannette finished up her paperwork. I looked at the rack of clothes that Marina, the seamstress, had pinned and marked for alterations. At least, I told myself, I was done until the fall.

When I got home Claudia was there, but she was behaving strangely. As soon as I opened the front door I heard her in her bedroom, bumping around and cursing.

"Claudia?" I called out. "Are you all right?"

Her reply was muffled, but definitely obscene.

When I reached her room, I saw her standing on a chair inside her closet, groping for something on a high shelf. She was wearing a backless sundress and a pair of cowboy boots. Except for the weekend that her parents had come to visit, I'd never seen my roommate dressed in anything but a set of surgical green scrubs. They were all printed with the words "Property of University of Chicago Hospitals" across the chest. Over time I'd come to accept that stamp as a fitting caption for this stage in Claudia's life.

"Oh, it's you," declared my roommate, extricating herself from the closet.

"What is going on?" I demanded, looking incredulously at the heaps of clothes lying on the floor. Claudia plunked herself down on the bed and sighed.

"I have hit an absolute low point," she groaned.

"What are you talking about?" I inquired with a growing sense of alarm. The Claudia I knew was a rock—a surgeon in training—leading a life consumed by work and stripped to essentials. She was always to be found at the hospital, asleep in bed, or occasionally sitting in a vegetative state in the living room, semicomatose from exhaustion, as a prelude to either of the aforementioned activities. Claudia in a dress represented a truly extraordinary turn of events.

"Claudia, what are you doing?"

"You're not going to believe it. I have a date."

"A date?" I echoed. Claudia did not, as a rule, socialize. The woman barely had time to sleep and eat. "If you have a date, that's great."

"I haven't told you the worst part. He's a dermatologist."

"Really? What's his name? What's he like?"

"What's he like? He's a dermatologist. The lowest of the low. A man whose entire medical specialty can be summed up by the axiom: 'If it's wet make it dry, if it's dry make it wet.' I can't believe I'd stoop this low just for sex."

"What has gotten into you?" I asked. I didn't know what else to say.

"I was having lunch in the cafeteria today. It was ten in the morning, but I knew it was lunch because it was hamburgers and mashed potatoes. Anyway, there was a group of us sitting together, too fried even to talk. I started to look at everyone's hospital I.D. We all wear them clipped to our scrubs—it's a rule. They take your picture the first day you arrive at the hospital.

"So there I was looking at these pictures—of people with tans, people who'd brushed their hair and were smiling, for God's sake. And then I looked at us in the flesh. Hell, we look worse than ninety percent of the patients. Here, look at mine." She scrabbled through the dirty laundry on her bed until she came up with her hospital I.D.

I looked at the picture. It bore a passing resemblance to my roommate, but this woman had rosy cheeks, wore mascara, and had the light of mischief in her eyes. Her hair, dark and shiny, hung loose over her shoulders. The Claudia I lived with had an ashen face, circles under her eyes, and a look of weary defiance. I had never once seen her wear her hair down. It was always in the long braid that hung down her back, out of the way.

"So?" I replied, handing the I.D. back to her.

"So when I got to thinking about what my life is like, I got really depressed. So depressed, in fact, that when this dermatologist I'd met once on a consult asked me to go to dinner with him tonight, I said yes."

"I'm glad you're going out," I said. "It'll do you some good to have some fun."

"You don't understand. I don't want to go out. That's a loop I don't want to be caught up in."

"What are you talking about? What's wrong with going on a date?"

"You don't understand. I'm a surgeon. Surgery is not a 'let's try this for a couple of days and see if it works' specialty. Surgery is full of absolutes. You either fix it, or you don't. In the operating room nobody cares if you're nice or compassionate or nurturing. You either can do the work or you can't, and the quality of that work is open to the scrutiny and judgment of the entire surgical team. There's no fudging. You are as good as your work. Period. I am a good surgeon, and I make a real effort to make sure that the people I work with think of me as a surgeon first and a woman second. If it gets around that I went out with a dermatologist I'll never hear the end of it. They'll be putting Clearasil and condoms in my locker in the surgeon's changing room. . . ."

"It's not fair to expect yourself to deny all the other parts of your personality for your work," I protested.

"I'm supposed to listen to advice on this from you?" Claudia challenged.

"What's that supposed to mean? I go out."

"Yeah. His secretary calls your secretary. You and Stephen see each other because you're both too busy to find somebody else. If Stephen weren't around, what would you do? Call Bloomingdales and have them send you a man?"

"Ouch, that hurt," I said. "Though I do know that I would draw the line at having them send me a derma-tologist."

I ducked just as Claudia's cowboy boot whizzed past my ear.

CHAPTER
19

Another Sunday morning. *The New York Times* lay unread on the coffee table, still sheathed in blue plastic. That was two in a row Bart Hexter owed me. Hard to believe he'd only been dead two Sundays. The sun was out, so I lengthened my normal Sunday run down the lakefront to the Shedd Aquarium. I was still feeling wiped from my dinner at Charlie Canter's with the Swedish chemist and his wife.

It had been a memorable evening. The chemist was urbane and charming. His wife, no doubt a lovely woman in her own language, was unfortunately possessed of not a single word of English. The minute we were shown to our table, the two men launched into an intense and technical discussion of the next generation of beta blockers and their application in the treatment of several neurologic disorders. His wife and I smiled inanely at each other for three hours.

Worse, I have always found Charlie Canter's to be totally pretentious. For one thing, the food is so much more fun to read about than it is to actually eat. For dinner I ordered a pork tenderloin wrapped in soft saffron noodles and stuffed with artichokes, roasted red peppers, sauced with an herb coulis and garnished with oyster mushrooms. It sounded wonderful—an adventure for the palate. The only trouble was that I should have ordered two of them. Maybe I really am a pig—or a prig. But I think there's something wrong with dropping close to a hundred dollars (without wine) for one meal and ending up hungry.

As I ran, I couldn't help but wonder how Claudia's evening with the dermatologist had gone. I found that my roommate's comments about my relationship with Stephen had also hit a nerve. Together Stephen and I made the kind of 'power couple' that made for good magazine copy. In bed we made fireworks. For many people that would be enough. But I had once had more, and I couldn't help but know the difference.

When Russell died I knew that a certain kind of love was gone for me as surely as an amputee knows he will not spontaneously regenerate a lost limb. I mourned that part of me as I had mourned Russell, and then went on to fill my life with the things that were still there.

When Elliott kissed me I began to wonder if what I thought was gone had instead just been pushed down so deep inside of me that I'd assumed it had disappeared. On the sidewalk in front of my office I had felt the prodding of some forgotten ember, an inkling that if not love, certainly attraction was possible again for me. Grimly sprinting by the lake I found myself wondering whether that was an entirely good thing.

I arrived at the office and immediately cracked open the first of the boxes that had come from Hexter's house. Cheryl had arranged for me to see Torey Lloyd at the Lake View Towers apartment at two, and I wanted to sift through as many of the papers as I could before then. I soon discovered that it wasn't going to be easy.

Hexter may have had a tremendous ability to manipulate numbers, but he clearly had no particular facility for accounting. It wasn't surprising that someone with Pamela's penchant for lists and order would have felt the need to keep an eye on him. In the boxes I found envelopes from six different brokerage houses—all unopened. Many held confirmations of the purchase or sale of stock, while others held account statements. After two hours of slitting open envelopes I had managed to unearth three uncashed dividend checks as well.

One of the boxes contained the statements from Bart and Pamela's joint bank accounts. They were neatly rubber banded together, labeled and chronologically arranged—no doubt by Pamela. I examined them with great interest. The story of our lives is written, at least in part, in the money that we spend. Almost all of the checks were written in Pamela's hand, and the story they told was an expensive one.

By the time I was due to leave for my appointment with Torey Lloyd, I'd learned several very interesting things. Among them: It cost more to heat Bart Hexter's house a month than Cheryl, my secretary, earned over the same period of time. That the Hexters paid dues to no fewer than seven different country clubs, including one in Palm Springs and one in Tucson. That Bart and Pamela gave Margot $10,000 a month, not including the $1,200 they shelled out directly to her shrink. And, most interesting of all, while Bart Hexter had died with $47,000 in cash in his desk drawer, he had never withdrawn more than $900 a month in cash from any of his accounts.

By the time I arrived at Lake View Towers I was convinced that I was the only person in Chicago working that afternoon. The parks that fringed the lake were filled with people, all playing. Parents were pushing strollers toward the aquarium and the streets were thick with cyclists. People were playing Frisbee with their dogs.

The apartment that Hexter rented for his mistress was on the thirty-eighth floor of the waterfront high rise. Torey met me at the door and, with little more than a nod for greeting, led me inside. I don't know what I expected—maybe red furniture and paintings on black velvet, but the apartment surprised me. It was large and modern, filled with light, and commanded a grand view of the lake. The floors were bleached oak, the walls and furniture white, all meant, no doubt, as a background for several pieces of daring modern art that dominated the interior and balanced the panorama beyond the window.

The floor plan was open, and in the dining room I saw a long glass table surrounded by high-back chairs reminiscent of Frank Lloyd Wright. Beyond it, I glimpsed a sleek Italian modern kitchen with counter tops of rose-colored granite. According to her personnel file, Torey earned $21,000 a year as a runner for Hexter Commodities. It was obviously not her salary that had paid for this apartment.

Torey motioned me into a large armchair of cream-colored leather. She, in turn, curled herself into a corner of the matching sofa. I hadn't seen her up close before, and I understood why Elliott had lingered in her doorway in order to catch a better glimpse of her. Her face was a magnet to the eye. Once you looked at her it was an effort to look away. And yet it wasn't a perfection of features that drew you in. Her eyes, it is true, were enormous—a cloudy violet that undulated between blue and gray as you watched. Her skin was perfect, her lips full, her teeth a study in white. But there was a bump in her nose and a hard set to her mouth that pushed her beyond Barbie good looks.

She wore a pair of gray cashmere stirrup pants with a tunic sweater to match. Around her neck she wore a long gold chain of unusual design. Her earrings were simple diamond studs, that—if real—constituted someone's serious investment in gemstones. On her left hand was an enormous, single diamond in a setting of modern simplicity.

"The family sent you here to make me go away," she said, making no attempt to disguise the steel in her voice.

"I can't make you go away," I said honestly. "I wouldn't even want to try. I came here to listen. Nothing more. Bart's son would be here himself, but he has more on his plate now than he can handle. Why don't you tell me when you began having a relationship with Bart?"

"Almost as soon as I started working for him. I think I managed to play hard to get for about three weeks. I was living with Carl at the time, and it was awkward. But Carl's a pig, and I knew that what we had together wouldn't have lasted. Besides, when Bart wanted something he usually got it. I know that everyone thinks I was after his money, but I have always been attracted by powerful, successful men. Bart just swept me off my feet.

"And right from the start I told him that I didn't want to spend my life being a rich man's mistress. I wanted more from my life than to sneak around while his wife thought he was out entertaining customers. That's why I never quit my job. I wanted to start trading for myself. Bart was going to lease me one of his seats in June."

"And did he start giving you money right from the start?"

"It wasn't like that. When I broke up with Carl I didn't have any place to live. Bart found this apartment for me. I said it was too nice, but he said he didn't want us to spend time together in a dump. He was a very generous man. He loved to give presents. He loved me to have pretty things. I never asked for any of it. I would have loved him if he had been a bricklayer."

"What about his temper?" I asked.

"My dad has a temper like that. I didn't let it bother me."

"So why did you call Barton? What is it that you want from him?"

"I want what his father promised me. He was buying me an apartment in the new complex that's going up by the river. He put the earnest money down, and he was supposed to make the first payment on Monday. I want the money to keep paying my rent until the new apartment is finished. I want money for furniture and to lease a seat to start trading."

"What you're asking for represents a great deal of money."

"It's less than what I would have gotten if that bitch, Pamela, hadn't killed him."

"You are assuming that your relationship with Bart was permanent. Who's to say how much longer it would have lasted? In any event, all that changed when Bart was murdered."

"It would have lasted," said Torey, locking me in the full beams of her violet eyes. "The last time I saw Bart, he came to the apartment after work on Friday and proposed to me. He said he had decided to leave Pamela. He gave me this."

In the tradition of brides-to-be the world over, Torey held out her left hand for me to admire her ring.

When I got back to the office I found Ruskowski waiting for me.

"Don't you believe in using the phone, Detective?" I asked as I unlocked the door and let us both in.

"I like to see who I'm talking to."

"Don't you waste a lot of time driving around?"

"There aren't that many homicides in Lake Forest. Now that Hexter's is closed, I've got time on my hands."

"So you feel satisfied that Pamela Hexter shot her husband?"

"What do you take me for? If I wasn't satisfied she'd have never been arrested, especially with the entire goddamn country looking over my shoulder. You'd better believe I'm sure."

"The reason I bring it up is that I was talking to Stephen Azorini. Since you know he sleeps with me I assume you also know that he's president of Azor Pharmaceuticals. We were discussing Hexter's medical history. Did you know that Hexter had suffered a near fatal heart attack?"

"Sure. The medical examiner said so."

"Did you know that as a result he developed a heart condition called ventricular tachycardia? It caused him to have blackouts."

"I knew he was taking medication for a heart condition, yes."

"He was taking a new drug called Ventrinome. People with Hexter's kind of history used to have to have a mechanical device called a defibrillator implanted in their chests. Ventrinome's a relatively new drug that makes that unnecessary."

"That's very interesting, Miss Millholland. So what?"

"The only drawback with Ventrinome," I pressed on, "is that the body becomes dependent on it. If you have a history like Hexter's, and you stop using it, chances are close to one hundred percent that you'll experience a fatal episode of ventricular tachycardia. Did you know that Ventrinome is dispensed in the form of a plain white pill—like an aspirin or a vitamin pill?"

"So?"

"So why would Pamela Hexter shoot her husband, risk discovery, and certainly endure the publicity surrounding his murder, when all she had to do was replace his heart medication with vitamins and wait for him to have a fatal heart attack?"

"You're assuming that shooting Hexter was a cold-blooded premeditated act. It didn't go down that way. Two days before he was killed he walked into Tiffany's and dropped eighty thousand dollars on an engagement ring. He asked a twenty-four-year-old runner at Hexter Commodities if she'd become the second Mrs. Hexter.

Problem was, Mrs. Hexter number one wasn't exactly thrilled with the idea. It doesn't take a criminal genius to figure out what happened next. He tells her. She gets mad. She cools him. A plus B equals C."

"Husbands leave their wives all the time," I countered. "If they all got shot, there'd be a lot more faithful husbands."

"Unhappy people shoot their spouses every day. People get mad, and they get even. Just because Pamela is loaded doesn't make her any different."

"That's where you're wrong," I insisted. "Pamela is different. She's never been inside a grocery store or scrubbed a toilet or been in a situation where she's felt her back against the wall. All her life she's solved problems with money. Why on earth would she start trying to solve them with guns?"

"Money is just money," protested Ruskowski. "Inside Pamela is just your average woman scorned."

"That's where you're wrong," I said flatly. "Pamela Hexter has about as much in common with the average woman as a Bushman from Borneo."

When Elliott called to say he wanted to see me, I told him to come to my office with some misgivings. I was still embarrassed about what had passed between us the other night and was unsure how to handle it. To fill the time while I waited I called Barton Jr., who agreed to see me the following morning at the offices of Hexter Commodities.

Elliott arrived wearing a blue blazer, jeans, and a white T-shirt. In one hand he had a bunch of scarlet tulips. In the other, a bag of oranges.

"These are for you," he said, laying both offerings on

my desk. "I stopped at Treasure Island to buy you flowers, but these oranges looked really good, too. I bet you don't eat enough fruit."

"Thank you," I replied, somewhat nonplussed.

"I wanted to apologize for the other night."

"It wasn't just you," I said carefully.

"I know you're involved with someone else. I just got carried away. I'm sorry."

I wanted to say that I wasn't sure I was involved with someone else, that I wasn't sure of anything these days, but the words got stuck somewhere between my throat and my lips.

"Apology accepted," was all I was able to manage.

"Do you have a second? I've just spent the weekend checking up on Hexter's kids. It's a very interesting family that you've hooked up with."

"So what did you find out?"

"First of all, Barton has no alibi for the murder. His wife was up in Wisconsin visiting her parents. She took the children and the au pair with her. He was alone in the house. The first time his mother called to tell him about the shooting she got the answering machine. He said he was in the shower, but who knows? He certainly had time to get to Lake Forest and back."

"I can't believe it was Barton."

"He's the person who gains the most from Hexter's death. He's inherited millions."

"You don't know Barton. He doesn't want millions. His whole world has been turned upside down by this—for Barton and his wife this has meant nothing but misery."

"You know him. I don't. I'm just saying he doesn't have an alibi."

"What about Margot?"

"Margot claims that she was home in bed. Her 'life partner,' Brooke Winkleman, claims to have been with her. I have no reason to not believe them except that Margot has a psychiatric history that would make Freud sit up and take notice. She makes no secret of the fact that she hated her dad even though he supported her completely. Did you know she's pregnant?"

"I heard."

"She told me that she's sure her dad was going to cut her off as soon as he found out. That smells like a motive to me."

"Did she tell you why she hated her dad so much?"

"I came right out and asked her. She said that when she was thirteen years old her father showed up at her eighth-grade graduation with a woman named Loretta Resch, whom he was having a relationship with at the time. Her grandmother had just died and her mother was in Palm Beach. I guess she was at an impressionable age. Talk about a troubled teenager—Margot did it all—sex, drugs, eastern religions, and two suicide attempts. Relatively speaking, she's straightened herself out. Believe it or not, she's doing very well in the psychology graduate program."

"Nothing the Hexters were capable of would surprise me."

"Wait until I tell you about Krissy."

"I'm listening."

"Well, you know, Elkin's been curious about the argument that Bart and Pamela had the night before the murder. The police have made a big deal of it. Pamela has refused to discuss it, saying that it was nothing, just Bart's usual bad temper. The other people at the party have been very close-mouthed. On Elkin's orders, I went out to their country club this afternoon to see if any of the waiters or waitresses who worked the party overheard anything."

"And?"

"And I found one little cocktail waitress who heard plenty. It seems that she was coming down with the flu and spent most of the evening in the employees' bathroom. The john shares a wall with the members' coatroom, where she says she overheard Bart and Krissy having a knock-down drag-out fight."

"Bart and Krissy!"

"Yep. Everyone assumed that the fight was with Pamela, but by the time he got back to the table he was just blowing off steam after letting Krissy have it."

"Why? What did they fight about?"

"It seems that Bart and one or two of the other men were planning to go to the smoking room for a cigar, but Hexter'd left his Cubans in his coat pocket. When he went to the coatroom to get them he practically tripped over Krissy, who was making out with some guy named Brad Cranshaw."

"I saw them, too!" I exclaimed. "After the funeral. I walked in on Krissy and some guy going at it on the pool table at Hexter's house. Where was her husband?"

"Saturday night he was in Baltimore playing polo. He didn't get back until almost noon on Sunday. According to the waitress, Hexter was furious. Called Krissy a slut and told her that if she didn't straighten up he was going to throw her out of her house and cut her out of his will."

"Really. And what did she say to that?"

"She said a lot of things, but she ended up by telling

him that she would make him sorry he'd called her a slut."

"Could she have killed him?"

"Sure she could have. She lives on the property. All she had to do was walk to the end of the driveway and wait for him to get the newspaper. Fourey was still in Baltimore, and their son was spending the night with his other grandparents."

"No wonder Pamela's being uncooperative. If what the police say about the gun is true—that the only person who could have taken it was a family member—then anything she says that exonerates her implicates one of her children."

"I've saved the best for last," said Elliott with a devilish smile.

"What?"

"Guess who the girl in the dirty pictures is?"

"Who?"

"Come on, guess."

"I don't know. Margot."

"Sick, but incorrect."

"Torey."

"Nope."

"Not Torey? Then who?"

"The maid, Elena Olarte."

CHAPTER
20

"He was sleeping with the maid?" I demanded incredulously.

"Not sleeping with her," replied Elliott. "At least not as I understand it. According to Elena, the pictures were more in the nature of a business proposition."

"You're kidding."

"I'm only telling you what she told me. It seems Elena wanted to trade up from cleaning toilets. She thought that since Hexter and his wife fought all the time she might be able to interest him in some extracurricular activities."

"So who took the pictures?"

"You're going to love this," replied Elliott. "Her sister. According to Elena, one sunny afternoon they just went outside and took some happy snaps. You'd better believe there were some guys in love with their jobs at the photo lab the day that film came in to be developed."

"But she says she and Hexter didn't sleep together," I interjected. "What a world. Do you think she's telling the truth about seeing the gun in Hexter's drawer? Could she be lying? An awful lot rests on that."

"Of course she could be lying," conceded Elliott reluctantly. "And you can bet that when she gets on the witness stand Elkin will do his best to make her look like a scheming tramp who would be capable of anything. But that's an old trick, using a woman's sexual history against her. You know that just because she wanted to sleep with Bart Hexter doesn't have anything to do with her being a liar. Besides, what would be the point? With Hexter dead, her hopes for any sort of arrangement with him were over."

"I still think she's a troublemaker," I said, "but I agree with you, I don't see the profit for her in that kind of trouble."

"Just think of what Hexter must have looked like to a penniless girl from Guatemala."

"Or a penniless girl from downstate Illinois," I pointed out.

"That's right. How did it go with Torey Lloyd? Is she on the level?"

"It was very interesting. On one level her demands seem quite reasonable ... considering."

"Considering what?"

"Considering that when Hexter came to see her the Friday before he died he told her that he was going to leave his wife. He asked her to marry him and gave her an eighty-thousand-dollar engagement ring."

"You're joking."

"Nope. She showed me the ring. Ruskowski's the one who told me what it cost."

"What a dunk. The prosecutor is going to have the jury eating out of his hand. Now that all this has come out, I wonder whether Elkin will try to cut a deal and get Pamela to plead to a lesser charge."

"I hope not," I said.

"Why?"

"Because I don't think she killed him." I told him what Stephen said about Hexter's heart condition and Azor's new drug, Ventrinome. I also confessed that Ruskowski remained unconvinced.

"I don't know," said the private detective when I'd finished. "I think I'll cast my vote with Ruskowski. You'd never be able to sell that heart thing to a jury."

"I'm not talking about what a jury will believe or not believe," I insisted. "Juries watch too much TV. I'm talking about what really happened. You've only got to look at Pamela. She's compulsive, a planner, a calculating woman, who, according to Carl Savage, was born wearing a green eyeshade. People like that don't just pick up a gun and start shooting."

"Maybe Hexter finally pushed her too far," countered Elliott. "Hexter wasn't any prize to live with. Maybe this thing with Torey was just the last straw."

"Assuming that he told her. Besides, she'd been on the receiving end of his temper for all those years. You don't think she'd thought about what would happen if he didn't take his heart pills? Come on."

"So you buy her story that she didn't know he had the gun? In her own house?"

"You've seen that house. It's so big there could be a band of gypsies living in the west wing and nobody would find them until spring cleaning. I bet there are rooms she hasn't been inside of in years. She told me that the study was the only room in the house where Bart was allowed to smoke his cigars. If she hated the smoke, she probably didn't go into the room. Besides, there's something else going on that Ruskowski isn't taking into consideration."

"What?"

"The day that Hexter was shot he was supposed to give me account statements for his soybean trades and for another account, Deodar Commodities. Those documents have disappeared. So have the office backup copies. The computer files were dumped the morning after the murder. And another thing. I found a wad of cash in Hexter's office. Pamela was incredibly cheap and Bart was a big spender. Just keeping Torey Lloyd was costing him a small fortune. Where was the money coming from?"

"I give up, where?"

"According to Carl Savage, Hexter was trading for himself in the name of Deodar Commodities. Deodar was just a shell company of Hexter's, a mechanism for hiding money from Pamela. My theory is that someone at Hexter Commodities found out about it and was blackmailing him. It just must have gone wrong somehow."

"But then you'd expect it to be the blackmailer who ended up dead, not Hexter."

"That's one of the details I haven't worked out yet. But I do know one thing. Ruskowski's solution only takes into account one part of the problem."

I spent Sunday evening alone, sitting in the rounded sun parlor of my apartment. When I first moved in with Claudia we lived on one of the safest blocks in Chicago. Harold Washington, the city's first black mayor, made his home in the high-rise across the street, and a police cruiser was stationed permanently outside his front door. After Washington suffered a fatal heart attack our little corner of Hyde Park slid back into the urban ooze from which it had briefly been wrested.

I sat for hours at the window, slowly drinking the better part of a bottle of red wine while I tried to sort out the events of the preceding week. On the table in the living room there were a dozen yellow roses jammed into a mayonnaise jar filled with water. Claudia had left the card lying next to them. It read: "You're wonderful—Jeff."

I watched the street theater playing itself out beyond the window as I strung together what I knew about Bart Hexter's death. Ruskowski assumed that when you stripped everything else away, Bart Hexter's murder was about sex. But there is a saying that businessmen are doomed to have their most interesting exploits measured by accountants. I was pretty sure that when you came right down to it, Hexter's murder would come down to a matter of dollars and cents. The trouble was, no matter how I juggled the profit and loss statement of Hexter's death, nothing I came up with came close to comparing to Ruskowski's case against Pamela Hexter.

When I arrived at Hexter Commodities on Monday I was surprised to find a bearded young man in a grotty flannel shirt and jeans sitting at Bart Hexter's desk with his eyes glued to the computer screen.

"Oh, gosh. You're here already," he blurted, looking up when I entered. "Professor Hexter said he was going to be using this room for a meeting, but I must have lost track of time. I'll be out of your way in a minute."

"Thanks," I said, extending my hand. "I'm Kate Millholland."

"I'm Kurt Loovis. I'm one of Dr. Hexter's Ph.D. students. You know this real futures stuff is far out. Exploring new frontiers," he laughed nervously as he gathered up his papers. "Going where no mathematician has ever gone before."

Barton Jr. arrived a few minutes after his graduate student had cleared out. He looked rumpled but relaxed. His eyes, I noticed, traveled immediately from the price board in the boardroom to the Quotron screen in the office.

"Did you meet the guy who was working in here?" asked Barton as his eyes followed the screen.

"Yes. He introduced himself."

"He's one of my research assistants. He's going to take a year's leave of absence with me. We're going to see if we can start applying what we know about chaos theory to developing a technical trading strategy for Hexter Commodities."

"That's great," I said. "I know you're busy, but I just wanted to fill you in on my discussion with Torey Lloyd."

"Who?"

"The young woman who claims to have been having a relationship with your father."

"Oh, God, yes. With everything else she just slipped my mind. That's a sad commentary on things."

"There's no question that she and your father had a relationship that had been going on for almost three years."

"So you think he was really buying the apartment for her? I don't know why not. When Dad did something, he did it big."

"Yes. I think he was buying the apartment for the two

of them." I paused and took a breath, "I don't want you to hear this from someone else. Friday night, before he came home for dinner, he stopped at Torey's apartment and told her that he was leaving your mother and asked her to marry him."

"That can't be true. She's making that part up."

"He gave her an engagement ring from Tiffany's. Ruskowski checked it out."

Barton let out a long sigh and ran a trembling hand through his hair.

"There's still the question of what to do about the apartment," I urged, quietly. "I think it's probably best if you make the payment as scheduled today. I can arrange it through Ken. That way at least the earnest money won't be forfeited. I'm sure I can put Miss Lloyd off for a while until things calm down a bit; then we can decide what to do. It can even be sold later."

"Do whatever you think is best," he replied woodenly.

There was a knock at the door, and Tim burst in breathlessly. "Sorry, but it's your wife on the phone. She says it's an emergency," he blurted.

Barton reached for the phone. He listened gravely for a moment. "Where are you? Don't worry. I can be there in ten minutes. Just don't do anything without me." He was on his feet before he hung up the receiver.

"What's happened?" I demanded.

"That was Jane," he said. "She's at the hospital. Her water broke during rehearsal. Her contractions are close together. I'm going."

"Good luck," I called, but he was gone so fast I'm sure he didn't hear me.

* * *

I sat at Bart Hexter's vast mahogany desk and looked through the record of checks that Hexter Commodities had issued to Deodar Commodities over the past three years. Loretta had sent over a young woman from the accounting department who explained to me that once the checks were cut they were, as a rule, taken straight over to Hexter's office where they were given to Tim, or more often, the great man himself. I sent her off to find the canceled checks, but I was pretty certain that she would not succeed.

"Excuse me," said a male voice. I looked up from the checks. "I'm looking for Mr. Bart Hexter." It was a bicycle messenger, one of the kamikaze cyclists who weave through traffic and pelt the wrong way down one-way streets all in the name of speedy deliveries. He wore a yellow jersey with his company name on the back, black bicycle shorts, and a purple helmet. In his arm he held a courier pack of documents.

"Mr. Hexter senior or junior?"

"I didn't know there was a junior," he replied, obviously puzzled to find me sitting in Hexter's chair. "This goes to the older guy who's always here in this office. I've got a delivery for him."

Tim Hexter appeared in the doorway with a sheaf of papers in his hand.

"Hi Gary," he said. "I can take those from you."

"You know better than that, Tim," admonished the messenger. "I've got to hand this to Mr. Hexter, personal."

"Don't you read the papers?" asked Tim. "Hexter's dead. Somebody shot him. You'd better just give it to me."

"No can do. I'll just take it back to the office. I'll have my supervisor call you."

"Oh, cut the crap, Gary," declared Tim. "Just give it to me."

"I can't do that," insisted the messenger, clutching the package to his chest as if he were afraid that Tim would snatch it from him. "Delivery is to Mr. Bart Hexter—hands only."

"His hands are six feet under ground," replied Tim, practically shouting with frustration.

"Why don't you let me handle this, Tim," I suggested. Tim gave me a dirty look and retreated to the doorway, a sullen onlooker to the proceedings.

The matter of the courier took much longer to resolve than it had a right to. The young man with the bicycle helmet was employed by a company called Couriers International, Inc., a firm that specialized in hand-carrying documents between countries. Bart Hexter had a regular monthly delivery contract with them and, as the supervisor patiently explained to me over the phone, the terms of their contract specified that all deliveries be made to Bart Hexter personally. Unfortunately, there was no contingency in the contract in the event of Bart Hexter's death. It was one of those idiotic situations that just suck up time. I knew that in the end the documents would rightfully be released to me. So did everyone I spoke to at the courier company. But that did nothing to assuage their fear of being sued if, in the end, trouble came of their making their delivery to me.

Finally, I succeeded in reaching the president of the courier company who agreed to release the documents to me if I drafted a waiver of liability that met with his attorney's approval. I dictated something that seemed appropriately impressive over the phone to Cheryl, who faxed it to the counsel for Couriers International. This was, I decided while I waited for the other attorney to review the release, just the kind of time-wasting problem that I didn't need if I was going to come up with some sort of reasonable plan for dealing with the CFTC.

Finally, almost two hours later, the forms were signed, and the documents changed hands. There was one large manila envelope with no return address. By that time, I was hopelessly late for the meeting I'd scheduled with two senior security partners, so I slipped it into my briefcase to pass along to Barton Jr.

When I got back to the office Cheryl was holding the phone up for me to grab. It's Barton Jr., she whispered.

"Well?" I demanded, taking the phone. "Is it a boy?"

"It is a boy," he replied. "But it's also a girl!"

"What?"

"It's twins!" exclaimed the happy father. "No wonder Jane was so huge and miserable. Jane delivered the boy first. We were all admiring him, and Jane kept on having these big contractions. The girl was delivered a minute and a half later."

"Four kids," I marveled. "A boy and a girl. Congratulations. How's Jane?"

"She's amazing. She says hi and ... what's that?" There was a pause. "She says to tell you that miracles happen every day."

I ran out of my office to the forty-third-floor conference room where I had arranged a meeting with two of

Callahan's senior securities partners, both of whom had a great deal of experience in dealing with the CFTC. I hoped that among us we'd be able to come up with some acceptable strategy for dealing with Hexter Commodities' regulatory predicament. Once I'd laid the whole thorny mess out for them, we all agreed that the best plan would be for the company to concede to the allegations in the Wells Notice. With luck I'd be able to convince the Commissioners that all the malfeasance occurred on Hexter's part personally, and then I'd push Herman Geiss to propose a settlement that was not too punitive. The trouble was, I wasn't feeling particularly lucky.

By the time we finished, Cheryl had already left for the day—on Mondays and Wednesdays she had her civil procedure course—but the receptionist had sent a clerk to drop off my messages. There, at the top of the pile, was a note from Carl Savage that read: "I have some documents you might be interested in re: Deodar. Meet me four-thirty on the seventh floor of the Merc."

I looked at my watch. It was already four-forty-five. I grabbed my briefcase and headed for the door. By the time I hit the reception room I realized I'd left my bag in the closet in my office, and I had to beg Lillian, the receptionist, for cab fare. Outside, a light rain was falling. The streets glistened, traffic snarled, and umbrellas popped up like wildflowers as the first wave of commuters hit the sidewalks heading for the train.

Together the CBOT and the Merc form the one-two punch that is the power behind the futures industry. While the two exchanges are careful to present a united front, in reality the two organizations are as different as the two buildings that house them. The Board of Trade

Building is an art deco masterpiece, a monument to capitalism and the old-boys' club of the futures industry. The Merc is the brash newcomer and its buildings— twin towers of sleek rose granite—are home to a market that is younger, louder, flashier, and more aggressive.

I entered the building battling the weary tide of humanity flowing out after the day's trading. Inside the elevator I pushed seven. When I got off at my floor I was surprised to step out into darkness. I stood, blinking in the faint glow of the exit sign, until I realized where I was.

The Merc had been built with expansion in mind, and one floor above the bustle of the pits sat another, still vacant, trading floor, awaiting the opening of trade in four additional contracts later in the year. There must be offices on the north side of the building, I reasoned. I'd obviously used the wrong bank of elevators. As if I wasn't late enough already.

The new trading floor was as big as two football fields and took up the vertical equivalent of three regular floors in order to be able to eventually accommodate the tiered risers of the pits. It was eerie to find a space that big and that empty in the middle of one of the busiest business districts in the world.

When he touched my arm, I jumped. Spinning around I expected to see Carl Savage. The sight of the figure in the stocking mask made me gasp. In the darkness I picked out a sweatshirt, black and hooded, and an arm raised, holding something that looked like a length of pipe, raised to strike. In an instant fueled by adrenaline I calculated that the odds were against flight— instinctively I understood that in the darkness of an unfamiliar place my attacker held the advantage. Instead,

I dropped to the ground and rolled—propelling myself into his legs, grabbing for his ankles, hoping to gain something by surprise.

He grunted as he hit the ground. I scrambled to my feet, grasping the handle of my briefcase with two hands and swung its hard frame with vengeance. It hit home with a sickening thud. I heard a muffled curse and the sound of something heavy hitting the ground. I hoped it was the pipe. I took my briefcase back for a second swing, hoping to land another blow before he got back up onto his feet. He caught it in mid-swing, and for a fraction of a second we stood there, breathing in each other's faces, each hanging on to one end of my briefcase like two-year-olds fighting over the same toy.

I ducked my head quickly and lunged into him, bringing the back of my head up fast and hard under his chin. I heard his jaw snap shut on impact, heard his startled exclamation of pain. His grip on the briefcase slackened for an instant. I yanked it away from him and made one last, ferocious swing at his head. I felt the satisfaction of impact before I turned and pelted toward the exit sign.

Frantically, I stabbed at the elevator button, then whirled around, desperately searching for a fire door or other means of escape. I found a door in a dark corner, but it was locked tight. I hammered on it with my fists, weak with frustration at my predicament. I stepped back toward the elevator and flattened myself against the wall opposite the doors, hoping that if he came after me, he'd go to the elevator and I'd be able to ambush him from behind. I listened for footsteps over the sound of my own breathing, rough and loud. I knew that he'd be coming after me, once he'd caught his breath and found the pipe.

My nerves were all over the place. Riding my body's tide of adrenaline, I willed the elevator to come. I imagined its halting progress, stopping at every floor, and my stomach cramped with fear. Stress dragged the seconds into what seemed like an age. When I finally heard the high ding of the bell, I jumped. My heart pounded in my ears as I frantically searched the darkness for a sign of my attacker. In the light from the open elevator doors I would be visible and therefore vulnerable. My heart was in my mouth as the doors slid apart silently in an ever-expanding sliver of light. I took a deep breath and hurled myself into the brightness of the car, straight into the arms of an astonished Elliott Abelman.

CHAPTER
21

I clung to Elliott as the elevator doors slid shut behind me, gasping for air and babbling. He pulled me close to his chest.

"What's the matter, Kate?" he demanded in surprise. "You're bleeding!"

I struggled for control of my breathing. My entire body was shaking as if I'd been suddenly plunged into icy water. I wanted to explain, but for the longest time no words would come out.

The elevator deposited us on the ground floor, and Elliott led me out into the bustling lobby of the exchange. I let the reassurance of the workday crowd envelop me. My chest was pounding. Taking stock of myself, I realized that my skirt was torn, my stockings were in shreds, and my hair trailed wildly in places. I patted it gingerly. My head was sore where I'd butted my assailant, and my hair was damp with blood. Fortunately it wasn't mine. Good, I remember thinking. I hope he bleeds to death.

Elliott dragged me into a relatively quiet corner, an alcove for the Federal Express box. He took me by the shoulder, and slowly I managed a fragmented account of the attack. Once I'd convinced him that I was shaken but unhurt, he vanished to notify building security.

"They've sent some men up to the seventh floor to look around," reported Elliott, who'd only been gone a minute, "but I'm sure whoever it was is long gone by now."

"What are you doing here?" I finally managed to blurt.

"I came to your office but I must have just missed you. The receptionist said you'd gone to a meeting. She was panicked because she gave you money for the cab there, but she didn't give you enough money for the return. It was raining hard, so I had her check your messages to find out exactly where you were going. I thought I'd try to catch you—play Sir Galahad. I didn't realize how much you'd need it."

"I was set up," I stammered, still struggling to regain my composure. "I got a message that Carl Savage wanted to meet with me—he was supposed to have papers that I wanted about Deodar, but when I got there, someone jumped me."

"Man or woman?"

"I don't know. I just assumed it was a man, but really there was no way to tell. I do know that whoever it was had a pipe in his hand. It all happened so fast."

"What did he want?"

"I think he wanted to kill me," I replied with a shudder. "It was only luck that I managed to get away. I don't think he expected me to fight back."

"Why would someone want to kill you?"

"I don't know. Oh God, Elliott, it was awful. I was so scared," I sobbed, as a sort of retroactive panic seized me.

"Hey," Elliott said softly. "You don't need to cry on

the mailbox when I've got a perfectly good shoulder. Come on."

I found relief in tears, but in a few minutes I felt ridiculous, weeping into Elliott's arms in the lobby of the Chicago Mercantile Exchange. With an effort I straightened myself up and took a deep breath. Elliott offered me a handkerchief, and I put it to good use. I knew that while some women look delicately vulnerable after they've cried, I look dreadful—red-eyed and blotchy.

"You know Kate, this could have ended up much differently," said Elliott gravely.

"I know. Thanks for coming to my rescue."

"Do you have any idea who attacked you?"

"Someone who knew I would be interested in documents related to Deodar Commodities. By now that's got to be half the population of Chicago. The whole thing doesn't make any sense. What were you coming to see me about in the first place?"

"Are you sure you're feeling okay?" he asked gently.

"Yes, why?"

"Pamela Hexter tried to kill herself this afternoon. She took an overdose of sleeping pills. It was just a fluke that someone found her. Krissy locked herself out of her own house. She keeps a spare key at her mother's. Still, it was just lucky that she decided to say hello to her mom."

"Is she going to be okay?"

"So far she's in critical condition, but that's just because she's still in ICU. Anyway, Krissy called Ken Kurlander at your office, who called Elkin. They're both anxious that news of this not get into the press. They're afraid that if the prosecutor gets wind of it, he'll try to get bail revoked."

"You better believe it," I said.

"We were trying to find Barton, but no one knew where he was. Everyone at Hexter Commodities had already gone for the day, and there was no answer at his house or at his office at Northwestern. Krissy'd been gone all day and didn't know where he was. Elkin called me to see if I could track him down. Under the circumstances, he didn't want to attract too much attention. I thought you might know."

"I do know," I said. "His wife had twins today. I bet he's still with her at the hospital."

"Do you know which one?" inquired Elliott.

"Northwestern Memorial."

"It's a small world." Elliott sighed. "That's where they've taken Pamela."

We broke the news to Barton Jr. in the brightly decorated visitor's lounge in the maternity wing.

"Don't tell Jane," was all he said when Elliott was through relating the details. "She's so happy. She's wanted a daughter so much. I don't want my family to spoil this day for her."

"The news will keep," I agreed.

"Did Mother say why she did it?" asked Barton wearily.

"She left a note," said Elliott. "Your sister had the presence of mind to keep it away from the paramedics. Elkin Caufield has it now, but he told me that it didn't contain anything that could be construed as a confession. He and Kurlander are working hard to keep up the impression that your mother took too many sleeping pills by mistake. I think her doctor is going along with it."

"Dr. Pollard is an old friend of the family," said Barton.

"Is there someplace private that you can make a phone call?" asked Elliott. "Elkin's anxious to talk to you. Then I'll walk you down to see your mother."

"Why don't you two go and see if you can find a phone. I'll just see if I can find a ladies' room and wash up. Then I'll stop in and see Jane," I said. "Don't worry. I won't mention this other thing. Come and get me when you're finished."

Jane sat propped up in bed, addressing birth announcements. "When James was born," she explained, "I was terribly superstitious. We didn't do anything beforehand. I remember, I wouldn't even let Barton put up the crib. He had to do it all himself while I was in the hospital. By the third time if you don't at least order the envelopes in advance, you'll end up sending the announcements out right before the kid starts kindergarten."

"The third and the fourth," I pointed out.

"I still can't believe it," sighed Jane. "Do you know how unusual it is these days to deliver unanticipated twins? You should have seen everybody in the delivery room—it was a madhouse. I don't think that Barton figured out what was happening until they handed him the second baby. I'll never forget the expression on his face as long as I live."

Elliott and I walked a few blocks north from the hospital to a Japanese restaurant called Hatsuhana. We sat in the serenity of blond wood and paper screens near the sushi bar, drinking Tsing Tao beer, eating California roll, and trying to figure out who wanted me dead. After three beers and half an ocean's worth of sushi, we still didn't have any answers.

"The problem," concluded Elliott, "is that when someone decides that it's necessary to crack your skull, they usually don't give up when they don't succeed the first time."

"So what do you suggest? I can't very well spend the rest of my life hiding under my desk."

"I don't want you to go home tonight. Your roommate probably shouldn't either."

"I'll call her. She can spend the night in the on-call room at the hospital."

"Is there somewhere you can go? A friend you can call?"

I excused myself and used the pay phone in the drafty entryway. Stephen's assistant, Richard Humanski, reminded me that Stephen was in New York until late the following afternoon. I went back to the table.

"Any luck?" asked Elliott.

"I think you're overreacting," I protested.

"Kate, you still have dried blood in your hair," Elliott pointed out.

"I'll check in at the Marriott down the road," I conceded.

"You'll spend the night at my place."

I shot him a look.

"I'm inviting you in my role as Sir Galahad," he insisted. "Do you really think you're going to be able to get any sleep alone in a hotel after what's happened today?"

Elliott lived alone in the top half of a pretty restored brownstone in the neighborhood near DePaul University. It was a well-proportioned residence with a large living room, two dormered bedrooms, and a turreted room that Elliott used as his home office. The kitchen was small, bright yellow, and looked as though someone actually cooked in it. I felt strange to be there, and Elliott, usually so at ease, seemed stiff and strangely unlike himself.

It helped that it was late and we were both tired. I admired his apartment while he scrounged up clean towels, a new toothbrush, a fresh cake of soap, and an extra T-shirt for me to sleep in.

"What time do you need to be in the office in the morning?" Elliott asked, his hand on the doorknob of the extra bedroom. The room was very neat and comfortably arranged with a bedspread on the bed and curtains on the windows. It even had its own bathroom, from which a shower beckoned. A whole new domestic side of Elliott presented itself to me.

"I'd like to get an early start. I still have to produce an answer for the CFTC by Friday. But don't worry, I'll just catch a cab in."

"Absolutely not. Until I find out what's going on, I'm walking you to your office door. What if we plan on leaving here at seven-thirty? Is that too early?"

"That would be fine," I replied.

"Well, good night then," said Elliott.

"Good night."

He closed the door behind him, and I breathed a sigh of relief. Even under the most innocent of circumstances, there is always an element of tension between a man and a woman. I'd noticed it whenever I traveled on business with one of the male attorneys at the firm. Nice men whom I liked, men whose wives I was friendly with, men who would never, in a million years, cross the lines of propriety with a colleague. And yet, there was still always that moment, late at night, slipping keys in the hotel room doors, when other possibilities seemed to linger near the surface.

Glad that moment was behind me, I kicked off my shoes and sat down on the bed. It seemed like a tremendously long time since I'd woken up that morning, ready to take on the day. The clock read 10:46. There was, I was sure, something rotten at Hexter Commodities, but whenever I felt that I'd gotten a grasp on an important piece of the puzzle, another one slipped through my fingers.

I took off my clothes and carefully laid them on the chair. In the mirror above the dresser, I admired the rapidly developing bruises on my arm and chest. Then I padded into the bathroom and took a long shower, luxuriating in the hot water and the glorious sensation of still being alive.

I washed my hair and rinsed it. The water ran red, then pink, and finally clear. I turned off the taps and dried myself, slipping into the clean T-shirt that Elliott had left for me. It was navy blue, and in white letters across the chest it read: CHICAGO POLICE.

I sat on the bed feeling battered and vulnerable. I looked at my briefcase. I realized, too late since I'd just dragged it all over town, that it might have been productive to dust it for fingerprints. I opened it up to have a last look at my calendar, but what stared me in the face was the long forgotten envelope that the courier had delivered to Hexter's office earlier in the day.

I could have kicked myself for not having remembered to give it to Barton when I saw him at the hospital earlier in the evening. With both Jane and his mother under medical care, with two new babies and a commodities firm to run, I wondered when I'd next have a chance to give it to him. Better, I decided, to open it up and see whether the contents were of any sort of immediate importance. I thrust my fingers beneath the flap and reached inside—more envelopes, three of them. I laid them on the bed. All three bore the logo of the Bank of Bermuda in the upper left-hand corner. All three were addressed to Mr. S. Bean. I opened the smaller envelopes one by one, laying the contents face up on the bedspread.

"Elliott?" I called with a growing sense of excitement. "Elliott, come here!"

He appeared in a flash, clad only in a pair of boxer shorts, a drawn revolver in his hand and a trace of toothpaste on his lips.

"What is it?" he demanded. "What's wrong?"

"I know what the man who jumped me was after," I replied. "He didn't want to kill me. He wanted to get his hands on these."

CHAPTER
22

I woke up feeling as though I'd been playing football. My arms, especially, were sore from the tug of war over my briefcase, and it was with an effort that I dragged myself out of bed and back into the clothes I'd worn the day before. As I reached for my blouse I noticed tiny splatters of crimson on the collar.

I found Elliott sitting at the kitchen table eating scrambled eggs, toast, and grapefruit sections. He was reading the sports page.

"There are eggs on the stove," he said, rising to his feet, "and I'll throw in some more toast."

"No thanks," I replied with a shudder. "It takes awhile for me to work up to food in the morning. Is that coffee in the pot?"

"Yes. The cups are in the cupboard above the coffee maker. There's cream and sugar on the table."

"Thanks, I just drink it black."

"Are you sure you won't even have a banana or something?" ventured Elliott. "I have cereal, too."

"Do you make yourself breakfast like this every morning?" I asked as I poured myself a cup of coffee.

"Not eggs every morning, naturally, but I like to sit down and have a real breakfast."

"I'm impressed. I don't even know whether the stove in my apartment actually works or not."

"I've lived alone since I left the Marines. You're going to laugh, but the thing I really hated about the military was eating that mass-produced food on metal trays. Since then I've always cooked and eaten off a plate. Living alone doesn't have to mean living badly."

I thought about that for a minute.

"I don't think I've made a conscious decision to live badly," I mused, pouring myself a cup of coffee. "But cooking, cleaning up, and going to the grocery store all take time, and right now all that time goes into my work."

"I'm surprised that it doesn't bother you," said Elliott, "considering how you must have grown up."

"Maybe it's rebellion," I offered. "I grew up in a home where living well was considered a full-time occupation. You'll have to see my parents' house sometime. It's a marvel. As soon as you throw something in the wastebasket someone comes and empties it. My entire life I never saw a ketchup bottle or a paper napkin or carton of milk on the table. When I was a child I used to play a game. I'd use a towel in the morning and spend ten minutes trying to fold it and rehang it perfectly. I'd come home after school and check. No matter how good a job I'd done, the maid would have taken it down and refolded it more perfectly. To me there's a certain freedom in not worrying about any of that."

"Freedom and bad eating habits," interjected Elliott. "Are you sure you won't try some grapefruit? They're

very good. My grandmother sends them up from Florida for me."

"No thanks," I said, smiling at this fussy side of him.
"Is there anything in the paper about Pamela Hexter?"

"I was reading the sports section," he said, handing
me the paper and beginning to clean up. "I spoke to
Elkin this morning. He said that Pamela has been
moved out of intensive care. He doesn't think her suicide attempt was in any way an admission of guilt. He
agrees with you that she finds herself in an untenable
position. If she didn't kill her husband, she realizes it
must have been one of her children. Under the circumstances, she saw the sleeping pills as the least painful
alternative."

"There's no mention of it in the *Trib*," I reported.

"That's something, anyway."

"So does Caufield want you to narrow your investigation to the kids?"

"No. I don't think Pamela wants to see her money
being spent to implicate one of her children. Elkin
wants me to concentrate on blowing the maid's evidence out of the water. I also thought I'd check who at
Hexter Commodities could have set you up yesterday.
What are you up to today?"

"I'm going to Bermuda."

Elliott stuck by my side all morning. First stop was in
Hyde Park, where I dropped in at my apartment to
change and gather up a few things. In light of our discussion that morning, I felt a little self-conscious about
our eccentric assortment of furniture and sorry state of
housekeeping in general. Much to my surprise, Claudia
had just come home and was sitting at the kitchen table

eating bagels with a nice-looking, fair-haired man whom she introduced, a bit sheepishly, as Jeff McConnell. The two of them had just come off their rotation, she explained, and had stopped in for breakfast.

While I went into my bedroom to change, Elliott sat in the living room and used the phone. I dug a suit of cream-colored linen out of the back of my closet, scrounged some light-colored pumps, gathered up some other clothes, and extracted my passport from the bottom of my underwear drawer.

After that we stopped at my office, where Elliott endeared himself to Cheryl, whom I'd called earlier and who had already procured my plane ticket and made my hotel reservations. I checked in with Ken Kurlander to make sure that he had no knowledge of Hexter maintaining offshore accounts, and asked him to have his secretary bring down a copy of Hexter's death certificate. In the meantime I culled the documents I thought I'd need to prepare myself for the CFTC, made sure I had fresh batteries for the small tape recorder I used for dictation and for the Walkman I invariably listen to when I travel, and shifted my wallet and passport into my briefcase.

Cheryl buzzed me and asked if I'd be back that evening for a chamber music concert I was scheduled to attend with Stephen. I told her to call and cancel while Elliott looked on with hooded eyes.

I felt out of place and slightly martyred on the flight to Bermuda. The only business traveler on a plane full of vacationers, I curled up in my first-class seat, popped a cassette into my Walkman, and attempted to forget that everyone around me was having a good time while

I tried to outline a response to the CFTC's Wells Notice.

Getting off the plane the air felt soft and warm and I
was seized with a sudden torpor. Everything about me
suddenly seemed incongruous and out of place: my
business suit, my briefcase, the panty hose that had instantly attached themselves to my legs in the humidity.
I stood in line at Customs, presented my passport, and
received my cheery, official welcome to Bermuda. Cir-
cumventing baggage claim—I had only a carry-on bag
and my briefcase—I stepped out into the brilliant sunlight and joined the queue for taxis.

Bermuda is a former British colony, and the flavor of
England is still pervasive—from the transmuted cock-
ney of the cabbies to the traffic that creeps on the left-
side of the road at the island's maximum speed of 25
m.p.h. For the most part the roads are narrow, twisting,
coral-walled lanes punctuated with hedges of hibiscus
and oleander.

Cheryl had booked me into the Hamilton Princess,
one of the large luxury hotels at the edge of the harbor.
My driver took me there via Front Street, proudly pointing out the best places to buy Shetland sweaters and
Irish linens. Traffic was clotted with tourists walking,
on mopeds, in horse-drawn carriages, and atop their bi-
cycles. Two cruise ships, leviathan and white, dominated the waterfront, floating worlds, separate and apart.

I paid off my taxi, surrendered my meager luggage to
the doorman who was clad, appropriately enough, in a
pair of impeccably white Bermuda shorts. Chicago and
its troubles seemed impossibly far away.

The formalities of check-in were accomplished
quickly and, after tipping the bellboy (U.S. currency

cheerfully accepted) I found myself in a sunny and spacious room with an ocean view. I kicked off my shoes, peeled off my panty hose, helped myself to a Diet Coke from the minibar and sat down on the edge of the bed to call the office. Cheryl picked up on the first ring.

"Ms. Millholland's office," she announced sunnily.

"It's me, Kate. You're sounding particularly cheerful."

"I know. I'm in a great mood. My boss is out of town."

"Nice to know I'm being missed. Anybody call?"

"Stephen, from New York, your mother, Barton Hexter, Roger Prendergast about Mascott Manufacturing—it seems they've finally found a buyer and he wants to talk to you—and Steve Potash from Overdrive."

"What did Barton want?"

"Just for you to call. Another thing, Elliott Abelman called about an hour ago. He said that if you called in I was supposed to tell you to be careful. What did he mean? What do you need to be careful about?"

"He just doesn't want me to get sunburned," I lied.

Everything about the Bank of Bermuda evoked the quiet dignity of the empire. The lobby was deep and cool and constructed of polished marble. Ceiling fans whirled mutely while tellers with clipped accents and disciplined hair ministered to the customers. After being passed through a couple of secretaries I finally arrived at the office of one Edmond Martindale, a sandy-haired Brit whom I was prepared to hate on sight. He pronounced himself at my disposal.

I thanked him for finding the time to meet with me

on such short notice, explained that I was an attorney from Chicago, and found myself on a rather delicate mission. "A client of mine named Bart Hexter died suddenly and unexpectedly ten days ago."

"Auto accident?" inquired Martindale in tones of well-bred concern.

"No. I'm afraid he was shot."

"Oh dear."

"Mr. Hexter was quite wealthy, but his affairs were left in some disorder. It came to my attention only yesterday that he maintained several accounts at your bank. Accounts," I added, "maintained in a name other than his own."

"Bit of a tricky situation," conceded the banker.

"I have with me copies of the most recent bank statements and a copy of my client's death certificate. I'm confident that this will be sufficient to begin the necessary steps for closing the accounts. I am also hoping that the bank will be able to provide me with complete records for the accounts, which appear to be connected with some transactions for which Mr. Hexter's company is under government investigation."

In reply, Edmond Martindale made a sound suspiciously like, "tut, tut."

"Why don't you give me those statements, and I'll pull the account records. In the meantime I'll buzz my girl and have her bring in tea. This should only take a few minutes."

Martindale retreated and a fiftyish "girl" in bifocals and a blue dress brought in a tray upon which rested a tea service that had been engraved with the crest of the bank. I was working on my second cup when Martindale returned. I knew from the look on his face that he wasn't going to give me what I'd asked for.

"I'm sure you are aware," he said, "that the banking laws of Bermuda are very strict. Indeed, inviolate confidentiality is one of our most valued assets—one that brings much banking business to the island."

"Surely," I countered, "the banking laws of Bermuda provide for the sudden death of an individual."

"They do. When Bart Hexter opened these accounts, he named his brother, William Hexter, as trustee. Now that we have been notified of your client's death, we will be sending Mr. William Hexter the appropriate notification form."

"Billy Hexter died in a car accident six months ago."

"Well then, there really isn't anything further I can do for you," said Martindale primly.

"Surely if I have his brother's death certificate faxed to you we can move on this. Your customer is dead, the account trustee is dead. . . ."

"Ah, but these are all joint accounts," interjected Martindale while I did a double take. "There is a co-signator on each of them, and to the best of our knowledge, that co-signator is very much alive."

"How do you know?" I demanded, as the cold hand of foreboding fastened itself around my entrails.

"Because a significant amount of money was transferred out of one of the accounts this morning."

CHAPTER
23

I tried everything I could think of to persuade Edmond Martindale to divulge the identity of the co-signator on Hexter's accounts, short of falling to my knees and begging. And I certainly would have tried that ploy if I'd thought there was a whisper of a chance that it would have worked. But with each approach, I came up against the Chinese wall of the privacy provisions of Bermuda banking law. No matter what tack I took, the response was always the same—Bart Hexter had set up the accounts so as to protect the identity of himself and the co-signator.

I left the bank discouraged and depressed. The information I had come to Bermuda to gain seemed even further beyond my ken, while the information I had obtained unsettled me deeply. I left the bank and walked aimlessly toward the waterfront, trying with little success to order my thoughts.

Even though it was late in the day the sun was still high, so I stopped at a garish little shop that catered to tourists. I bought myself a big T-shirt, plastic thongs, a towel, and a bathing suit. The shop stocked only bikinis. I chose the most modest one I could find, but even so, I was sure that I could have folded it up, top and bottom, and mailed the whole thing to Cheryl in a letter. My purchases made, I hailed a taxi and instructed the driver to take me to Horseshoe Beach.

The cabby dropped me off at the end of the path to the Pavilion and agreed to come back for me in an hour and a half. Amid tan and sandy bodies preparing to return to their hotels, I slipped into my new bathing suit. I rolled up my business suit and put it in a rental locker along with my briefcase and headed for the ocean.

It was as wonderful as I remembered: white sand as fine as powder, crystalline sky, and water of impossible, heartbreaking aquamarine. I laid out my towel and, feeling a little self-conscious with my white skin and microscopic swimwear, ran splashing through the surf into the water. I swam out beyond the breakers, feasting on the huge, uninterrupted vista of ocean, comforted by my smallness in the scheme of things. I dove down into the water, felt my hair shake loose like silken seaweed along my spine. I flipped over onto my back, blinking in the sunlight. I had come to Bermuda for answers and found instead another dead end. Hexter was turning out to be a bigger pain in the ass dead than he was alive. I floated on my back, bobbing on the surface for a long time, carried by the gentle motion of the waves.

Screw Hexter, I thought to myself.

When I got back to my hotel room, there was a message for me to call Edmond Martindale. I phoned him immediately.

"I've been giving your problem a great deal of thought," he said in his cricket-fields-of-Eton voice. "It's been discussed at the highest levels of the bank as well. My wife and I are having some people round for dinner tonight, but I was rather hoping that afterward you'd be able to drop in and continue our discussion."

"I'd be happy to," I replied eagerly. "Where do you live?" He gave me the address.

"Let's say ten-thirty, if that's not too late for you," continued the banker. "I'd rather that all our guests had gone before you arrived. Actually, I'd rather we agreed to agree that our little meeting never happened at all. . . ."

Martindale lived inland, if there is such a thing on an island that is less than three miles across, in the parish of Somerset. He had a large, traditional house of pink stucco. Its roof was white and sloped, like all those on the island, to gently direct rainwater into the cistern. It sat at the end of a lane that dripped with bouganvilleas. A short distance away I could see a cemetery, eerie in the moonlight with its concrete crypts, whitewashed and in rows aboveground. The night air was filled with the rhythmic chirping of tree frogs.

The banker was waiting for me on the porch, genial and apologetic for the hour. He was dressed in linen trousers and an open-necked shirt. I followed him inside and allowed myself to be introduced to his wife, Polly, who was overseeing the washing of the dinner dishes by two teenage girls. I accepted Martindale's offer of a whiskey and soda which he mixed, British style, with soda from a siphon and no ice. He led me to a terrace overlooking a deep and narrow garden. He pulled up two wrought iron chairs, and we got down to business.

"Despite the rather overheated notion in the press that we overseas banks are havens for drug money and

God knows what else, we are actually very sensitive to any hint of wrongdoing," began Martindale confidingly. "We can't be responsible for the actions of our clients—no bank can. You said when we spoke this afternoon that Mr. Hexter was the subject of a government investigation. Does this involve the accounts he maintained in our bank?"

"Yes, but only in a tangential way. I believe that Mr. Hexter maintained these accounts for purely personal reasons. His children, who have inherited his business, would like to normalize the firm's operations. Until they discover the identity of the co-signator, they can do nothing. Certainly if the accounts were maintained jointly it must be assumed that Bart Hexter meant to share the assets in them with the co-signator. Yet I would be hard pressed to believe that he'd approve of the co-signator's emptying of those accounts without the knowledge of his heirs."

"It isn't the bank's responsibility to second-guess our customer's intentions," pointed out my host.

"It is a great deal of money."

"Yes, it certainly is a great deal of money," drawled the banker.

"You said on the phone that you might be willing to assist me," I prodded. "Off the record."

"Oh yes. Definitely off the record. If ever you should acknowledge this conversation to anyone I would deny it absolutely. Under oath if necessary, and with a completely clear conscience."

"I understand."

"I'm afraid that I will not be able to give you that which you desire most."

"You mean the second name on the account," I said, deflated.

"Such a revelation would indeed constitute a gross breach of trust—one that might be traced back to the bank and leave us open to prosecution and certainly to the loss of many accounts."

I didn't waste my breath telling him that I thought it unlikely. Bankers were all the same. They acted like whores and were as careful of their reputations as virgins. There was no changing them.

"So what can you tell me?" I asked.

"I have decided to give you information about the accounts themselves, in the hopes that it may help you uncover the identity of the co-signator. I have copies of all of the account statements, which I will give you, unattributably, of course."

He went back into the house and came out with a sheaf of copies.

"The three accounts were opened on May 4, 1988. I had just joined the bank, and by chance I was the officer who opened the account for them. I must confess that, even by Bermudian standards, their requests for privacy were extreme."

"Of the two of them, who did the talking?" I asked.

"Mr. Hexter."

"Is the co-signator a man?"

"That would be a safe assumption," replied Martindale. "But that is all I will say about him. The accounts were to be numbered, and all correspondence from the bank was to be sent through an international courier company. Deposits were either made in check form through the courier or by wire transfer. Transactions could be affected by phone, provided the caller identified himself as either Mr. Silver or Mr. Bean and a nine-digit code number was provided to the bank."

"A nine-digit number? No letters?"

"No letters. Cash withdrawals, of course, could be made only in person by either of the signators."

"How were they identified," I asked, "apart from the code number?"

"We have photographs on file."

"May I see them?"

"I'm afraid not," replied Martindale with regret. "Though the management of the bank would be more sympathetic to that request if it were accompanied by the code number."

"You said that money was transferred out of the account on Monday. Can you tell me where it was transferred to?"

"To another account in the bank, this one in the name of Mr. Silver alone."

"When was that account opened?"

"Six months ago."

"Have any other transfers been made from the joint accounts to Mr. Silver?"

"Yes, three in the last three months. All transfers in excess of one million. We also have been instructed to have a withdrawal of five hundred thousand U.S. dollars cash ready this Friday."

"When was this instruction received?"

"Last Friday. You can understand that it takes us five business days to ready a withdrawal of that much foreign currency."

"Is there anything else you can tell me?" I asked.

"From the day the accounts were first opened, Mr. Bean has never set foot inside the bank. To my knowledge, all of the cash withdrawals have been made by Mr. Silver."

I stayed up late that night going through the bank statements that Martindale had given me, looking for patterns. The accounts had been opened simultaneously, each with a modest initial deposit of nine thousand U.S. dollars. After that, deposits had been erratic, always large and interspersed over the year with no particular regularity. Withdrawals seemed more regular, roughly every other month, between fifty and sixty thousand dollars at a crack.

There were, I knew, regulations about bringing cash into the country. Customs required that currency or negotiable securities in excess of ten thousand dollars be declared in writing. But five hundred one-hundred-dollar bills could be easily concealed, and it was my experience that U.S. customs inspectors were much more interested in looking for drugs than money.

From the records it appeared that from the time the accounts were opened the money had traveled—wire transfer or deposits of checks from Hexter Commodities, Inc., cash withdrawals every sixty days—in U.S. dollars. Within the last six months the pattern changed dramatically. There were, in addition to the previous day's wire transfer, two other transfers of funds, each in excess of one million dollars, going as far back as four months before, all from the same account. The Friday before Bart Hexter's death, a five hundred thousand dollar wire transfer had been attempted from the same account and denied for insufficient funds.

The money in the Bermuda accounts was certainly a motive for murder. From where I sat the most likely suspect seemed to be Carl Savage. The accounts were opened after he'd been with Hexter Commodities long enough to have gained Bart Hexter's trust, and he would be a logical accomplice for the internal trade allocation. Then there was the fact that Hexter had stolen Torey Lloyd from him.

There were, I realized, only three minor glitches in my theory. The first was that if Savage intended to empty the Bermuda accounts into his own, why did he pull the stunt with Barton Jr. about extorting a higher salary? Did he just assume that inexperienced Barton would be willing to pay anything to keep Savage's expertise? Was it true that there was no limit to greed? Second, if he wanted to kill me, would he risk using his own name in the message luring me to the Merc? More troubling, of course, was the minor problem of how Carl Savage could have gotten hold of Bart Hexter's gun and shot him.

CHAPTER
24

My plane touched down at O'Hare a few minutes after four, and I rushed to catch a taxi back to my office. I spent the cab ride into the city turning everything over in my mind for the thousandth time. During the last few days of Bart Hexter's life, he'd ricocheted from one confrontation to another. According to Mrs. Titlebaum, he'd spent his last day at Hexter Commodities in a foul mood, fighting with whoever had the bad luck to cross his path. That afternoon he'd called Ken Kurlander to urgently make an appointment—presumably in order to change his will. The only person he didn't tangle with on Friday was Torey Lloyd; indeed, he came to her apartment and presented her with an engagement ring. But by the time he arrived home to Lake Forest he was back in form, and Pamela's family dinner had disintegrated into harsh words and hurt feelings. By all accounts he'd managed to keep civil during Saturday's golf outing, but that night he'd caught Krissy groping in the coatroom with another man. His youngest daughter had received a tongue-lashing, and he'd left the party in a bad temper and alone. Sunday morning the cook heard Bart and Pamela arguing. Within hours he was dead.

What changes had Bart wanted to make in his will? Had Margot, perhaps, called her father with the news of her pregnancy? Or maybe he wanted to reallocate the disposition of his property to include Torey. Deep down I feared that Ken Kurlander was right—most likely Hexter's reasons had died with him. And yet I couldn't help but wonder.

The issue of the withdrawals from the offshore accounts was even more puzzling. Martindale had confided that the recent wire transfers had been made to a relatively new account listed solely in the name of the mysterious co-signator. The statements showed that the first transfer was made on the same day as a $60,000 cash withdrawal. It seemed a fair bet that the co-signator had gone to Bermuda on one of his cash runs and taken the opportunity to open a separate account.

I was pretty sure that the wire transfers had been made without Hexter's knowledge. That would explain the transfer that had recently been denied for insufficient funds. No doubt Bart had wanted to wire the money for the condominium payment. Whoever had been moving money out of the account would have known that there wasn't enough money in it to cover the transaction. Bart, notoriously lackadaisical about opening and examining his account statements, had instead relied on the running mental tally that he believed was more accurate than the bank computers—accurate, that is, unless someone is stealing from you.

I arrived at the office just as Cheryl was leaving. She handed me my messages and agreed to call over to Hexter Commodities before she left for class in order to make sure that someone would still be there when I arrived. I scanned my mail and flipped through my phone messages. There was nothing that couldn't wait until later.

I was just pulling my raincoat and purse out of my closet when Cheryl came in to say that she'd made the necessary arrangements for me at Hexter Commodities.

I arrived at the commodities trading firm long enough after the market close that the office was empty. The receptionist waited for me sullenly, coat in hand.

"Barton Jr. said to tell you that he's bringing the babies home from the hospital," she reported, locking up her desk. "But he said he'd be here as soon as he could. In the meantime, you should just do whatever it is you have to do."

"Is Mrs. Titlebaum here?" I asked.

"She's already gone."

"What about Tim?"

"He left. Are you going to be needing me? I mean, I usually catch the five-forty for Schaumburg. . . ."

"Is there anybody else in the office? Is Loretta here?"

"Nope. You've got the place to yourself until Barton gets here."

I made my way through the empty trading floor to Bart Hexter's office. I'd spent a lot of time over the course of the past week sifting through the dead man's things, but this time I was looking for something specific—the nine-digit code number that would unlock the offshore accounts.

At his desk, I looked through his address book and his papers, jotting down numbers that looked possible. His social security number, copied from some bank papers, seemed promising—nine digits. I would try it out on Martindale in the morning.

After I finished with Bart's office, I moved into Mrs. Titlebaum's. I tried not to be discouraged. Hexter, after all, had had a photographic memory for numbers, and had most likely never needed to write the code number down, but there was a chance that he'd given it to his secretary or his personal assistant. Rifling through Mrs. Titlebaum's desk I uncovered a few possibilities, including two numbers written next to each other on a rolodex card. They were probably her lottery picks for the week, but I made a note of them anyway.

As I made my weary way to Tim's office I realized that I was clearly not cut out for the painstaking nature of investigative work. Besides, going through other people's things made me feel like a thief. I was also worried, as my list of possible numbers grew, about how much patience the Bank of Bermuda was going to have for playing "is this the code number?" with me.

With a sigh I took a seat behind Tim's desk. Everywhere I looked there was the familiar red, white, and blue of Cubs memorabilia. On one corner of his desk he'd taped the team's spring training schedule. In the margins he'd penciled the scores of the games that had already been played. In front of me lay a stack of material all related to an elaborate fantasy baseball league, of which Tim Hexter appeared to be commissioner. I opened the top middle drawer of his desk and began my search. For a moment I just stared. Stacked in one long, neat row, was an assortment of matchbooks—each from a different restaurant on the island of Bermuda.

I sat for a moment, contemplating my own idiocy. Detective Ruskowski's words rang in my ears. Lawyers—we take what's easy and make it hard. Of course. Take my brains, boil them, mash them, and serve them with butter. Of course. It was Tim, the gofer, who had been making the runs to the Bank of Bermuda. Tim, the trusted nephew who'd been trusted with the joint accounts. I'd assumed it was Savage, but Tim made so much more sense. It would be hard for Savage to be away from the office for any length of time. Besides, Tim was family, and by all accounts Hexter believed in family loyalty.

Family.

I was so stupid. The police said that the only people with access to Hexter's gun were members of his family. Elliott and I had assumed that meant his wife and three children. But Tim was his nephew. Mrs. Titlebaum had even told me that Tim went to Hexter's house on Saturdays to drop off the final tally of the week's trades. I had just been too stupid to put two and two together. Last Saturday Bart and Pamela had been on the golf course, but that didn't mean that Tim hadn't used the opportunity to go out to the house, remove the Deodar statements from Hexter's briefcase, and take the gun from the drawer.

My new theory explained so much—Hexter's bad temper, his wanting to change his will. Presumably he'd decided to disinherit his nephew after he'd tried to transfer the funds to pay for Torey's condominium and discovered that money had been siphoned from his account. No wonder Bart had gone home Friday complaining that everyone was trying to stab him in the back.

I heard the click of the lock as the door handle turned.

"Barton?" I called out, flushed with excitement at my discovery.

The door opened.

"Afraid not," replied Tim grimly from the doorway.

"Your secretary told me that you were in Bermuda yesterday. Did you have a nice trip?" he asked, coming around beside me. He sat on the edge of his desk, looking down at the still open drawer in front of me. He towered over me. In his hand was a hunting knife.

I didn't speak.

"I hope you enjoyed yourself, since it's probably the last trip you'll be taking—well, the second to last."

"I've already called the police," I lied. "They're on their way here right now."

"I don't think so," replied Tim mockingly. "I think you're bluffing. Once you're out of the way my problems are over."

"You're wrong," I said with a growing sense of alarm. "Getting rid of me isn't going to solve your problems. Whoever takes over my files will pick up right where I left off. You would be making a terrible mistake."

"By the time they figure out what's happened to you, I'll be long gone. There are a lot of places a man can hide with four million dollars—warm places, with palm trees. I'll be thinking of your rotting corpse while I sit on the beach drinking piña coladas."

"I can't believe you'd be stupid enough to steal from Hexter. How did you expect to get away with it?" I demanded, switching to the offensive. "I could tell you were a loser when you jumped me at the Merc. I bet you felt like a tough guy sitting there with blood in your mouth."

"Shut the fuck up," he hissed.

"And you rode to a murder on your bicycle," I continued, keeping my eyes on the knife. "I bet the papers are going to have fun with that. You know the cops found your footprints by the road where you waited for Hexter. That's the kind of physical evidence that killing me won't change."

"Shut your stupid mouth."

"Everything you touch you botch, Tim. Hexter asked you to spread his trades across the different accounts, and you couldn't even do that right. You allocated too many trades to Deodar and brought the whole CFTC down on Hexter Commodities. I bet Hexter had some choice things to say when he figured out what your carelessness was going to cost him. But that was nothing compared to what happened when he found out you were stealing from him. That was a bonehead move, Tim."

"It would have worked," shouted Tim defensively, "if that bitch Torey hadn't gotten greedy and wanted that fucking apartment. Bart never even looked at the junk they sent him from the bank. How was I to know he'd pick the one account he never touched for that damned apartment?"

"And so you killed him."

"He fucking deserved to die. Before his accident, Dad went to him crying, begging him to lend him money. The loan sharks were going to bust his kneecaps. But my fucking uncle told him that he didn't get where he was by backing losers."

"So why did you take the money? To get even?"

"To get the fuck out of here," he answered, breathing fast. Adrenaline surged through me as I readied myself.

"Do you think I wanted to spend the rest of my life taking his abuse while his fucking kids got rich? Do you?"

"I think you're going to spend the rest of your life in jail. That's where losers like you end up," I shouted as I jumped to my feet, grabbing hold of his wrist with both of my hands, trying to knock him off his feet. We struggled for a moment in the stillness of equally balanced opposing forces. I focused on the hand with the knife, holding it away from me. I did not see him grab the baseball bat from the display on the wall until it was too late.

I came to in a small space, curled in the fetal position. My head hurt so much I thought I would throw up. As I pulled myself more solidly into consciousness, it became clear that I already had. I shuddered miserably for a few minutes, trying to get my bearings. I tried to sit up but hit my head almost immediately. I groped with my hands in total darkness.

The reality of my predicament came to me in fragments. I felt some sort of rough, cold fabric against my skin that felt like carpeting. There was a noise as well, a constant rumble, but it was awhile before I decided that it was coming not from my throbbing head, but from some outside source.

I had no room to move. Panicked and disoriented, I thrashed around in the tight confines of my prison. Finally I realized that I was inside of something and that something was the trunk of a car. I groped around again, struggling to orient myself. I felt the sharp ends of something metal under my shoulder that frantic fingers revealed to be the ends of a set of jumper cables. Scrabbling in the dark I brushed up against the familiar bulk of my purse, a towel that smelled like gasoline, and the sleeve of my Burberry, slippery with blood and vomit.

"Tim!" I shouted. "Hey, Tim! Can you hear me?"

"What do you want, bitch?" came his muffled reply.

"Where are you taking me?"

"It doesn't matter, does it? Wherever it is, you aren't ever coming back!"

"Killing me isn't going to solve anything. Just the opposite. The police will come after you even harder. Do you really think you were able to get me out of the Board of Trade Building without being seen? The cops are probably right behind us."

"Dream on. I stuffed you in one of those deep mail carts, spread some mail bags on top. And besides, there isn't anybody coming looking for you." Suddenly the car slowed and changed direction. We'd turned onto a different road, one with a rougher surface. We drove for a few minutes in silence. It's going to be soon, I thought, willing myself to stay in control. I knew that at some point Tim was going to stop the car and that when he did, he was still going to have the knife.

Tim cut the engine, and we drifted to a stop. I held my breath, and time stood still. I heard the door open. Everything else disappeared, the sounds of my breathing, the rank smell of my appalling fear—it all gave way to something else.

I had squirmed around in the cramped confines of the trunk, turning myself so that I was lying on my side with my feet tucked under me. My knees were pushed up against the inside of the license plate wall. My head was jammed up against the back of the car's backseat. At the moment I heard the click of the key in the lock of the trunk, I found myself praying that the overhang wouldn't get in the way.

I don't remember what Tim said when he opened the trunk. All I remember is the flood of moonlight, bright after the darkness of the trunk, and the slow-motion impact of the bullets as they tore their way into Tim Hexter's chest as I pumped the trigger of the almost forgotten .38 automatic I'd managed to extract from the bottom of my purse.

I had planned to shoot every bullet in the gun, but after the third shot he staggered and fell over on top of me, dead. I felt the warmth of his body, the sickening wetness of his blood as it gushed on top of me, warm and sticky.

Suddenly I was suffocating. I was screaming. After the moments of calculation and control in the trunk, something inside of me broke loose and I scrambled, starved for air, heaving the dead weight of him off of me.

I stumbled away from the car. My legs were cramped from what must have been hours in the trunk and trembling so that the ground seemed to pitch beneath me like a boat at sea. I staggered until my hand felt something rough. The bark of a tree.

I grabbed it with both hands and threw up.

CHAPTER
25

When I think back on the murder of Bart Hexter, I always begin with our aborted Sunday morning meeting and end with the bullets tearing into Tim Hexter's chest. That is where the story ends in my mind, in my dreams, and sometimes even in my nightmares. But, of course, that wasn't the end of it. Events dragged on over hours and days—macabre, tedious, and with flashes of burlesque.

It took me some time before I was able to convince myself to return to the car. There was, of course, no other alternative. It was dark. I had no idea where I was. I was covered with Tim Hexter's blood. I'd thrown up on my shoes.

I walked around the front of the car. There were no keys in the ignition. I went to the trunk and looked in the lock. It was empty. Tim's body had fallen head first into the trunk, but his legs hung out grotesquely. I looked away and got down on all fours, groping through the grass in the hopes that he'd dropped the keys before he fell. No luck.

Screwing up my nerve I forced myself to go through his pockets until I finally found what I was looking for—the keys to his car. Then, without allowing myself to think about it, I shoved his dead legs into the trunk and slammed down the lid—just like he must have done to me.

I got behind the wheel of the car and followed the road until I came to a gas station. There, while the teenage attendant looked on, aghast, I dialed 911 from the pay phone and told the dispatcher I had a body in my trunk.

I was not feeling well at all. I was dizzy and freezing cold, and I felt like I had a thousand butterflies dancing in my stomach. Within minutes there were policemen everywhere—sheriff's department, highway patrol, squad cars, and the paramedics. Everyone, it seemed, wanted to get in on the excitement.

They took me to the sheriff's department where I used my one phone call to dial Stephen Azorini. I may not understand my feelings for Stephen all the time, but I knew that when Russell lay dying in his hospital bed, it was Stephen who kept me sane, holding my hand and that of my husband down the darkest road I ever hope to travel. If I ever needed that kind of unfailing friendship, I knew that he would be there.

The rest of that night is all a blur. There were detectives and doctors and district attorneys. At first they couldn't decide whether I was a crazed killer or a brave victim who'd foiled her attacker, so they tried treating me both ways. I explained the whole convoluted mess until I was shouting with frustration. After I'd been through it a dozen times, Ruskowski showed up, and I had to go through it all again.

It was close to four in the morning when they finally let me go. Stephen was waiting for me, alone on a folding chair in the hall. I was so glad to see him that I felt weak in the knees.

"They said you'd need a ride home," he said, almost apologetically. "Do you want to talk about it?"

I looked into his handsome face, and a tremendous weariness came over me. First thing in the morning, I knew, I would be calling Elliott to tell him everything that had happened. Right now it all seemed too much to begin.

"No," I replied gratefully. "Not now."

Also by Gini Hartzmark...

PRINCIPAL DEFENSE

A heart-pounding thriller
Available in bookstores everywhere.

Katharine Millholland may be an heiress, but she works hard for her money as a mergers and acquisitions lawyer in Chicago's most aggressive firm. When Azor, the high-tech, high-profit pharmaceutical company founded by her sometime lover, Stephen Azorini, faces a takeover, Kate will do anything to stop it from happening.

But the stakes get higher when Stephen's teenage niece, Gretchen, is killed. Everyone knows that if Gretchen's shares go to the corporate raider, Stephen will lose all control, so Kate plunges into an investigation of the murder. An as family fights simmer and mob ties threaten to smother, Kate works against an impossible deadline to find Gretchen's killer. Unfortunately, the closer she gets to the answers, the closer she moves to becoming the latest victim of a corporate bloodbath....